# SHERIFF
## of
# HANGTOWN

*A Western Duo*

# LAURAN
# PAINE

CENTER POINT LARGE PRINT
THORNDIKE, MAINE

This Center Point Large Print edition is published
in the year 2014 by arrangement with
Golden West Literary Agency.

The text of this Large Print edition is unabridged.
In other aspects, this book may vary
from the original edition.
Printed in the United States of America
on permanent paper.
Set in 16-point Times New Roman type.

ISBN: 978-1-62899-029-4

3 1969 02243 9540

Library of Congress Cataloging-in-Publication Data

Paine, Lauran.
  Sheriff of Hangtown : a western duo / Lauran Paine. — Center Point
Large Print edition.
     pages cm
  ISBN 978-1-62899-029-4 (Library binding : alk. paper)
  1. Large type books. I. Paine, Lauran. Outlaw's hide-out. II. Title.
PS3566.A34S493 2014
813'.54—dc23
                                                              2013045998

# TABLE of CONTENTS

# OUTLAW'S HIDE-OUT

They called him Hap Thompson but his name was Carlysle Thompson, and, as a deputy U.S. marshal had once said, someone named Carlysle should have been called either Cal or Carl. He was no more than average in height, compact and powerfully put together; he looked deceptively youthful considering he was somewhere in his forties and except for a streak of gray over each temple could have passed for a man ten years younger. He was a good-looking man, bronzed from exposure, perfectly co-ordinated, and even without the ivory grips on his holstered Colt would have immediately impressed other men as a person capable of looking after himself and his particular interests.

He had been a top hand, a stage driver, a blacksmith, and for one riding season he had scouted down through the Chiricahua country where it got so hot a man could fry an egg on just about any flat rock. For twenty years an inherent restlessness had driven him. The ironic part of this was that just when he became very good at something, was on the verge of becoming successful at it, he wearied of it and drifted on.

But a man changes. Hap Thompson sat by his

green-twig spit with a brace of prairie chickens slowly turning above a dry-oak, smokeless fire, thinking of many things but mostly about a future that was not very promising. His latest profession had provided excitement enough. It had also given him another opportunity to prove his cleverness. And it had also put him outside the law. Robbing a bank was a challenge, but that was only the beginning. It also made the robber a fugitive with a price on his head and with tireless pursuit on his back trail.

He peeled off a piece of roasting prairie hen, found it cooked through, and allowed the green twig to turn a few times before removing it. He had a perfect hide-out in the hushed and timbered mountains and he was wise enough never to ride out and back until he had a promise of rain ahead. Hap Thompson was that most difficult of all outlaws to apprehend, the kind who leaves no tracks.

He had been in the Dogwood Mountains since early spring. It was now approaching late summer, early autumn. He had only moved out three or four times, to ride down to a town upon the grassland bench southeastward, load a sack at the general store, and ride back. Always with black clouds threatening overhead. Twice he had got caught but he'd had a slicker both times. The cabin he'd been erecting, more to pass the time than because he needed a shelter, now had three sides of peeled logs, a solid roof, and a stone combination oven and fireplace. He had worked neither fast nor hard. Some days he went to the blue-water lake a couple of miles northwest under the black rims of the highest peak and fished. Other times he went even farther back on horseback and hunted. The cabin was more a hobby than a necessity.

His horse had feed for his belly in the fifty-acre meadow out front of the cabin. He had been getting too fat but there was little Hap Thompson could do about that until he peeled pine logs for a corral to one side of the cabin and he hadn't done more than snake in the saplings and skin them. They were lying over there ready to be notched into the posts. They had been lying there most of the summer.

There were comforts. A steel mirror for shaving hanging upon a tree in front of the cabin. A fresh-water creek less than a hundred feet away that bisected his glade. Game and fish enough to keep tallow under a man's hide and all the peace and quiet and safety a person could ever want, plus some magnificent mountains in three directions without sign of another soul anywhere throughout them.

He ate prairie hen until he felt stuffed, then lolled back to watch the day follow its ancient sequence of drawing to a close. His horse was a couple of hundred feet off, standing contentedly, hip-shot, in the beauty of a waning, perfect day. To the northeast a few soiled clouds pushed up over the rims and hung there. Hap studied them. Like most range men who had reason to be concerned about things such as weather, he was a fair judge of the portents. If those clouds fleshed out in the night, there could be rain the following day. But if they were simply the farthest edge of some great storm center lying beyond the peaks, there was a better than even chance the rain would go somewhere else to drop.

It did not matter. He rolled and lit a smoke, eyed the cabin, and decided he might as well commence completing the front, now that he had the stonework inside completed. The way Hap Thompson did most things was after thought and deliberate planning. He was not an individual who acted often on the spur of the moment or who was given to sudden bursts of activity. A cowman he had once worked for in Idaho had categorized Hap Thompson as one of those men who rarely did anything hastily and, as a result, rarely did anything halfway. It was a sound judgment. Even when he had robbed that bank in Nebraska he had not afterward fled south for Mexico, which was how the pursuit went in search of him. Nor had he just walked in with a gun in his fist demanding their money. He had first worked for three months on a cow outfit near the Flint Hills country to learn everything he could about that bank. Then he had robbed it—the evening of the same day that a bullion shipment had arrived.

Hap was a calm, shrewd, sagacious man with a world of experience in a lot of different fields. He also happened to be deadly fast and accurate with that ivory-stocked six-gun. For about six months now he'd had plenty of time to practice, when he felt like doing it. Gun thunder up here was smothered by the rearward black barrancas, in most other directions by a land of silent, ageless emptiness. But Thompson had been highly proficient with weapons before he'd ever found his hide-out in the Dogwood Mountains, primarily because he was perfectly co-ordinated but also because he'd often practiced. But he had never sought a fight. It was contrary to his nature to fight, unless he absolutely had to, and then it became a different story.

Men he had ridden with used to shake their heads, hard put to decide whether Hap was lazy or whether maybe things just came so easily to him he looked as though he never used any effort doing them. But robbing the bank was a mistake and he knew it now. He probably suspected it might be while he was considering it but that was water under the bridge. As for the challenge—there hadn't been any. Not even the guard inside the bank challenged him. Even getting them to open the safe and sack the money for him had been easy. He was not sure to this day what he had expected them to do but in retrospect it had been a dully routine experience from beginning to ending. There was one thing he was sure of now. Whatever had originally motivated him, he had done the most foolish thing of his life.

They had a description of him without a picture and they had backtracked to the outfit he had worked for last, in the Flint Hills, to get his name and previous points of origin. He had been a fugitive for more than a year now. He thought another year had ought to see his dodger get buried beneath a whole batch of fresh Wanted dodgers of other outlaws. Then, with caution, he could head on out and start over.

He'd had lots of time to ponder this. He had decided he might go over into the Oregon high desert country; it was rumored a man could lose himself among those cow outfits over there without a bit of trouble. Also, it was a little-known territory. After a year or two over there he could conceivably begin working back again.

He smiled at the firelight. Grow a beard, maybe. A few riders wore them. Or go south, down around the Mexican border. Or maybe even out to California where they had some big cow outfits, too.

He yawned, looked out where the horse was back grazing, and beyond, over where solemn sentinel firs and pines bordered his glade and finally up at the sky, which was as tantalizingly magnificent as it always had been and was equally as mysteriously uncompromising as it also always had been. Most of the mountain predators had learned over the months to give Thompson's clearing a very wide berth. The first big black bear to be drawn by the delectable smell of horse sweat had not quite got clear of the last tree stand.

For a while Thompson had tolerated a scarred old bull elk but when he started making rushes at the horse, taking over the entire glade, Thompson ran him off. Wolves and a big cat or two had come stealthily—right down a gun barrel each time. By that peculiar moccasin-telegraph wild animals share, it became general knowledge throughout the mountains that one of those two-legged creatures had established himself at the big meadow below the barrancas and he did not tolerate four-legged visitors.

There was one disadvantage to this. Now Hap had to saddle up and ride a couple of miles when he went pot hunting. But it was worth it. If he had allowed a predator to kill his horse, he would be just as crippled as though he lacked legs, not just because he was miles from anywhere in the primeval mountains but also because, as a fugitive in a world of mounted men, he could be run to earth very easily—providing, of course, they first discovered his lair.

He went inside the partially completed cabin, tested the wall bunk he had just completed, then bedded down and slept better than he had slept before in this secret place.

What awakened him was the cry of blue jays, raucous and blatant, but the pitch and tone told him the birds were simply abusing each other, which was a different sound from that which they made when a trespasser was in the forest. He went to the creek to wash. Because that water came right off an ancient snowfield, miles distant and lying necklace-like around the base of a giant peak, it was very cold. Sometimes he heated it first but most often he did not bother unless he intended to shave.

The world was slow to light at this place; there were too many easterly rims to hold back the sun for an hour or so after it had risen elsewhere. But the glow of it reached Thompson's meadow, making the place softly and beautifully gray-blue-pink as the moments advanced.

The cold usually did not depart until around 10:00. At that elevation, in such an isolated, forest-sheltered, hidden place, even during the hottest midsummer time it was chilly in the early mornings and sometimes, if it was overcast, it got chilly early in the evenings. This particular morning there was an overcast, thin and veil-like, pale and weightless as ancient silk. As Hap started back to the cabin, he studied the high sky. Those clouds he had noticed yesterday seemed to have spread during the night, to have spread and thinned out, become diluted as they sought to cover all the vast firmament that was visible to him. It was a peculiarly diaphanous overcast. It did not inhibit the sunlight, when eventually it arrived, but it seemed to add a sense of moist, faint grayness to the day, combining its own soft diffusion with direct sunlight.

Hap shrugged and went about making his first meal of the day. He burned only dry wood—in the morning and at midday, if he cooked at midday—because with dry wood there was hot fire and no smoke. For his evening meal he was not that careful; nightfall would conceal rising smoke.

He knew where the cow outfits were, south and east and west of his mountains. He also knew they did not come up this far into the Dogwoods. But curiosity was a powerful segment of human nature; let him show enough white smoke above the high treetops and not only would someone notice, but, if they saw it several times, they would ride up to investigate.

The only other person he had encountered this far into the miles-deep, rugged highland country was an old trapper who had a shack about five miles east and he had his fixed route to run his trap line, had evidently had this fixed course for many years judging from the signs Hap had studied. Once he had watched the old man for two full days to satisfy himself the trapper was no threat, but now, since hot weather had arrived, the old man had left the mountains. Hair slipped and hides were worthless once the heat came. Now, with autumn close, perhaps the old man would return, at least to look over his territory before moving up for the winter season.

Sometimes the weather played tricks. As the day advanced that odd veil-like mistiness seemed neither to decrease nor increase. It hung up there as though the world were stationary. The sun too acted oddly. Unless Hap simply ignored it for hours at a time, it did not seem to move. And the warmth steadily increased, which came as no surprise at the nearing close of a warm summer, but it continued to get hotter until about noon it was as hot in the hidden meadow as it had been during the peak of summertime.

Hap thought all these harbingers might presage a final burst of summer heat that could run well into the autumn, bringing on an Indian summer, as those irregular hot last autumn days were called. But there was something else he noticed. Not only were the blue jays quiet for a change, there was not a sound anywhere.

The air got heavier and breathlessly still. Along with the silence came a sensation of expectancy. It was this that made Hap finally abandon notching logs for the cabin's front wall, go to the creek to sluice sweat off his bronzed, naked upper body, and kneel there, looking and listening. If a storm was coming, it was not following the customary patterns of storms in this hidden country. He had seen a lot of them up here in the past year or so. He could tell when rain was coming, when wind or sleet was coming. This time the pattern was quite different. It was also debilitating; the heavy, breathless air sapped a man's energy very quickly. His bay horse was standing indolently beneath a huge pine half-heartedly switching his tail at mosquitoes and gnats, eyes almost closed, lower lip sagging. He showed sweat at the chest and flank.

Hap packed in an armload of dry wood to the combination oven fireplace and during the course of the mid-morning went several times to the creek to drink and sluice off. That very cold water was a blessing this morning.

By early afternoon a subtle change began. The veil-like high mistiness congealed a little, thickened and deepened and broadened until sunlight came through with a watery, diffuse haziness. The heat, however, lingered without seeming to grow less or more.

Hap had a smoke in the shadow of the cabin's solid south wall where he had made a rough log bench. It was here that he had strung his lariat as a clothesline. There were a number of giant trees close by. It was almost always cooler on the south side of the cabin than it was anywhere else.

The change continued, slowly, until by mid-afternoon a welcome little cooling breeze came from due north. Even his bay horse shook off the lethargy as the breeze cooled things by several degrees. He walked down, drank at the creek, then wandered off, grazing his way back in the direction of the trees. Hap went back to work, notching and fitting peeled logs. He had already set split cedars for the doorposts, so all he had to do now was axe-out the notches so that they would fit tightly and perfectly. He had become very adept at doing this by the time he got to the front wall.

The little breeze did not turn into a wind, which so often happened. It blew gently as the sky steadily underwent a gradual, prolonged change and the first indication Hap had that there might be a storm coming was when he had just completed setting in his fifth log and a distant cannon roll of deep thunder made the mountains reverberate. He stepped back and scanned the faraway ancient peaks. There was indeed a storm up there. Massive, soiled clouds were building against one another, their centers swollen and thick.

He had seen storms form that far up many times and they seldom came down south but went off in one of the other three directions. But as he watched now he could distantly make out a great, ponderous southward drift, as though the storm were coming down the south slope of the black-rock barrancas to cover the mountains and perhaps also eventually to ride out over the lower range country. But slowly, since evidently there was no high wind to propel the storm as there ordinarily was.

He shook his head and turned to go to the cold-water creek again. It was a storm, no question of that, and he would not escape it this time, but it was also an odd one. Finally, after wasting most of the day forming its ragged high ranks and ordering its lines, the storm received some high impetus and started southward, darkening the world as it advanced.

The temperature dropped, but it did not plummet. In fact, the day did not ever turn actually cold. And the benign little breeze suddenly faded altogether. Hap was meticulously notching in his sixth log, ignoring what impended, when another great, ominous drum roll of thunder shook his upland world. This time, as he twisted to glance toward the scowling black cliff faces, a blinding, wide flash of jagged lightning made a crackling sound and momentarily blinded him.

He waited a moment for visibility to return, saw his horse moving, head up, nostrils distended, toward the area of the cabin, his tail hair splayed out from electricity. Hap sank the hand axe into a log and went to get his laundry and bring it inside. He did the same with everything else rain might damage, including his saddlery, booted Winchester, and the other odds and ends, thinking irritably as he made a number of trips back and forth that, if the cabin had been finished, if he had been living inside it instead of still camping near the creek where his stone fire ring was, he would not have to go through all this.

Several more of those violent lightning flashes *crackled,* each as wide and blinding as the first flash, and each had little vein-like off-shoots of lightning from the main jagged columns. He knew now why this storm had been different. It was less a downpour than it was an electrical storm. Most storms did not especially bother him but he had seen evidence of the murderous violence of true electrical storms, especially in a forested country where summer-long drought had everything tinder dry. He began to watch the sky with a trace of misgiving. That kind of lightning would eventually hit tree crowns. Unless the drenching rainfall came immediately afterward, or even earlier, there would be that deadliest of forest fires—a crown fire. Not even fire breaks could win against crown fires, but that would not matter where Hap Thompson was, since there were no fire-break crews armed with axes and shovels to create fire breaks. And if there had been, a crown fire could leap from treetop to treetop. With wind, it could leap as much as a half mile, farther than any man-made fire break Hap had any knowledge of.

He tried to discern whether the veil-like failing darkness up yonder, which meant rain was heavily falling, was in front or behind the lightning. A gust of cooling wind came—dry as a bone. He let his breath out slowly. The rain was not in front of the storm; it was farther back. Still, if there was enough of a deluge, it could quench a crown fire. He had to hope this would be the case.

It was much farther from the ancient peaks to Thompson's vale than it looked to be. Hap had time to get his things inside. He guessed there would be no direct assault against his hide-out for perhaps another couple of hours, although those vagrant gusts of cool wind came now and then and seldom from the same direction twice. Waiting was worse than doing nothing, so he pulled loose the hand axe and went back to work notching logs and sledging them to make perfect fits. Afterward, when things were back to normal, he would chink between the logs, but for the time being he simply strained every muscle once he got higher than his chest in order to get the logs into place. On the other walls he had used a fulcrum of his own devising for this, utilizing his saddle, lass rope, and his bay horse. This afternoon his horse was as nervous as a cat; he would have been useless for lifting logs.

The lightning struck once, directly overhead, and the bay horse lunged over where Hap was standing, shaking from head to tail. Hap laid a hand on the beast's neck and talked to him. Usually this made all the difference; this afternoon it made some difference, but not very much. The horse rolled his eyes in fear so Hap led him over and through the half-completed doorway. Inside it was dark but the horse seemed to feel much safer in there.

More lightning came, splaying in two directions simultaneously. The horse softly snorted in his dark place but moved very little, feeling safe no doubt, at least for the time being. Hap flinched at those lightning flashes, not particularly from fear, although he was very conscious of what might happen if a huge tree was struck close to his cabin. He flinched because each time the white tongue of lightning struck beyond his view, he expected a red glow of burning treetops to follow. If that happened—when it happened—being surrounded by a dry forest of great density, he and the bay horse could very well be cooked to cinders.

The rain arrived, each droplet as large as a spur rowel. They struck with solid force and upon the cabin roof they sounded like small fists beating in mindless anger. The horse seemed to mind them less than the lightning; as time passed he even became resigned to the steady racket.

Hap stood in the doorway, watching. Within

moments, it seemed, his creek was rising to its highest point, the trees looked sodden, rivulets ran not in trickles but in miniature rivers from each pole rafter end. An awful lot of water was being dumped in one place in a short length of time. Hap had to retreat a little as several gusts of wind drove rain onto him.

The horse was back there, standing motionless, but without showing all the whites of his eyes and without snorting. But he could have snorted and Hap would not have heard him. The deluge, however, gave Hap peace of mind because not only was his roof tight, but now, if the lightning started fires in this kind of downpour, they would not last long.

He twisted to look at the horse. For a moment they exchanged a non-committal gaze, each of them brought to the same level of intelligence, their concern identical in both instances—the storm. Later they would revert to animal and master again.

Hap could have stepped outside to watch the progress and direction of the storm but within thirty seconds he would have been drenched to the skin. Nor was he as anxious now as he had been. He rolled and lit a smoke, stepped up to where only back splash reached, and peered out. Those massive cloud bellies were directly overhead. Nor did it seem they more than barely cleared the tallest treetops.

The sound was deafening but once, just before retreating from the spray, he thought he heard an alien sound. It came only once and evidently was wind-borne to him from the east side of his meadow—the high whinny of a horse.

He waited for it to come again, and, when it didn't, he decided it may have been the sound of a tree grating against other trees as it fell. Or, for that matter, it could have been rocks rattling in the overflowing creek. One thing he was certain of was that it was *not* a horse. He had been up here a year and had neither seen nor heard another horse than his bay and had detected no sign of one.

Sometime in the night the rain stopped but the wind continued until just before daybreak, and it was this that allowed Hap's monitoring subconscious mind to permit him to sleep through until first light, secure in the knowledge that he and the bay horse were safe. But after sunrise it was easy to see the wreckage; tree limbs had been torn loose; grass had been beaten flat; the creek was silted, muddy, and still out of its banks; the sky was a washed-out pale blue, and the place where Hap had been cutting wood out through the northeast end of the meadow offered one redeeming element—of all the uprooted trees that had toppled during the height of the storm, three had fallen exactly where he would have dropped them to be cut up. The third one, however, was several yards outside the stumped-over perimeter of his cutting ground. Not too far, but when he walked over, exulting because it was a huge sugar pine, he got the surprise of his life. There was a battered, head-hung horse entrapped by his reins in among the tree limbs, wearing a saddle.

The horse hardly responded. He had stood like that, evidently caught when the tree fell and very fortunately just far enough out so that the main force of that toppling giant had not caught or crushed him. But even so he was scratched and battered and he had stood caught and exposed like that throughout the storm.

It required a half hour to get the beast free and to lead him over into the clearing. He obeyed listlessly. His mouth was cut from fighting the bit in his terror. All four legs were scratched and cut and he had a gash on the right shoulder that had bled a lot. He was a blue roan gelding but rain-diluted blood had made parts of his body more nearly strawberry roan. Hap mouthed him; he was six years old. He was a stocky, short-backed, good quality animal under other circumstances but now he looked like a half-dead beast that would serve wolvers as bait. He was stiff and humped up. Hap took plenty of time to get him over into the sunshine of the meadow where the bay horse was back grazing as though nothing had happened the previous late afternoon and night. He showed quick interest in another horse, followed Hap to the creek where Hap washed blood off, removed the saddle and bridle, and, using drying swatches of tall grass bent double, rubbed hard to restore the battered horse's circulation and body heat.

He worked all morning with the blue roan horse. Used buck fat to salve the injured right shoulder and by the time the humid heat was high enough to aid the restoration of the horse's renewed circulation, the animal started to graze a little, gingerly because of his swollen, battered mouth.

Hap's bay, who was neither belligerent nor bossy by nature, grazed alongside the blue roan acting as though they had been friends for years and this too helped. What people had recently discovered, animals had known for centuries: the best medicine for the injured was a friendly and sympathetic but healthy companion.

It was early afternoon before Hap hauled the gear from the injured horse to the south side of the cabin where he draped the blanket over the saddle so that, as the leather underneath dried, it would do so very gradually, minimizing the stiffness that otherwise would result.

It was here that he noticed the narrow seat and the shallow depth. It was a woman's saddle. He tested the stirrups and also found them shorter than most men would ride their stirrups. For a moment he stood gazing at the saddle, then turned and studied the blue roan gelding. Beyond, over where the strange animal had been trapped by tree limbs, there were soft shadows among the drying timber.

He spoke aloud. "Hell!"

Without bothering to scout out and around, he walked directly and swiftly back to the wood lot, studied wet earth where he had found the blue roan, then began slowly and carefully to walk down the back trail, much of which had been washed out during the recent deluge. But in the forest, rain did not strike directly downward to the ground. This deflecting of the rain's force allowed tracks to show fairly well in the places where huge tree limbs blunted the rainfall. Nonetheless it was slow going. Hap halted twice, once where the blue roan had crossed a clearing —there were no readable tracks out there—and again where the horse had found a game trail that had been sheltered from above, but which was depressed sufficiently from centuries of use so that it resembled a slight trough, and here rivulets had changed everything.

He picked up the trail again, though, where a washout had diverted the runnels, and from this point for about a half hour he had almost no difficulty. The blue roan had been running, probably in panic, so he had struck hard down with each hoof, which helped, too. Finally he came to a low, thick knoll with a grassy top-out amid hardwood trees and found her.

She had blood on one shoulder and down both the front and back of her blouse from a torn ear. Her hair was black and filled with mud. She had dragged herself to the shelter of a tree and was propped there, unconscious and inert.

He thought she was asleep but could not rouse her as he sank to one knee and spoke, louder each time, then lay a hand upon her arm and gently shook her. She sagged away from the tree and would have toppled, but he held her upright and looked for injuries. From the torn, muddy condition of her clothing he guessed she had been dragged. Or perhaps she had been knocked from the saddle as the panicked horse stampeded by a low tree limb, something that happened in forested country.

He could find no broken bones but she was badly bruised and had cuts and scratches. He guessed she might have hurt her head in falling. The tree had sheltered her during the storm as had her hat and coat, but both those latter items were now lying beside her. Hap surmised that she had taken them off probably only an hour or two earlier, since the sunshine had created morning warmth. Of course that meant that she had only recently lapsed into unconsciousness.

He rocked back on his heels, studying her. She was an exceptionally attractive woman, perhaps in her twenties, perfectly rounded, muscular, and tanned. Who she was, what she was doing this far back in the mountains, he did not think about. His concern was whether she could stand being carried back to his cabin. Without knowing the extent of her injuries it was dangerous just to pick her up and start back. He had this decision to make when she slowly opened very dark blue eyes and looked directly at him without blinking, without showing either surprise or apprehension.

He said: "How do you feel?"

She sat there, looking at him without opening her mouth. It made him uncomfortable, so he smiled this time as he repeated it.

"How do you feel, ma'am?"

Very gradually her eyes filled and tears coursed down her soiled cheeks; she slumped and wept, leaving Hap uncertain as to what he should do now. Crying women had always unnerved him; this woman was no exception since he suspected she might be internally injured and in pain even though she seemed more dazed and disoriented.

He pushed back his hat, pulled forth a bandanna, and gently wiped her face as he said: "You'll be all right. The storm's gone. The sun's out again. . . . And I have your roan horse . . . cut up some, but he'll mend in time." He leaned back and waited. It took moments but eventually she raised her face and in that very direct manner she had, stared at him.

"Who are you?" she asked.

He grinned. "I reckon it's decent etiquette to introduce ourselves but right now it's more important for us to get you down to the cabin. Can you stand?"

She listened to him—he knew that from her rational expression—but she lapsed back into silence again. This time he did not yield to her but asked again if she could stand. She finally, softly said: "I don't know. . . . What happened?"

"My guess is that your horse spooked, maybe from the lightning, ran away with you, and either jumped you off or maybe a tree limb knocked you off. I think you may have got hung up and dragged for a short distance."

She said: "The lightning . . . I remember lightning striking some trees behind us. It was a . . . terrible, blinding moment."

He nodded understandingly. "And the horse bolted."

She did not deny or confirm this, just sat gazing at him. "Where is this place?"

He gestured vaguely. "High in the Dogwood Mountains, one heck of a long way from anywhere. . . . What interests me is how you came to be here."

She rocked her head back, resting it against the tree trunk, and closed her eyes. "I'm tired and hurt all over," she murmured.

The afternoon was moving along. It was a long

hike back to his meadow. "Don't pass out again, lady. We've got a heck of a walk ahead of us."

Still without opening her eyes she said: "I can't. I can't even stand up."

"Where are you hurt?"

". . . Please, if you have some blankets . . . leave me here with them. . . . I'm weak all over."

He had no blankets. All he had was a pelt-lined rough-out vest and that was useless under these circumstances. He put a hand upon her blood-soaked shoulder, gently squeezed. "I'm going to pick you up, but first you've got to tell me if you hurt inside somewhere." His gentle squeeze sharpened slightly. "Lady, fight against passing out."

She responded sluggishly to his grip, opened her eyes, and softly said: "Just leave me. Please. . . ."

"Does your chest hurt, your stomach, your back?"

She would have closed her eyes again but he gently shook her. ". . . Weak," she murmured. "Weak all over. No hurting pain, just can't move my legs or arms . . . just want to doze off."

He could not avoid the decision much longer if he expected to reach the cabin before nightfall, so he positioned himself, slid both arms under her, and straightened up. She was surprisingly solid for a woman no taller than she was. He had already guessed her height at about five feet and two or three inches, but having estimated her weight at about a hundred and maybe five or ten pounds, once he had her cradled in his arms, he revised that upward to perhaps a hundred and twenty-five pounds. Fortunately he was power-fully muscled and in excellent condition after so much log lifting at the cabin. Even so he stopped to rest each time he found a deadfall that he could lean down and place her upon without having to bend all the way down to the ground.

It took twice as long going back as it had taken to find her. Shadows were lengthening upon his meadow by the time he saw the blue roan and his bay grazing along contentedly together, but from that point to the cabin was still a fair distance and this time there would be no deadfall to rest against, so he waited at the last halt until he was fully prepared, then hoisted her, and started forth again. She had not said a word. In fact, he thought she had passed out again the way her eyes were closed and her head rode loosely upon his shoulder.

The horses saw him at once. Both of them turned with a considerable show of interest, then moved warily out of his path. They continued to watch as he trudged steadily across to the cabin and, finally, when he disappeared through the doorless front opening, they went back to grazing. The blue roan was evidently making a swift recovery but then he was a young, sound, and sturdy horse and none of his injuries, including the gash on his right shoulder, was actually very serious. His biggest problem had been loss of blood. But he must not have lost as much as it had seemed; otherwise, he would not be eating along out there; he would be feebly and listlessly standing.

Inside, the cabin had less light, now that two-thirds of the front wall had been put in place. What sunlight reached through came either from the long open slits between the logs, which Hap would eventually chink, or from the doorless front opening. It was warm inside but not as warm as it was outside.

He put the woman on his bunk, removed her boots, got a basin and water, and washed her face, then her hands, and finally examined the torn ear. He knew what was required—stitching—but he had neither the implements nor the knowledge, so he instead created an intricate bandage that held the torn flesh together and wrapped her head so the ear was kept immobile and in place.

The abrasions on her cheek required cleansing, then salving. Otherwise, she seemed to need rest and quiet. Whatever else might be wrong with her, Hap had no idea. He hoped she was simply dulled by the punishment her body had taken while she had been dragged, and, as he went over to start a fire in the stoned-up combination oven and fireplace and after that to start preparing a meal for them both, he worried and wondered what would be required of him if she did not recover as he wanted her to or, worse still, if she died.

He made hot broth from venison, laced it with black pepper, trickled a little precious whiskey into it, not enough to taste, and went over beside the bunk.

She was staring at the ceiling of peeled logs above. He slid an arm under her shoulders and lifted, then he held up the tin cup, and said: "This'll put a bow in your neck."

She tasted it first, then took two swallows, and finally drank the cup empty. As he eased her back and said he would get her another cupful, she said: "Where is this place?"

He smiled at her. "It's somewhere between Taos and Fort Collins. Don't worry . . . when you and the roan horse are ready, I'll see to it you get back." He paused. "Back to wherever you started from."

She turned her head to watch him go to the fireplace, did not take her eyes off him even when he came back to hoist her up again. This time she drank the cup empty without pausing. He laughed, pleased and relieved. "You eat like a horse," he said to her, easing her head and shoulders back down. "I'm going to go hunting twice as often from here on. How come you're not as big as a horse since you eat like one?"

She kept watching his features, his eyes, his wide, good-natured mouth, the lines at the outer edges of his cheeks when he smiled or laughed.

Without warning the tears came right when he was beginning to believe by smiling and laughing he was lightening her solemnity a little. As before, he sat on the edge of the bunk feeling awkward, clumsy, but most of all helpless.

# IV

After the third day he knew three things about her. Her name was Mary, she was not internally injured, and she was making good her loss of strength, which, like her horse's difficulty, seemed to be due mostly to shock and loss of blood. What he had been unable to discover was what her last name was, how she had happened to be so deep into the primeval wilderness, and what it was that seemed lurking just below the surface to prevent her from speaking much, from taking much interest in anything, and that evidently was responsible for the sudden tearful interludes. He had listened to her stifled crying in the middle of the second night. But he asked no more personal questions after she told him her name and gave him a blank look when he had asked how she had got this far back into the Dogwoods. She seemed to be a reticent, very close-mouthed woman.

She was extremely attractive even under these adverse conditions. When he propped her up the third day to change the ear bandage, she asked if he had any soap. He had several chunks of it purchased at that town southeast of the mountains. He also tactfully told her he would be off hunting most of the day, far to the northwest, and, as he tied the fresh bandage, he said: "That buck grease I used for salve on your face and arms is in the saddlebags on the peg by the fireplace." He settled her back and they looked at one another. He smiled. "Just go slow and easy. I don't want to come back and find you've gone and overdone it."

She did not return his smile. In fact, she had never smiled, not even once, since he had brought her to the meadow. Even her conversation to this point had been minimal. But that very direct way she had of looking at him implied trust— wariness, but trust.

She said: "I'll be careful. . . . You haven't told me your name."

"Carlysle," he said.

"I'll be careful, Mister Carlysle. You do the same. Men hunting alone in the mountains can have accidents."

It was the first personal thing she had said to him. He had arrived at the conclusion that she was by nature very reserved. Maybe that had been a premature judgment. As he sat looking at her, it occurred to him that whatever deep-down problem she had probably made her seem other than she really was.

"I'm usually careful, Mary, and men alone in this kind of country have to be careful even when they're chopping wood. If you get hurt up in here, you're pretty much on your own."

She agreed with that, then she said: "But I suppose there are advantages to living alone and apart, Mister Carlysle."

As their eyes held, he got a feeling that she had been doing some private appraising of her own—about him. Nor was it difficult to guess what conclusions she had arrived at, by this comment she had just made. She thought he was hiding out.

"If I have a little luck today," he told her, arising from the edge of the bunk bed, "we can have prairie chicken for supper and talk a little."

She nodded up at him. "I suppose it's time for that, Mister Carlysle. I owe you for saving my life."

He snorted softly. "You weren't dying, Mary, you were cut and scratched and set afoot. You'd have made it all right."

"To where . . . up in these big mountains, on foot?"

He reached and adjusted her head bandage. "We'll talk tonight. Keep this bandage in place. The ear is healing in pretty good shape." He straightened back again and winked at her. "I'll be back sometime this afternoon."

He did not take the bay horse, nor did he take his six-gun, but the Winchester with a full magazine rode lightly in his fist as he skirted out behind the cabin through the trees walking in loose, easy strides.

He knew the country in all directions probably even better than the Indian hunters who had at one time maintained camps this far back. He knew prairie hens were at the lower elevations rather than up along the higher plateau; they were seed eaters and the bunch grass at the higher glades, while going to seed this time of year, did not offer the diversity that other undergrowth offered down closer to the cow country, so rather than head over where he usually hunted for large game, he angled downslope. He was strong and tough and perfectly conditioned to this life he had been living for so many months now. He could cover a mile or two in a steady fast gait without any strain on his legs or his lungs.

By the time he got four miles lower down, in among the interspersed meadows where sage chickens fed and roosted, he had pretty well decided what questions he would ask her tonight during supper. He was also sure she intended to go out to the creek and bathe today. Nor was there any reason why she shouldn't go out that far if she wished to, for, while she was still stiff and sore and slightly unsteady, her strength had been returning for the last couple of days and, providing she did not overdo it, as he had cautioned her, there was no reason why she should not begin taking an interest in where she was and what the area was like. He felt it was really her inner trouble that was keeping her spirit from recuperating in pace with her body, and, while he was naturally interested in this secret of hers or whatever it was, he had no intention of prying. He simply wanted her to recover fully, and today, as he reached the meadows where he would hunt, it occurred to him for the first time that he had not thought beyond her recovery. What, once she was strong and capable again, was he going to do about her?

He did not dwell upon the problem as he stepped up beside a huge dark fir tree to become motionless while gazing out across a big sunshiny clearing because something unexpected distracted him. There was a camp out there with a wisp of smoke rising from a fire along the southwest curve of the open large meadow. Four hobbled horses were peacefully grazing, switching their tails as they kept their heads to the ground, moving very slowly along. This was the first time he had encountered people this far into the mountains. They were barely five miles from his own higher, more secluded meadow. But that was not a great distance to mounted men if they were up in here exploring or perhaps even looking for something—or *someone.*

He forgot the prairie chickens and crept around through the forest fringe like a stalking fox until he had a good view of the camp. The men had axed off limbs from which to suspend saddles by their stirrups. They had a clean camp among the trees at the very edge of the meadow, over where a seepage spring filled a small stone basin with clear, cold water. But there was no sign of the inhabitants of that camp, which made Hap uneasy. He did not want to be caught from behind while spying on the camp. In fact, he did not want to be caught at all.

The telltale sounds were absent; no blue jays were anywhere close. None of the other treetop denizens were around, either. Hap studied the saddlery, the weapons draped from low limbs, the bulging saddlebags full of supplies, and decided that whoever these intruders were they were not novices. What particularly bothered him was trying to surmise their reason for being this far into the Dogwoods and their ultimate goal. If they were outlaws fleeing northward, fine, then they would most probably ride by eyesight, meaning they would have selected the lowest notch in the yonder skyline and set a course to pass over up there, in which case they would not come within miles of his cabin. He knew they had not come down from the north. There were no tracks upon the soft ground from the north. They had come up from the south or perhaps inland from the west. If, however, they were perhaps posse men, seeking a fugitive wraith named Thompson up in here—he would be interested in knowing how they could have located him. He had felt right from the start that, as he had spied on that old trapper miles to the southeast of his meadow, now and then other men, always hunters, might have stumbled upon his clearing and seen his horse and his cabin up there and might have stealthily slipped away to pass along the information that someone was actually living back where people almost never went. These strangers might be seeking his camp out of sheer curiosity, which would be bad enough since, if they found it, his secret would no longer be a secret, but if they happened also to be lawmen or bounty hunters . . .

He faded back through the trees, grateful that he had not seen any sage hens to shoot at. One gunshot would have done all the damage he preferred not to stir up.

Back a half mile and poised to move again through deep, slanting forest gloom, he heard a man's high, keening whistle off somewhere to his left. For a time there was no reply, then the second keening whistle came. Clearly all four of those men had not gone off together; they had scattered out in the manner of hunters. But—what were they following, game or the boot tracks Hap Thompson had innocently left all the way down here from his meadow?

He wanted to leave, simply to choose a fresh route, a very circuitous one this time, and get back to his highland glade, but his curiosity was stronger; he particularly wanted to know who these men were and why they were riding this far into the depths of the wilderness. They certainly were not cowmen or wild-horse-hunters; there were no wild horses up here and no cowman in his right mind would consider pushing a herd into this predator-infested primeval territory.

He decided to go back, find a hiding place and at least see the strangers, hopefully even to get close enough to hear them. But until he was satisfied by those whistles back and forth where the strangers were, in which direction they had been exploring, he slipped northward and finally waited in a thicket where he could see the big meadow as well as the distant camp. There he remained hidden until two men strolled forth to look at the four grazing horses. Farther back the coals of their fire were being stirred to life; thicker gray smoke was rising. He did not believe outlaws would have used punky or half-cured wood; they would have wanted to avoid visible smoke. Still, four armed men did not have a whole lot to fear.

He took his time going around the meadow along the north curve, and, although he finally saw all four of those strangers lolling in their camp, smoking and drinking coffee, hats back, bodies slack in tree shade, he continued to be extremely careful. If they saw him, or even heard him . . .

Someone gruffly laughed, and another man at

the camp loudly said: "You'll likely eat bear meat before you eat fat beef again." Again there was laughter. Evidently someone had mentioned killing a bear for camp meat, and someone else had complained.

Hap crept closer and finally had to stop in place because there was a thinning stand of second-growth timber on ahead. They might not see him creeping through there but on the other hand they might, and he preferred not to take the risk.

They were rough-looking men; two had thick, close-cropped beards, one was tall with a wedge-shaped, coarse face, a small, fat, selfish mouth, and the fourth man was thick-set, making him seem shorter than he was. Their outfits included booted saddle guns, bedrolls, and capacious Army saddlebags. There was not a badge showing among them, but that did not necessarily preclude the possibility that someone had a badge in a pocket. They seemed to have been together for quite a length of time for, while they did not discuss why they were in the mountains, they occasionally referred to something they had done elsewhere, down in one of the cow-country towns or out in other camps or among the cow outfits. They looked as though they were range men, but if indeed this was so, then they should have been down in range country. They could not have got into a more alien element if they had deliberately tried to, than to be up where they were now.

Hap waited for some word to define their status with the law. He was inclined to believe they might be outlaws, perhaps one of the rustling bands that infested every cow range. But the riding season was well advanced. Usually by autumn the outfits had completed their drives to rail's end, and with the choice beef gone the rustlers drifted on or turned to other varieties of law-breaking such as stealing horses. Maybe they had robbed a stagecoach.

The longer he waited for the commitment that never materialized, the more he was inclined to believe they were fugitives who had fled into the primitive uplands for the safety the Dogwoods offered. He had to give it up eventually for, although he had seen each of those men closely enough to recognize them again, he knew little more after wasting an hour and a half scouting them up than he had known before he had got close to them.

He slipped rearward until he was far enough to turn and hasten back in the direction of his cabin. He did not even remember that he had promised to bring back some prairie chickens until he had a covey of them burst awkwardly out of a sedge and go bumbling aloft in ungainly flight. He did not raise the carbine. He simply stood watching the birds. Sage hens were easy to catch even without a gun, providing the hunter would wait until they went to roost in the late evening among low tree limbs. Otherwise, since they could fly only in short bursts and would then drop clumsily to the ground and squat low as though to hide, a hunter could stalk them with rocks.

Hap considered taking the time to bring in a couple, but in the end abandoned the notion and went along to the edge of his meadow where he paused a moment, smiling at the sight of horses peacefully grazing and the snug log cabin in its forest fringe setting. He had come to like this spot very much, more, in fact, than any place in which he had ever spent this much time before.

He came down behind the cabin, saw laundry draped from his lariat on the south side, saw where someone had used his homemade broom even to sweep the hardpan out front, and whistled.

The reply came belatedly, as Mary came around the north side of the cabin. She no longer had the big bandage around her head. She had created a much smaller one over the injured ear. She had washed her close-cut curly very dark hair and even her blouse looked fresh, unironed but fresh and clean.

As he came closer, he could see that she had scrubbed her face, then had re-applied salve to the scratches. Nearby his bay and her blue roan lifted their heads to watch Hap come down behind the house and around the north side of it. The roan's shoulder showed a fresh application of salve.

She had been busy today. He shook his head as

47

he came down and halted in front of her. She looked around. "Where is supper?"

He answered a trifle ruefully. "It's a long story." Their eyes met and held. "You overdid it, didn't you?"

"Just a little. And I rested between chores." Her eyes fled, then returned slowly to his face. "I . . . cleaned the cabin and . . . re-arranged things. You'll have a fit." She studied his features for a moment before also saying: "And in case you got skunked at hunting, I have some trout ready to fry."

"Trout?"

She twisted to point to the creek over where the horses were standing. "Didn't you know there were trout down a ways in some of the deep holes?"

The only fish he had ever seen in that meandering little watercourse were trout minnows and he had been here a year. "Didn't know there were any big ones," he told her, and, as she turned back facing him, he faintly wagged his head. She understood that gesture. Before he could scold again she led the way to the cabin.

Darkness was close. It had already reached the lower elevations. She had three lighted candles inside, the table he used as a catch-all cleared with two tin plates and cups on it and two sets of eating utensils. The earthen floor had been swept down to the hardpan and most of the things he had been leaning or piling or simply tossing aside for months now hung suspended from pegs driven between higher logs of the back and both side walls.

It did not look like his shack; it resembled an actual home. She had the cleaned trout in his iron skillet beside the dry-wood fire. He leaned to examine the size of them. He'd had no idea pan-size trout were to be had in the creek. As he straightened around, she pointed. "The wash basin and things are out back. I took that bench from the south side and put it near the back door for a washstand."

They stood looking at one another for a long time before he turned and without a word went out back to wash. Before he had finished, he could smell frying trout. He draped his old towel upon a nail driven into the back wall above the wash-stand and shook his head again, for about the fifth or sixth time.

She had been wan this morning. Not as listless as she had been the previous couple of days, but he never would have suspected she could have accomplished all that she had done today. Not and still be standing up. He rolled a smoke and stood in the soft autumn evening, watching his part of the world slowly darken, the moods, like the sights and sounds, subtly changing. Even the night fragrances were different from the daytime fragrances.

Then he discovered that she had also brought his steel mirror from the tree where he had hung it months ago and had placed it near the improvised washstand. He ran bent fingers through his thick brown hair, killed the smoke, and entered the cabin.

# V

She had rolled the trout in some sage, some kind of herb anyway. He had never eaten fish that had such flavor and texture. She had sanded out his dented little graniteware coffee pot. His first cup of coffee brought up a direct stare at her.

"I don't see how you managed it all," he told her.

"Some of it I did while sitting down. The coffee pot, for example . . . it was . . . well . . . unbelievably foul. I sat beside the creek in the sun and used the sand over there to scour it clean." She held his eyes. "You didn't say anything about my re-arranging . . . about the way I hung your things up."

He looked around, then back. He thought she meant he had not noticed. "It looks great, better than I would have done if I'd ever got around to it." He smiled.

"You're not angry?" The way she asked this,

with candid surprise, was to stick in his mind.

"Angry? Mary, I think you did a great job. A person can actually walk around in here and not be careful he don't fall over something." He smiled at her again. "You're a regular wizard. The cabin looks wonderful . . . Mary . . . you look wonderful, too."

She stiffened, reminding him of a doe ready to flee. He growled inwardly at himself for being stupid. But he really had had very little experience with women. He rushed right on. "You sure know how to cook. This is the best trout I've ever eaten."

There also were baking-powder biscuits, something he *did* know how to make. But her biscuits were lighter, more golden and fluffy. He held up a biscuit as though it were a jewel. "Feel the heft of that thing. Don't weigh as much as a handful of duck down. And the shape and color . . ." He glanced sidelong at her. She was relaxing a little. He put the biscuit upon his plate. "Were you ever a cook for a living, maybe?"

It was difficult in poor candlelight to notice changes as they came and went across her features, but he was sure, when he asked this question, something dark passed softly across her face. She dropped her head and resumed eating.

"Every woman learns to cook if she . . . is around other people. That's what men expect from women. And not just men."

51

He knew she was back down in her memories again, even before detecting the faint bitterness in her voice.

"Well, anyway," he reassured her, "you're about the finest cook I ever ran across. And that reminds me of something. . . ." He told her of the four strangers five miles southwest of their hidden meadow.

She looked up at him, listening to each word, and, when he had finished speaking, she said: "What does it mean?"

He did not want to frighten her. He knew that something, sometime, had frightened her badly. What he wanted now was for her to learn to relax and loaf and soak up sunshine and get back to feeling perfectly normal again—if it was possible—so he hedged with his answer. "Maybe grubliners, maybe pot hunters, maybe just drifters crossing the mountains."

"And maybe outlaws, Mister Carlysle." She paused, ready to make another suggestion when their eyes met and held. He could almost feel her thoughts so he said: "Go ahead, say it. Maybe outlaws or . . . ?"

Her voice was close to a whisper. "Or man-hunters."

"After me?"

Their eyes held. "Would they be, Mister Carlysle?"

He side-stepped a direct reply. "Lots of folks

like to live apart, Mary. It's beautiful up here. Peaceful and clean and fragrant and . . ."

"And . . . a perfect hide-out, Mister Carlysle."

"You've got your mind made up, then?"

"Whoever you are does not mean a thing to me, Mister Carlysle. My father taught me never to make judgments based on what other people say . . . only on my own personal experiences. You saved my life."

He drained the cup of coffee before speaking again. "I told you, Mary, you weren't dying and you wouldn't have died. You might have missed a few meals stumbling around until you got back down out of here, but you were never close to dying. I didn't do a darn' thing more than haul you here to my hide-out and smear salve on you. Lady, you don't owe me a blessed thing." He suddenly smiled to break the solemnity of this hard turn in their conversation. "Anyone who could cook me a supper like this one . . . hell, it's the other way round. *I* owe *you*." He arose from the table before she could speak. "Let's go out and watch the moon come up."

From the door he turned to watch her cross the room. She was solidly muscular, delightfully rounded and full-bodied. He stopped outside, fishing forth his tobacco sack and papers. The moon was already up. They stood a moment gazing at it, then she turned to look out where the horses were drowsing.

"It is a beautiful place, isn't it? It's just so far from town." She looked at him. "I mean, if you got sick or had an accident."

She was right, of course, but then his original view when he'd come across the high peaks and had first found this secret meadow had been that it fit perfectly into his plans—for a year or two anyway. The trouble was that the longer he was up here, the less inclined he was ever to ride on, even though he knew someday he would have to.

"If I get sick someday," he told her, watching the moon and the rash of tiny stars around it, "I'll ride down out of here to that town northeast of the foothills."

"Curranville," she murmured.

His eyes dropped to her. "You know that town?"

She knew it. "I grew up not very far from Curranville. I left there . . . five years ago. Until . . . recently . . . I hadn't been back."

He could tell now, on their third day together, when she was going back down into her memories. He was also learning how to jolt her out of those brooding moods. He did it now by lightly touching her shoulder as he said: "I don't care. I don't want to hear the story of your life." He gently turned her, then removed the hand as they strolled together across the moonlit meadow over as far as the creek, beyond which their drowsing horses had come fully awake to turn and watch.

He stopped suddenly. "What the hell am I thinking of! You're tired and you're not yet up to snuff and you worked like the devil today." He took her hand to turn back, but she planted her heels flat down and, clinging to his fingers, hauled him back around. "Let's go pet the horses." She freed his hand but did not turn to step across the creek. He smiled at her and turned around.

He offered her his hand. She jumped the creek as though she did not have a sore muscle or bone in her body. On the other side she slipped slightly in wet grass. His arms caught her. He laughed, and for the first time she smiled at him. She was a beautiful woman. Laughter or a smile made it more than ever apparent. He freed her, and they walked on.

The horses were willing to stand and be stroked. Hap examined the wounds on her blue roan and gently explored the bruised, torn mouth. There was still plenty of swelling but the horse was clearly recovered in spirit. "Another week," he told her, "and you can bit him again. That gash in the shoulder, though, is going to take a long time to fully heal. You've got to keep it greased all the time it's healing so scurf don't form . . . dry, scaly scar tissue. Keep it greased every blessed day and in time the hair will come back. He'll have a scar but it won't be very noticeable." He turned and caught her sidelong appraisal of him. He straightened up. "I guess I sounded like a know-it-all. I was just thinking out loud, is all."

"You sounded concerned, Mister Carlysle. A lot of men know how to care for injuries on horses, but not very many sound as genuinely concerned as you just did."

He patted her roan, scratched its withers, ran a gentle palm down over its rump, and stepped around to his bay horse and ruefully pointed to the fat gut. "Grass colt," he said to Mary, and grinned. "But I don't have the corral finished to hold him in over night and I don't have any time to go riding around to exercise the horse, when I'm trying to finish the cabin and all."

"I'll do it," she said, looking past him at the bay horse. "I looked him over today. He's really a splendid horse. Barrel, forearms, rump, head, eyes. Mister Carlysle . . . ?"

"Yes'm."

"If I were an outlaw and I would naturally want to own a fine, strong, swift, and durable horse to keep me from being caught"—she did not once lift her eyes to his face as she said all this—"that is exactly the horse I would spend a lot of money to find and own."

He studied her profile in the silvery light. "Sometimes, Mary, folks just naturally delight in owning the best horseflesh they can afford. Even honest folks, sometimes."

"Mister Carlysle . . ."

"Mary, that's my last name, not my first name.

56

Folks call me Hap. Just plain Hap and no mister."

She turned from admiring his horse. "Hap . . . do those four strangers you saw down yonder today worry you very much?"

He shrugged. "They're rough-looking men, Mary. Each one owns two guns, which adds up to eight guns. I've got two guns. Yes, they worry me a little. I don't want to lose my horse or my grub. I don't want them to see you. . . ." He took her hand and turned back with her at his side. "There's no law up here. It'd pay us to look out a little. At least we know they're in the mountains, so they're not going to just ride down onto us."

At the creek she held out her hand although, after he took it, she cleared the creek without needing his help, and afterward they strolled along in the direction of the cabin with her still holding his fingers. She had small, broad, very strong, tanned hands.

She hauled him sharply around when they were in front of the unfinished front wall. "Hap, it's very unmannerly to ask questions straight out. I know that. I grew up knowing that. Least of all personal questions."

He was sure where this was heading, so he freed his hand and began shaking his head as she spoke. She paused then long enough for him to say: "I don't ask and you don't ask, and we get along right well for perfect strangers, don't we? Now come along."

Inside, he heated water for the dishes while she was busy at the table. Several times he felt her studying him.

This third day of their acquaintanceship was different from the previous days. He had returned to the meadow today to discover an almost entirely different woman. True, she still slipped over the edge and went down into her solemnity now and then, but she had smiled, actually smiled at him, and she was no longer reticent. He sighed. Reticent? She was almost at the other extreme from reticent now. He grinned as he worked.

She suddenly said: "What are you smiling about?"

He faced her. "You. It's like knowing two different people. You today and you the two days before today."

"That amuses you?"

"Well, yes, I guess it does. You're nicer today. So much easier to be around. And that first day I worried like the devil that you might be hurt internally and might need a doctor or might even die." He leaned against the wall, looking at her. "I should know you better, eh? You're as tough as a Texas steer."

She leaned to douse their tin plates in hot water. "What a charming compliment," she droned, and he laughed aloud at her.

# VI

He *did* worry about those strangers but he did not mention them to her the following morning before he left the meadow to go prowling, on foot again as he had done the previous day. She was busy in the cabin until the sun was half high, then she went out to salve the roan horse and to explore the meandering creek farther southward in case there was another deep hole or two where large trout lived.

The day was magnificent, but shortly after high noon a faint, high haze hovered around the uppermost rims. Probably no one heeded it because it was thin and diaphanous, scarcely noticeable unless a person looked directly up there. By mid-afternoon, though, it was spreading outward and downward while at the rims it was also assuming thicker, less gauze-like substance.

There was heat. Not as depressing or humid as it had been the time of the electrical storm, but this late in the season even dry heat was noticeable to animals with two or four legs who had been conditioned by a long summer to expect a cool autumn. The creek where Hap knelt to drink and sluice off had the tracks of shod horses going up it. But he had already determined from hiding that there were only two riders and that, although they had both passed along with saddle guns as well as their belt guns, they were traveling without saddlebags, meaning they were not expecting to leave the country. They were instead making a larger version of that on-foot exploration he had seen all four of them indulge in yesterday.

He sat in mottled shade, deciding that at least from appearances these men were not just passing through at all; they were in the mountains for a particular purpose. After watching their exploratory side trips, it was an inescapable conclusion to suspect they were not looking for a particular place—they were looking for a particular *person*. There were actually only his observations coupled to his acute suspicions to base this notion upon and yet, as well as he knew the mountains and much as he had studied the strangers, he could not imagine a single other purpose for them to be up here. They were no wild horses. They were not range cowmen, nor was this cow country. They were not hard-rock miners, nor to his knowledge was there gold or silver up through here. But there *was* a fugitive hiding from the law up here, whose secret hide-out they had not located yet, and those four rough men, hard-looking and thoroughly capable, did indeed resemble manhunters.

He paralleled the course of the two scouts riding up the creek, but was careful—so careful in fact that most of the time even after he caught up with them he was hard put to see them and they never saw him at all. But he had left tracks and the day before he had also left tracks. Maybe the strangers would not find his sign right away but eventually they certainly would—if they were worth their salt as manhunters. It was downright hot and hushed in the heart of the forest. He perspired until his entire shirt, back as well as front, was soaked and dark.

Shadows lengthened and deepened, reflecting the limited loss of daylight above. Hap saw the pair of strangers dismount, slip their bridles and loosen cinches so their animals could drink while the men rolled smokes.

It was not necessary to get close to hear them. Even normal conversation carried in the total silence of the forest. One man said: "God damn' hot, considerin' we're in the shade all the time. Likely goin' to rain or something."

The other man was indifferent to both discomforts. "Heat don't bother me. Not after fifteen years on the south desert near the Mex border. If it rains . . . then it'll just up and have to rain."

"It'll wash out tracks," grumbled the first man, scratching a bearded face.

That indifferent individual also had an answer for this. "We ain't found any so far anyway. . . . I'll tell you what I'm beginnin' to think. This here is a wild-goose chase. The whole darned thing is a wild-goose chase."

The second rider seemed unwilling to commit himself. He in fact changed the subject by saying: "When you come through Curranville, did you see the pretty girls they got at the pool hall and dance floor?"

"See 'em!" exulted the self-assured, detached-acting man. "I done stopped overnight there and played pool, and danced, an' I'm livin' proof to tell you, partner, dancin' ain't all they'll do."

The other man's entire attitude changed. "Really?" Tracks, possible rainfall, and uncomfortable heat suddenly became affairs of such minor relevance he had forgotten them entirely.

The casual individual, a clean-shaven, bold-faced man in his thirties cast a sly, knowing smile toward his companion. "Hey, let's finish scouting this lousy creek, then get back and see if the other fellers'd like to take a day off maybe and lope down there. You ready?"

"Ready! Christ's sake I been ready all season and I ain't even got a single lousy smile from no lady yet."

They snugged up, bitted their animals, and struck out following the creek again. Hap knew this particular little veined waterway. Its source was beneath an enormous black-rock escarpment about six miles north and west. If those two riders persevered, they would not get back to camp before dark but, whether they went all the way to the creek's source or not, they were riding in the opposite direction from the hide-out, which was sufficiently reassuring for him to conclude his own exploration and spying for one more day. He did not have to gain much elevation in order to be upon the level of his hidden meadow and this permitted him to make good time returning.

From the same round knoll covered with thick timber he had crossed the previous day and from which he had a good view of the meadow he saw someone far out, riding his bay horse. He stopped to smile and watch. She had evidently been over through the easterly brakes putting a few miles on the bay to make him lose some of the grass gut. She did not see him even after he had come down the slope behind the cabin, then went over through the shadows on the south side to walk out front. She was at the creek when the bay jumped. He had a particular aversion to water except to drink. He never stepped over a creek; he invariably jumped each creek as though it were the Missouri River.

She was not expecting such a leap, yet not one inch of sunlight showed beneath her and the saddle seat. Hap shook his head. Not many men, let alone many women, would have done that well.

Then she spied him over there, grinning, and eased over into a lope. Some women—even some who rode well—vibrated like jelly when a horse trotted or looped. Not this woman; she was solid and firm all over. When she reined to a halt and slid off to hoist the stirrup leather and begin pulling loose the latigo, she said: "I didn't want you to be mad." She looked up at him. "I guess you didn't really tell me I could ride him. You just said he needed riding. . . ."

He leaned against the cabin wall, watching her off-saddle. "Yeah, lady, I'm mad," he said. "In fact, I'm in a towerin' rage."

She turned, watched him a moment, then softly said: "Care to know something, Hap? You really don't get mad, do you? Care to know something else? I never before knew a man who didn't get furious, and most of the time very easily and quickly. You're an . . . unusual man, Hap."

"Just hungry," he told her, and stepped over to take the saddle and bridle from her as she turned to free his bay horse.

She followed him inside, watched him drape her saddle from its wall peg, and, when he turned, she said: "You forgot your carbine when you went hunting today."

Her gaze was stone steady. Nor did he make any effort to avoid it. "I didn't exactly go hunting today. And you suspected that."

She came closer. "Are they still out there?"

"Yeah. They're making a hunt."

She twisted to look over her shoulder from

where she was stripping kindling to start their supper fire. "Hap . . . a manhunt?"

"I think so, Mary. So far, at least today, they followed the wrong watercourse. Maybe within a few days they'll have backtracked them all . . . including the one that crosses our meadow."

She continued to stand, leaning slightly, watching him. "And when they get here, Hap?"

He shrugged and went over to help her light the fire. "We've got at least tomorrow to figure something." He also leaned, got fire, and carefully nursed it among the shavings. Then he turned his head a little. They were facing one another at very close range. "Mary . . . ?"

"Yes, Hap."

"You're fully recovered. Well, you've still got the scratches and the healing ear, but I mean you are strong and healthy again. You can ride. I watched you a while back. You can ride all the way back down out of here. The roan horse is pretty well recovered, too. His mouth and shoulder are going to need babying for another couple of months but . . ."

"Hap, are you sending me off because those four strangers are in the mountains?"

They straightened up, facing one another. "I'm telling you, Mary, that you're well enough to go back to your folks . . . or your husband . . . I don't know and I never asked. I just know you're strong enough now."

"To ride out of here before they track you down!"

"Mary, they're not going to track me down. Not by a darned sight."

"Because you're going to strike camp and disappear?"

He nodded. "Something like that."

She looked slowly past him at the handsome little cabin, then out over the beautifully serene, sparkling large meadow. "Just . . . leave it all, Hap?"

He said: "Yeah. I love it. That's kind of funny, isn't it? It's been nothing but a hide-out right from the first time I saw it, but I'll tell you something strange about this place . . . everything I ever thought I needed or wanted has come to me here. It's sort of strange how this has happened. Maybe a little spooky. Good weather and water and plenty of feed, straight timber for a house and corrals, isolation and good hunting, even pretty fair fishing, peace . . . and you, Mary. It's kind of uncanny. Like maybe I been all my life aiming to get here and, by golly, I finally made it."

She put her head slightly to one side as she said: "And now you're going to saddle up, turn your back on all of it, Hap, and just ride away and never think of it again?"

"No. I'll think of it. I'll remember it as long as I live . . . Mary . . . all of it." He stood looking steadily at her and this time she did not stiffen, did not give him that impression of a doe poised for flight. She waited as though expecting him to have more to say. When he remained silent, she turned back toward the fire and only spoke to him once again during the course of preparations for supper, when she asked if he could fetch a bucket of water. He went outdoors to do that and stopped over beside the creek to turn slowly and admire his hide-out place in the somber beauty of another fading day.

Then he filled the bucket and started back. She was working at the table and acted as though she had neither seen him nor heard him as he brushed past to set the bucket in its place, then go out back to wash.

It was the first time this particular kind of mood had ever existed between them. He could not define it. He thought she was angry with him or maybe exasperated with him or perhaps just plain disappointed in him. Well, he did not really fear those four manhunters as much as he just did not want to have to fight them. The actual advantage was his; he knew where *they* were and they had no idea exactly where *he* was. But he still did not want to fight them, perhaps even kill one or two of them. And he had always thought this hide-out was a temporary place for him and the bay horse. The trouble was that now, after a year, he knew the area well, had been comfortable here, had in short grown attached to the place.

He was drying his hands when he decided maybe it was more than that. Maybe it was simply that he was at the age of life finally, when moving, riding into new territory every few months, making fresh camps was no longer enough. He had seen a lot of new country. From Fallen Timber to Socorro, from El Paso to Hangtown. It was all different and yet it was all pretty much the same, too.

He draped the towel and turned. She was watching him from the doorway, her face gentle in the shadows, her eyes darker and her mouth set softly. He smiled at her. "Might even miss you a little," he said, and waited for her to move out of the way. "Only woman I ever knew who had an ear mark."

She raised a hand to the healing ear. It would look normal again but close inspection would show a scar from the top halfway down with a tiny V in the rounded top of the ear. She turned without a word and went to the table. As they were eating, she finally said: "When will you leave, Hap?"

He hadn't really thought up to that yet so his answer was vague. "It'll take a little time to get ready. In the past, I just took down the shaving mirror, tossed things into the pack bags, saddled up, and rode off. I've been here since last fall." He did not meet her gaze as he was speaking. "Maybe in a day or two."

"When will those manhunters get here?"

He had to guess about that, also. "I'd say late tomorrow at the least, and day after tomorrow at the most. I saw what they were doing. They're not greenhorns at their work. They're following up the creeks. They know a man up in here has his camp near water."

She said no more until they had finished supper and he was helping her at the washing up, then she dried both hands, put them on her hips, and looked at him. "I guess you're right."

He said—"Yeah."—half-heartedly, believing she meant he had been right about riding on. Then she elaborated and that was not what she had meant at all. "I guess I'm able to ride again, and I've been up here long enough."

When he went out front for his final smoke of the day, to watch the soaring silver moon and the grazing horses and listen to the soft sound of the creek some distance across the meadow, she did not join him. It was a little as it had been before he'd found her—he was alone again.

# VII

In the morning it was more than ever as it had been before. She was gone. So was the blue roan horse. His bay was out there, picking his way closer to the creek. Now and then the bay would lift his head and look all around. A couple of times he nickered. He missed the roan gelding.

Hap had coffee for breakfast. He knew how the bay horse felt. He would have stepped to the unfinished doorway and looked around, too, except that he knew he would not see her, so he finished his coffee and this time, as he left the hide-out to go scout up the manhunters, he took along the Winchester.

He did not expect to find them in the same camp. Nor were they that far southwest. They had moved north a mile or perhaps a mile and a half and now they had established their camp upon the correct creek—the one that led up to his hide-out.

He shook his head over that. They were better at their trade than he had thought they were. Evidently while the two riders he had kept track of yesterday were scouting up one watercourse, the other men were doing the same thing to other creeks. He was sure that by now they had found his old tracks, too.

They were still in camp when he got upon a high slope where he could see down through the clearing to the glade where they were slowly making breakfast, caring for their horses and talking loudly back and forth. The impression they gave Hap Thompson was thoroughly experienced, unhurried, unrelenting men who, like a mountain avalanche, persevered without haste knowing exactly where they were going and taking all the time they wanted to take in getting there. He decided to return, bring in his horse, and start breaking camp. He had no fear of their catching him once he was moving. He would ride directly west, up under the black-rock barranca where eons of sloughing shale would hide his tracks to all but the sharpest eyes.

For a few minutes, though, he hunkered on the side hill, watching the manhunters, feeling bitter over their efficiency, and, as he arose finally to head for the meadow, he also felt bitter over his own damned idiocy in robbing that bank. For all he'd got out of it he might just as well never have entered the building. There was $13,000 in a soiled canvas pouch with leather corners and a broken top hasp under some flat rocks behind the cabin. So far he had not had a chance to spend any of it and in fact so far he hadn't really felt any need for more money than he'd already brought up here with him in his britches pocket. There wasn't a single squirrel, deer, elk, bear, or catamount that would accept a single scrap of greenback currency from him. He sighed, arose, and turned back, carbine cradled loosely in one arm as he took long strides along the homeward trail.

Behind him, the manhunters finally finished eating, tossed their tin plates aside in the grass, and went out to saddle up, to sling gun boots under their fenders and walk back to camp to finish the coffee before riding out.

Now they said very little. One of them carved off a chew from his tobacco plug and spat into the dying fire. Another one, bearded and black-eyed and weathered to the color of ancient leather, swung up, evened his reins, and said: "Jaybird distance apart." He gave a perfect imitation of a scolding blue jay and turned his horse up the hill and across the small meadow.

They had several miles to cover but they were on horses, their animals tough and accustomed to this kind of rough usage. Hap Thompson, albeit with a head start, was on foot.

The sun was misty this morning, which Hap had first noticed when he had gone out back to wash and shave, but the heat was strong again, although up the farthest slopes turning leaves created the effect of a golden, russet, red, and tawny-tan soundless explosion, and that haziness would mean a change in the weather. But this was something to bear in mind only in an incidental way. Hap's foremost need now was to rig up and ride out. And yet as he topped out over the forest hillock behind his cabin, he paused, as he usually did, to look out over the hide-out, the big rich meadow with its watercourse, the dark circlet of big softwood timber, the endless sweep of marching hills and farther mountains. It did not sit well, thinking this was to be the last time he would see it all. Being a range man he summarized the pain of loss and the self-reproach in one word of heartfelt profanity. Then he started down the slope.

His horse was two-thirds of the way across the big meadow, having drunk earlier and being now perfectly willing to graze farther out as he had been doing for a year now. Even when he saw Hap striding toward him the bay horse did not anticipate anything in particular. He was a friendly, docile, wise, big animal. In the years he and Hap had been together he had not once been struck or abused. He was willing to wait and be caught. Even so, it took time to get out there, slip on the tie rope, and start back. The sun behind its haze continued to climb steadily. By the time Hap was back in front of the cabin there was an almost direct flow of brilliance from overhead.

Nor did Hap hurry. But even if he had, there was much more to do striking this camp, as he had told Mary, than there had been before, at any of his other camps, so the sun was slightly off center when he finally went back into the cabin for a final look. He lingered, against his best judgment, to roll and light a smoke, to admire the clean fit of the logs he had slotted so meticulously into each wall. In many places he would never have had to chink them. And the roof. It had just the right pitch to slough off even heavy snow and like the walls it had been put together by a man with all the time in the world. It was strong and plumb and perfectly even from wall to wall.

He dumped the cigarette, said—"God damn

it!"—and turned to step through the door opening. He'd had no way to plane lumber, so that door would have been a challenge. To make it of logs would have been pointless since it would then have been so heavy the stoutest hinges a man could hire some blacksmith to make would never have prevented it from sagging. He had pondered this problem for months. Now he would not have to think about it ever again.

The bay was drowsing as Hap went over to reach for the reins. Suddenly the horse threw up his head, looking up the slope southward of the clearing where the cabin sat. He froze in his tracks, both eyes fixed on something up there, little ears pointing. Hap started to turn, started to step away from the horse to twist and look, when a solitary sharp gunshot sounded from the tall timber some distance farther south than where the horse was peering.

Hap felt the breath of a bullet and sprang clear, aiming for the front of the cabin as his astonished horse shied when dirt exploded upward from the ground, raking his undersides with tiny stones and hard-packed soil. The bay whirled and fled out across his familiar meadow—with the booted Winchester buckled in place, with the laden saddlebags and Hap's bedroll.

A man's strong shout from down where the gunshot had come from elicited a response from another man almost directly behind the cabin up that same low, timbered hill where Hap usually halted on his return to the hide-out each time. A third man sang out, making a hooting sound from on around to the southeast at the narrowest part of the big meadow, over where the creek left the meadow to head down through timber to the grassland miles below. Hap stepped inside, halted, and listened, but if the fourth one was somewhere close, he did not reveal it by making a sound.

He palmed the ivory-stocked six-gun wondering aloud how in the hell they managed to get here so swiftly. Unless, of course, they had scouted up this far before dusk yesterday. He decided the two he had not seen yesterday must indeed have done this. Then a shrinking sensation came over him as he looked out across the meadow where the bay horse was now placidly grazing, fully rigged out. Hap's one box of extra charges for the gun in his right fist were in those distant saddlebags along with the Winchester and the extra loads for it. He had exactly six bullets to use.

The silence returned, settling more ominously than ever before throughout the entire area. Hap cracked the rear door to peer up through the clearing into the big trees for movement. They had him boxed in as neatly as though he had willingly co-operated. Nothing like this had ever happened to him before. But then, as he stood there waiting, listening, and looking, he decided that he had never before been face to face with professional manhunters, either. He had no idea how much of a reward was on his head. He had never seen a single dodger with his name on it, yet he had never doubted but that there were plenty of them. And evidently his feeling that as time passed, as the Wanted posters gathered dust, his chances would improve was quite ignoring the fact that for professionals like those four men, closing their surround today, the rules of the game were different. They, too, were satisfied for time to pass, for everyone, including the fugitive, to grow lax and careless.

A magpie squawked back up the side hill behind the cabin. Hap had a glimpse of vivid white and black as the big bird flung itself furiously off a perch and went hurriedly out over the meadow. Magpies were usually raffish, bold birds. They did not frighten easily. Hap eased the door closed a fraction more and eased up along the nearside log wall to wait. But whoever he was, up there, he did not show so much as a hat brim. Yet without much doubt he was creeping closer. Hap had cut back the nearest trees for cabin-logs as well as for firewood, so the manhunter could only get just so close without sacrificing his cover. Even so, by the time the man got that close, he would have a perfect sighting all along the rear of the cabin and meanwhile the other three would be edging in from other directions.

It was a long wait. The sun was sliding midway

along the afternoon sky before a sound of any kind came to Hap, sweating inside his house, safe enough from bullets, at least from *most* bullets. A man's voice sounding surprisingly close and seeming not to be raised at all suddenly said: "Carlysle Thompson! There are four of us. It's up to you. We been at this business a long time. You aren't goin' anywhere except out of the shack . . . standin' up or flat out, feet first. Take all the time you need to think about it. We're in no hurry and sure as hell you aren't in any hurry."

As though to lend emphasis someone fired a saddle gun. Hap heard the bullet strike solidly into the logs of his incomplete front wall. He guessed that one, whoever he was, had to be somewhere out in the tall grass of the meadow. Prone, no doubt, hidden as well as though he were back in the timber. One in front, one behind, and the other two probably on each end of the cabin. He dried sweat from a clammy palm down the seam of his britches. With six bullets he could not afford to waste a single slug. Answering their gunfire was of course what they would want to bait him into doing. But even if he'd had the cartridges and his saddle gun, he would not have done that. He'd never had to fort-up like this before, but by instinct he was not a furiously hostile individual. He was calm and careful. He was also a very practical man; if he got out of this without being shot, it would be simply because those bounty men out yonder figured he was more worthwhile alive than dead.

"Thompson? We always offer a fair proposition . . . first. There's six thousand bounty on you. Come out arms in the air, make no trouble on the ride down out of here, and we'll give you one thousand of it for a lawyer. That's our only offer. We figure it's fair, and we're businessmen just like a storekeeper or a blacksmith . . . or them bankers you cleaned out. How does that sound to you?"

Hap believed the calm-voiced man, for some reason he could not have specifically defined, except that the man spoke firmly and resolutely. Nor was such a proposition unheard of. Man-hunters, too, were vulnerable to gunfire. Any way they could avoid risk, within reason anyway, they were commonly willing to take.

The odds were completely against Hap. Whether this was entirely his fault—and he thought that it was—or not did not alter a thing. He had six bullets and one gun. There were four men out there, professionals at their trade, with two guns each, a carbine and a handgun, and plenty of ammunition. The only advantage Hap had was cover. He could keep them out, maybe all tonight and maybe even tomorrow as well, but there was another factor worth considering. They were probably not the most patient individuals on earth and the sod atop his cabin roof had cured, dead grass growing like the hair on a dog's back all over it. One firebrand flung up there could possibly turn his cabin into a blazing over-size coffin.

He barred the rear door without a sound and stepped carefully over to the front wall to look out. There was nothing to be seen, nor had he thought there would be even though one of those men was out in the grass somewhere, more vulnerable to lead poisoning than the others.

"Thompson?"

Hap waited, but this time the strong-voiced man had nothing to say; he seemed simply to want an acknowledgement that Hap was in there. Hap did not answer, so that man tried again.

"Hey, Thompson!"

Hap waited but he was not called by name again.

A bad hush settled. Far out his horse was serenely grazing; otherwise, there was nothing to be seen but sky and grass and distant timber and that misty, hot sunlight that seemed to be cooling just a little as the afternoon wore along. Finally a horse nickered, but that was all, and he had not done it loudly enough for the bay to have heard him, so Hap's animal went ambling out of direct sunlight to the forest fringe, full as a tick, to stand in tree shade and doze away what remained of the long, silent afternoon.

Hap drank water twice and finished a piece of cold fish left over from the day before. He smoked a cigarette, holstered his Colt, and sweated.

There were thin little forest shadows emerging when that strong-voiced bounty man called to him again in the same detached-sounding, impersonal tone of voice.

"Got a decision yet, *amigo*? It won't get any better waiting for night. You aren't going to slide out of there in the dark. We got some decent grub back in camp. Come on out and let's all of us head back for some coffee and supper."

From behind the cabin a different, more gruff and unpleasant voice said: "Thompson! You ain't worth a damn to yourself dead. But you're worth just as much to us that way. Use your damned head. You got a chance with a lawyer, and with a gun you ain't got a single chance at all!"

It was a convincing form of logic. Hap had another drink of water and kept silent.

# VIII

His strategy had evolved out of necessity. Because he had not decided upon a course of action yet and also because he was not entirely sure there was any way out of this except *their* way he had nothing yet to tell them. They seemed to accept his silence the first hour or so as the result of his surprise at finding himself caught or at least cornered. They had sounded persuasive and impersonal, willing to reason with him and even to negotiate to the extent of giving him part of the bounty money. But midway through the second hour his silence seemed to trouble them, to stir doubts to life, and, when they called to him now, they were more menacing although they persisted in their earlier offer. But as the shadows began to darken, at least up among the timber stand, the manhunters evinced a creeping form of anxiety about his silence. One man called to another one suggesting that, somehow or other, the cabin was empty. It was this hint of doubt that gave Hap an indication that being silent had helped him in a way he had not anticipated. He did not have them on the defensive but he had them wondering and worrying.

How he might be able to exploit this he had no idea but there had to be a way. It and six slugs were all he had going for him as the afternoon steadily waned. When nightfall arrived, he might have that on his side, too, but the manhunters were also going to be protected by darkness. If they decided to fire his cabin, that would be the one time when they could successfully get close enough to throw firebrands atop the roof. Could he get out of the cabin *before* they got close? He considered the idea. There were two particular perils. One, of course, was that they would be watching both doors like hawks, and, as darkness came, they certainly would move in closer in order to be able to keep a better vigil. The other peril was that he had deliberately cleared an area around the cabin for some little distance. Originally he had been motivated in this by his need for handy timber for building but also he had done it to create a fire break all around the house. Now, unless it was very dark and unless he could slither snake-like and unless they were not close by and intently vigilant, he would be unable to escape this way. The alternative, of course, was to remain inside and pray they did not try to burn him out.

Their advantage, aside from numbers, was maneuverability. While he had to remain stationary inside the cabin, they could move almost at will. He would have no idea where they were in darkness until one of them saw him or until he stumbled upon one of them.

He drank water, peered out back, carefully looked out front, paced the cabin from end to end, and perspired. Otherwise the silence ran on and on. Maybe the manhunters would welcome the darkness. They were knowledgeable at their trade, he knew that, and they would no doubt have experienced similar situations before.

A blue jay squawked south of the cabin but not very distant. Behind the cabin up across the clearing in among the trees another bird scolded. Hap shook his head. He had spent hours imitating the jays for no particular reason except that they had been his most persistent and raucous critics ever since he had arrived here and he had amused himself scolding back at them, something that invariably threw them into a rage. He knew an imitation when he heard one but mostly because he knew the habits of blue jays. They would not be up there in the timber as long as people were close by.

As time passed the blue jay calls seemed to serve as a means for the manhunters to let each other know where they were or where they were moving to. And they were closing in. Hap could have guessed that without bird calls simply because it was the reasonable thing to do; as the shadows crept closer, so did the men who were utilizing them for protection.

The rear door was barred and Hap stood longest where he could see out the front doorless opening. Fifty yards from the cabin the tall grass began. It was rank and in most places it was also waist-high. If he could get out that far undetected, he could crawl on all fours without being visible. There was a man out there. Maybe there was more than one man by now, but earlier, when they had first arrived, he had heard one out there.

If he left the cabin, he had to do it by either the front or back door. The manhunters knew this by now as well as Hap knew it. If they were positioned to be able to watch both doors, his chances were two-to-one against success. He wondered if they would be content to wait him out until daybreak. If he could feel fairly certain of this, he would not have to try to escape, at least not tonight, and he rather thought they probably would not risk their lives in the darkness by an attack on the cabin when they did not have to. His fullest impression of those four men was that they did not take unnecessary chances at all, that they were professionals with all the detached knowledge and experience of men who did not try to bring in fugitives because of any love of the law, just of bounty money, and, when manhunting was reduced to that level, it became a business exactly as they had called out to him. They would know every option available to Hap, would know every way to thwart his limited capabilities, and would kill him in a moment if they felt this was necessary or maybe even just convenient for them.

He made a smoke, his last for the day, and leaned along the front wall, straining to detect sound of any kind as the fading light turned slightly amber. There were not even any more blue jay calls. He could have called out. At least one of them would have replied. But his lengthy silence was a weapon by this time. Not the best imaginable weapon but then he did not have very good weapons of any kind. As though this were a free-traveling thought and had infiltrated a second mind, that strong-voiced man called out again.

"Thompson! Listen to me! You can't get away

when it gets dark. There's no way for you to do that. You can't even poke your head out a door without us bustin' it like a punky melon. And you won't have any better chance come daylight again. By now you know we got you. Just toss out the gun and walk out, hands high. You'll get guaranteed passage down to the jailhouse at Curranville. We got not a damned thing against you personal. Our job was to find you and fetch you in and get paid for doing it. That's all. And we already give you a darned fair chance. We'll pay you one thousand greenbacks out of the reward money for just comin' along without no fuss. Otherwise, Thompson, we're going to fire the shack and shoot you by firelight when it gets so hot you got to run for it. Thompson, this time you got ten minutes to make up your mind. Walk out or roast. Answer within ten minutes!"

It had been a lengthy, unimpassioned statement, the kind Hap could believe in, and he did; that spokesman out there had sounded absolutely sincere each time he had called to Hap. Maybe, if he surrendered to them, he might be able to escape in the forest on the ride down to Curranville. Or possibly escape from their custody on their way down to the camp. He grunted derisively at himself for thinking such things. They were clever enough to corner and perhaps capture him; they were clever enough to make certain once he was in their custody that he would not escape. It was pure wishful thinking to entertain ideas of escaping from them.

The ten minutes came and went. He did not call out and for another ten minutes that strong-voiced man did not call back. But eventually he did.

"It's your funeral, Thompson. We been patient all afternoon. That's long enough."

There was no grisly threat, no profanity arising from fierce resentment or frustration. Hap had by this time come to the conclusion that they were a coldly practical foursome. If they had decided they had been patient long enough, Hap was now going to be introduced to whatever second phase of manhunting they had in their bag of tricks. He could guess what it was. Fire the cabin as the spokesman had said and drop him by the light of his own burning house when heat drove him out. One thing was becoming more evident with the passage of time; he had to make some kind of move, had to take the initiative. Darkness would help, perhaps not as much as he hoped, but it would help some. But whatever he did had to be motivated by desperation. He had to get out of the cabin. Of course they also knew that. Nevertheless he had to do it, so he knelt by the rear door, opened it a fraction, and watched the darkening gloom across the stumped-over clearing. There was a man up there. He was as certain of that as he was of anything. If it would be possible to reach the trees his chance of escaping would measurably increase. But he was certain that manhunter up the slope had the clearing and the rear of the house under constant surveillance. And there was a moon. Most of the month there would not have been. It seemed, the longer he crouched there thinking, that nothing was in his favor, not even the likelihood that if they saw him and opened up, that they would miss. They were not the kind of men who missed often. A regular posse or a band of irate range men or townsmen or farmers would miss more often than they would connect, but even in this the odds were stacked against him.

He got a long piece of firewood, opened the door more, leaned down as low as he could, and eased his hand, then his arm, far out until he felt the touch of the bench Mary had placed out there for a washstand. He waited, then roughly shoved and the bench grated over hardpan making a distinct sound. The very next moment a gun flashed orangely up the slope no more than two hundred feet away and a bullet splattered with a meaty sound inches above the bench.

Hap left the kindling out there, pulled back, and softly closed the door. For someone making a sound shot, that manhunter was either awfully lucky or awfully accurate. Hap surmised it was the latter and leaned on the wall for a moment before crossing to the front wall to sink to one knee, ease around until he could see out and listen.

No one called inquiringly about that gunshot. There was no sound outside at all. After a while he got two more pieces of firewood from over by the stone fireplace. One he pitched to his left as far as he could fling it. It struck and rattled along the ground. Nothing happened over there. He waited a long time, then tried it again, hurling the second piece of wood even farther. Where it landed, there was matted grass and the sound was more like a series of rustling footfalls against dry under-growth, but there still was no reaction, at least none that he could detect.

While he was concentrating on the area northward, something solid rubbed the opposite corner of the front wall. Hap sucked back on instant reflex but again nothing happened. He pulled back, then stood up. That had sounded like someone's hip holster rubbing against wood, as though perhaps someone had been along the south side when he had hurled the sticks and had brushed close to the south wall as he advanced to the corner to peer around.

He moved soundlessly across to the opposite side of the unfinished front wall, got close to that far corner, then leaned and tried to peer through the unchinked logs. There was not much daylight left but it was brighter outside than it was inside and he was able to see fairly well within the limited scope of the slit he was peering through. But there was nothing moving. A man could have been standing a foot from him out there, but as long as he did not move, Hap could not make him out, so he waited, scarcely breathing and with apprehension increasing with each passing moment. They were up to *something,* he was as certain of that as he was of their presence as dusk settled and the mountains on all sides of his hide-out meadow descended steadily into a scaling darkness.

It was a long wait. He was about to abandon it when a soft blur of soundless movement occurred just beyond the crack between two wall logs he was peering through. The movement was to Hap's left, in the direction of the doorless opening. There may have been time for speculation, but he did not indulge in it; he simply straightened up, also moving soundlessly toward the door hole, but he stopped two feet south of the doorway, raised his six-gun, thumb on the gnarled flange of the hammer, and scarcely breathed. The man upon the opposite side of the log wall from him still did not make a sound. Hap had to guess he was also flattening upon the outside wall but perhaps a foot closer to the door opening.

Moments passed, the tension drew out almost to the breaking point, then someone out back moved the bench just enough so that it would make a faintly abrasive sound upon the hardpan and Hap almost succumbed to the instinctive reaction of anyone in his position—he was almost momentarily diverted. At the very last second he steeled himself to watch the doorway.

A man's thick, crouching body came weaving to the left just enough to show chest, head, and shoulders, and a gun hand swinging as one of the manhunters strained slightly from the waist to peer through the interior darkness for his target. Hap's gun barrel came down hard on the gun wrist; his other hand lunged and caught a fistful of cloth. The manhunter made a deep, wrenching sound of pain, like a cough, then Hap dug in both heels and hauled the man inside, off balance so that, as he dropped his six-gun from the broken wrist, he struggled to hold his balance by flinging out his right hand and arm. He encountered bone and muscle.

Hap swung the gun barrel a second time, much higher. The stranger was falling, head forward as he catapulted through the doorway. The gun barrel came down across the man's neck just below the skull in back. Hap released his grip of his shirt front and the manhunter fell in a heap.

For ten seconds Hap waited, listening for others, then he leaned and rolled the unconscious man onto his back. Very dark and sightless eyes stared past him at the dark ceiling. The manhunter was deeply unconscious.

Hap dragged him clear and left him outflung on the floor, picked up the six-gun, shoved it into his britches front, and stood motionless, half expecting another attacker to come through the doorway.

No one appeared. The night was as silent as ever, and, as the moments passed, Hap decided the other manhunters were waiting for a gunshot that they expected would signal the killing of Carlysle Thompson. He obliged them. He aimed at the ground and squeezed off a shot that sounded cannon-loud in a muffled way inside his cabin.

Then he went over by the doorless opening and continued to wait. If they thought that stalker had killed him, they would come. If not, they would stay out there trying to imagine what had happened.

They did not come, so evidently the stalker was supposed to call out after he had killed Carlysle Thompson or perhaps signal with another gunshot. Hap eventually went over to peek out back, but the man who had moved the bench to distract him was gone. Just trees and shadows and cooling night air greeted him.

He was damp with cold perspiration. Clearly, since he had not responded to their offer as they had thought he should have, they decided not to waste more time but to take him back down out of here belly-down across his saddle.

As time passed they were bound to reach a conclusion that had to be accurate—*their* man had not fired that solitary gunshot, which had to mean

*Thompson* had fired it. Perhaps that would inspire fear or at least respect; they might decide now either to wait for daylight to finish their work at Thompson's hide-out—or to fire his cabin.

# IX

He squandered a little water by trickling it upon his injured manhunter, to no effect. The man was breathing, his right wrist flopped, and he did not respond to cold water or to anything else. Hap had struck him hard.

He searched the manhunter, came up with a Bowie-style boot knife and a .41 under-and-over Derringer. He also found a flat packet of greenbacks in what seemed to be large denominations. Evidently Hap was not the only outlaw these men had tracked down lately.

He used the man's trouser belt to lash both ankles tightly together and left the man's arms free. One wrist was broken and the man was disarmed.

Time passed. Hap tried to conjecture what they were doing out there. If they had all crept to a rendezvous to discuss what had happened, he could probably escape. At least it seemed they might have done this, so he went back to open the rear door and listen. It was too dark to see anything. Then he swore under his breath, closed and re-barred the door. There was still a man up there. He had picked up the faint, unmistakable aroma of tobacco smoke.

What seemed like a lifetime but was in fact about an hour passed without incident, and Hap speculated on their reasons for not firing his cabin. At the end of the hour he made an interesting discovery. His prisoner groaned and weakly moved on the ground. Hap went over and watched the man struggle up out of his feelingless void. It took time and the first thing the man-hunter did when consciousness returned was grit his teeth against the pain in his right wrist.

Hap sank to one knee so the man could see him better. Even then he could not have appeared very distinctly. It was as dark inside as it could possibly be, except perhaps on a night when there was no moon at all.

He said: "Just keep quiet, mister. Don't move your right arm and it won't hurt so much. You've got a busted wrist. I can't set it because there's nothing in here to use. You hear me all right?"

The manhunter stopped moving his right arm and he did not speak, so he had at least understood the admonitions.

Hap leaned a little closer. "That was pretty stupid, trying to shoot me from the doorway."

The man groaned and ground his teeth. "My head," he murmured.

"You'll make it. You're not shot. You just got hit. Why don't they fire the cabin?"

The manhunter closed his eyes in pain, then gradually opened them again as Hap leaned a hand upon the man's shoulder, shaking him a little. "I was out there . . . to light a piece of pitch pine and fling it up there . . . when I heard someone . . . sounded like someone was north of the cabin a few yards. I eased around to see if it was you. . . ."

"And you saw the door?"

"Yeah. Figured I'd have a look inside."

"What will your friends do now? They know you didn't shoot me."

The manhunter gritted his teeth again. He was in bad pain, probably less pain in his right wrist than in his head. "I don't know what they'll do. But come daylight, they'll smoke you out. They're going to kill you now, Thompson."

Hap left the man and returned to the front wall. The night was hushed the way it normally would have been except that now there was a distinct feeling of hazard. He considered rolling a smoke but neglected to do it as the prisoner groaned again. Hap went back over there. Without much doubt the pain was very bad. He had nothing to alleviate it, but he wished he did have. He had nothing really against the manhunter—as an individual—and he had never enjoyed watching people or animals suffer. He said: "The whiskey's out in my saddlebags on the bay horse."

His captive looked at him, then slowly closed his eyes.

It was beginning to turn cold. He had wood enough over by the fireplace to warm up the cabin, but he made no move to go over there. The glow from an open hearth would be an invitation to someone out yonder to try a few exploratory shots.

Still, as the hours dragged along and the cold increased, he thought several times of trying to build a fire small enough to minimize the glow and still warm the cabin. There was nothing wrong with the idea; it just would not work was all.

His prisoner waited until Hap was close, then said: "You know who Spade Leggett is?"

Hap had no idea. "No."

"He's the feller out there who's going to execute you for puttin' us to all this trouble. That's who he is. He's the best bounty man between here and Council Bluffs. You maybe eluded all the others but not Spade Leggett. We been on your tracks for two months."

"How did you know I was up in here?"

The suffering man might have shown some sign of triumph if he had felt better. All he did was look steadily up at Hap. "Ain't no fugitive alive who don't go into a town somewhere sooner or later. Folks remember faces of strangers, Thompson. A storekeeper in Curranville recognized you from the pictures Spade and the town marshal showed him. And we wasn't really lookin' for you. We was trackin' down a feller named Farnham for stage robbin', but you're worth as much as Farnham, so we commenced huntin' you down. Thompson, you should have taken Spade's offer. Now . . . it's too damned late."

"If they fire the cabin, you're goin' up with it."

"They won't fire it. Not with me in here. An' they don't have to fire it. All they got to do is set around here and wait. No one's comin' along to help you and there's nothin' around here to keep you goin' very long. You got to go out of here. Sooner or later, Thompson, you're goin' out that door."

Hap shook his head. "Not when they aim to kill me anyway."

"Sure you will," averred the prisoner. "Even if you try to do it with a gun in each hand, you're goin' to try it, because when the water runs out, you can't hang on for more'n maybe another three, four days. Sure you'll go out of here, Thompson."

Hap and the manhunter exchanged a long look. The manhunter was right. Sooner or later, one way or another, Hap had to go out of here. He smiled thinly. "When I do, *amigo*, you and I are going out together . . . but with you in front."

He returned to the front wall. The silence outside was as solid and deep as ever. It troubled him that they could play their game of cat-and-mouse with him and there was nothing he could do, at the very least, to worry or harass them.

Behind him the prone captive huskily said: "Water."

Hap got him some and supported him while he drank, then eased his back down. The manhunter surprised him by saying: "Thanks."

Hap continued to lean there, down on one knee. "What's your name?" he asked.

The manhunter answered easily: "Lew. But it won't mean nothin' to you, Thompson."

"Maybe not, Lew. What are they doing . . . just waiting?"

"Sure. That's the best thing we do, once we run a feller to earth . . . wait him out. Why do something stupid and maybe get shot?"

"Like you did when you came to the doorway?"

Lew did not like that. "I did it because I heard something. It could have been you sneakin' along the front of the house to nail me when I lit the pitch wood to fling it on the roof. I had to be sure."

Hap said: "And suppose they decide to burn the cabin now?"

Lew was firm about that. "They won't. Not with me in here."

"You're sure? Maybe they think you're dead."

"Naw. There was no shooting."

"Yes there was. After I cold-cocked you, I fired once into the ground."

Lew watched Hap's face. "What the hell did you do that for?"

"Because I figured they expected it. They figured you'd shoot me. So I helped the idea along." Hap smiled but it was not very clear in the darkness. "I wanted them to come and look inside, too. But they didn't come. So, maybe they think I nailed you."

Lew lay, staring straight at Hap. For the first time in their talks Lew had no answer. He evidently was beginning to believe his companions might fire the cabin after all. Eventually he said: "It ain't going to do you any good at all, holdin' out like this. It's not too late to make terms with Spade."

Hap gently wagged his head. "I got a hunch it is too late and I'm not going to put it to a test . . . throw out the guns and go out there to be blown down."

He waited, but if Lew wanted to protest or argue, he did not get a chance. There was a thin rind of pearly dawn light over against the eastern rims and somewhere outside a jay bird answered, this one north of the cabin.

Hap said: "The war's startin' again. I hope they don't ground sluice through the doorway or they'll kill you sure as hell." He started to arise.

Lew squawked: "Move me, damn it. Drag me over away from the doorway!"

Hap turned and crossed to the front wall to listen

but now the silence was fully down again. He could detect a faint paleness. Up here at the hide-out, though, sunshine did not reach into the big meadow until nearly mid-morning. Daylight would arrive, gray and softly bright with fair visibility, but real sunshine would not reach here for another two hours. Hap was accustomed to this, knew what it was like beforehand, and also knew when the sun would finally climb higher than the rims. He had no objection to a cool, prolonged morning without eye-squinting brilliance, for while extensive visibility was not forthcoming, he could see all the way across the meadow and that was good enough. But when he leaned to peer through cracks in the front wall logs, although he could see his horse out there, still wearing the saddle and bridle, that was all he saw. If one of those manhunters was still low in the yonder tangled tall grass, he was not visible from the cabin.

He shook his head. These had to be the most casual manhunters he had ever heard of. What confirmed this, about an hour later when daylight was firmly over the mountains, was an aroma he detected that seemed to come from the south-westerly hillside. Well, maybe that was the way to do a job of manhunting, after all. Certainly he had never heard of anything like this before, and yet, according to Lew, Spade Leggett was a very successful manhunter, so perhaps Leggett's system was the best. And the aroma made his stomach growl; it had been a very long while with nothing but water in it. Very probably it was going to be another long while in the same condition. He rolled and lit a smoke, got Lew another drink of water when he called for it, and offered Lew the smoke but Lew turned it down. Then he said: "How's your headache?"

"Better'n it was but my neck's sore as a boil."

Hap could appreciate that. It had been his neck, not his head, that had caught the force of that overhand blow. "What the hell ever got you started in this business?" Hap asked.

Lew changed his mind about smoking, so Hap rolled him one, lit it, and handed it over. Lew smoked left-handedly. His right hand, wrist, and most of his right arm were badly discolored and hugely swollen, but the pain did not seem to bother him much, or, if it was troubling him, he refused to let Hap know about it.

"More money in manhunting," he explained to Hap, "than there is in ridin' for cow outfits or toolin' stagecoaches, or swampin' for freighters or blacksmithin'." He blew smoke and regarded Hap stonily. "More money than there is in robbin' banks, some of the time, and my way you get to spend it. *Your* way, you don't."

"They haven't buried me yet, Lew," Hap stated, dropped his cigarette, and ground it underfoot. Outside, one of those blue jays squawked again, and this time it was daylight so it could have been a genuine bird but both the men in the cabin knew otherwise.

Hap returned to the front wall, leaned, and peered out. Someone was riding down through the trees to the northward. Hap remained glued to the wall, staring. All he could make out at first was that it was a solitary horseman. He had no idea who would be coming from that rough country climaxed by these forbidding black-rock barrancas. It was certainly not impossible for a rider to cross over from the far side of the rims—Hap had done it last year—but a man would have to be particularly motivated to try it and this rider did not appear to be straddling a tired horse. Also he could not possibly have crossed over this morning, so he had either come part way before dark last night and had camped up there somewhere, or else he had not come over the rims at all but had perhaps angled around the hide-out from some other direction and was now coming straight down into the meadow.

Hap was certain he was not one of the manhunters, but to satisfy himself on this point he called back to Lew. "Which one of your friends rides a big chestnut horse with a light mane and tail?"

Lew answered promptly: "None of them. Why?"

"There's someone coming out through the trees from the north on that kind of a horse."

Lew considered this before saying: "It won't do you no good. Spade'll nail him before he can cross over to the shack."

The big burnished-copper horse cleared the last row of dark trees; his rider, heading out into the brightening daylight, saw the cabin and reined to a halt out there. He was too far for saddle gun range and the way he remained that far out made Hap wonder about him. Of course, he could be just a grubliner, a drifter, or maybe some range man who had been pot hunting, but whoever he was, one thing seemed evident, he had sense enough not to ride any closer.

A blue jay called twice rapidly, paused, then did the same thing again. From behind Hap the injured manhunter said: "They see him. That's the call to palaver. Is he still coming?"

"No. He's sittin' out there beyond range, just looking things over."

"You recognize him?"

"He's too far off, but I wouldn't know him anyway."

Lew was unperturbed, curious and interested but not at all worried. "Spade'll settle with him."

Hap grunted over that. If Spade Leggett was going to settle with the well-mounted stranger, he was going to have to ride out into the open to do it because the stranger showed no urge to ride closer to the cabin.

Lew said: "What's goin' on?"

There was nothing going on. The stranger on his handsome big horse was still out there as motionless as a carving, and, as far as Hap could see, no one had as yet moved forth from the forest to intercept him. Then the stranger saw Hap's saddled horse and veered at a slow walk over in that direction. Hap's bay was a friendly, gregarious animal; he not only did not turn tail, but, after watching the big chestnut horse for a while, he decided to meet him halfway and went ambling toward him, dragging his reins to one side after the manner of many bridle-wise horses so as not to step on the reins and yank the bit against his teeth and tongue.

Without a doubt the three remaining manhunters were watching all this from hiding. What their reaction might be Hap had to guess and he thought perhaps Lew was right, Spade Leggett, or one of the other manhunters anyway, would eventually ride forth to meet the stranger.

The sun was coming. Its flaring rays shot upward all along the uneven eastern horizon. Warmth was increasing and that haziness that had been lingering for the past day or so was no longer in evidence. It was going to be a typically golden, Indian-summer day. Like all days—good and bad ones—the universe seemed not in the least concerned over the tribulations of individuals. Nature followed out her seasonal sequences with a calm and magnificent indifference. Men might be crouching inside an uncompleted log cabin, hungry and gritty-eyed, soiled and unshaven, and neither the approaching sun nor the soft-pale high heavens knew it or cared about it.

Lew's curiosity about the interloper prompted him to ask several times for information, but when Hap simply grunted or answered curtly, the injured manhunter finally ceased asking. What held Hap's interest was the way the stranger out across the meadow had dismounted to free Hap's bay of its bridle and saddle, dump the equipment in the grass, and allow the horse to continue grazing unburdened. Only one thing did the stranger retain as he swung back up across his saddle—Hap's saddle gun. With this balancing across his lap, the stranger finally turned back toward the cabin and within moments Hap saw two riders emerge, walking their mounts out toward the stranger. One rider was coming from the south, the other from the east of the cabin. Both were mounted on bay horses and both also had saddle guns but neither man had removed his Winchester; they were still butt up in the saddle boots.

Hap was satisfied that those two were part of the manhunting crew. He could not see them well enough to relay a description to Lew but their identity did not really matter to him as much as their purpose. He had misgivings. Unless that stranger on the handsome chestnut horse was careful and experienced, he might be riding into trouble. One thing Hap felt confident about was that those manhunters would try and get rid of the interloper. They could hardly attack the cabin while an uninvolved stranger was around to watch. At least they dared not do this if they intended to kill the forted-up fugitive. At least these thoughts, groundless or not, filed through Hap's mind as he watched.

The stranger suddenly halted and raised Hap's saddle gun in one hand to wave off the manhunters with it. He called something to them. Hap could make out the deep call but not the words. The manhunters halted. The three of them were beyond six-gun-range. At least they were beyond any hope of *accurate* six-gun-range.

They spoke loudly back and forth. Again, although Hap could distinguish sound, he could not make out words. The distance was far too great. It occurred to him that, while his foes were concentrating upon the stranger, two of them anyway, he could conceivably slip out the back way. But when he turned to glance back there, Lew said: "Hell, I figured you'd have tried it long ago. And you go right ahead. You figure Leggett's a fool? Go ahead, open the back door."

Hap hesitated, then crossed the room and lifted the bar. He set it soundlessly aside, reached to ease the door open, and within seconds a drawling voice said: "You ready to come out and give up, are you, Thompson?"

He replaced the bar and saw Lew watching as he started toward the front wall again. Lew wasn't smiling but he surely would have been if he hadn't still been in considerable pain. He said: "Who's out there with the stranger?"

Hap did not answer but went close to the doorway where he could see. They were still palavering out there as he watched. The stranger gestured again with Hap's Winchester. Both the manhunters turned back toward the cabin. Hap began to have a poor feeling about this. The stranger would not allow either of those manhunters to ride beside him, but, as they progressed, he did allow himself to get close enough for six-gun range, which Hap suspected might be a bad mistake. Then all three stopped again. This time it was the manhunters who refused to get any closer to the cabin. They pointed and gestured, the stranger listened, then said something, and urged his horse directly toward the front of the cabin, the saddle gun riding loosely across his lap.

Hap had a good look at the stranger. He was wearing a pelt-lined leather vest, had a gray Stetson canted down to shield his ruddy features, and was gray enough at the temples to seem to be more than perhaps forty. He was a medium-sized man but thickly made with powerful shoulders and arms.

He halted a few yards out front, sat gazing at the cabin, then called out: "Thompson!"

Hap heard authority in the strong voice. He did not answer but he straightened up and moved closer to the door. Behind him Lew asked who had called. Evidently Lew knew the voices of his companions and had not recognized this man's voice.

"Thompson, if you're in there, answer me, because I'm comin' in!"

Hap still said nothing. A moment later the burly man stepped to the ground, draped the Winchester from a bent elbow, and walked forward. Hap palmed his Colt. In the shadows Lew said: "Is he really coming?"

Hap answered without taking his eyes off the stranger. "Yeah, he's coming."

"Who the hell is he?"

Hap did not reply. The stranger was less than a hundred feet away with morning sunlight on him when he halted and spoke less loudly this time.

"Thompson! Hold your fire." The stranger leaned and put Hap's saddle gun on the ground. He was still armed with a worn six-gun showing scarred walnut grips as he hooked both gloved hands in his shell belt. "Answer!" he snapped.

Hap had listened to them all in dogged silence up to this point. Now, because he knew the stranger was going to come inside and because he had no desire whatever to shoot the man, he said: "Toss down the six-gun, too, mister!"

The burly man did not even hesitate. He pulled out his Colt and leaned to place it also on the ground, then, as he straightened back, began tugging off his rider's gloves. Next he walked slowly and purposefully to the doorway of the cabin.

Up close he looked a little older and somewhat heavier than he had at a distance. He had a square-jawed face with a wide, tough-set, lipless mouth and the eyes in hat brim shade were as direct and steady as blue-washed creek pebbles. He neither moved nor spoke when his eyes became sufficiently adjusted to the interior gloom to make out Hap, standing directly ahead, ivory-handled cocked Colt at his side. Then the man saw Lew and grunted, either in sympathy or surprise, and stepped inside.

Hap aimed the gun. "Hold that vest away from your body!"

The burly man obeyed, his eyes drifting again from Hap to the injured man.

Hap said: "Have you a boot knife or a belly gun?"

The stranger shook his head, showing something like disdain as he said: "I don't need things like that." He pointed. "How bad off is he?"

"Broken wrist and a neck ache." When the burly man started to move, Hap halted him with a short question. "Who are you?"

"My name is Henry Blondell. I keep an eye on cattle down along the foothills. That answer you?"

"Not by a damned sight. What did you and those other fellers talk about when you finished off-saddling my horse?"

"They told me who you were. Showed me a Wanted poster on you and said you'd killed one of their crew." Henry Blondell's voice was gruff and curt, but it did not seem particularly hostile. "I guess they just figured you'd killed this feller. But he sure don't look very good."

Lew said: "He caught me from behind, clubbed me down, and broke my wrist. He'd have killed me if he'd dared. Mister, did you talk to Spade Leggett out there?"

Henry Blondell sauntered over and stood gazing at the immensely swollen and discolored hand, then he knelt, fished forth a pocket knife, and neatly slit the straining cloth and made a little clucking sound at the sight of the bluish-mottled swollen arm. "Yeah, I talked to a feller out there said his name was Leggett. Cowboy, that arm looks like hell." Henry Blondell twisted to glance up at Hap. "You got anything to make splints with in here?"

"No. And he's not going to die, so for now forget about him."

Blondell continued to kneel, gazing up at Hap, then he shook his head and lumbered back upright. "You're not goin' out of here, Thompson, if those men outside have anything to say about it."

Hap did not consider this a major revelation. Not after being forted up since yesterday morning. "I think you'd better stay in here, too," he told the cowman. "Did you come up here alone?"

Instead of replying, Henry Blondell fished around for some cut plug, gnawed off a corner while studying Hap and the ivory-gripped Colt aimed at his chest, put away the plug, and sighed. "Let 'em take you," he said around his cud of chewing tobacco. "I'll ride down to Curranville with you. Make plumb certain you get there."

Hap showed a bleak small smile. "You against those three? I reckon not."

"You got food in here?" Blondell glanced around and shook his head. "Don't look like it. How long you figure you can hold out?"

Lew spoke up waspishly. "I been reasonin' with the pig-headed damned fool and he won't listen."

Blondell did not take his eyes off Hap and for some reason Hap began to wonder about Henry Blondell. He did not seem hostile even though he knew who Carlysle Thompson was—a fugitive from the law, an outlaw with a bounty on him.

"Then stay," the cowman said, slowly ruminating and continuing his study of Hap Thompson. "But you're sure fightin' a losin' battle. Up to now you have been, anyway." He shoved fisted, big, work-scarred hands into trouser pockets and went over where he could see out the doorless front wall opening. "They're gone," he mused aloud but more to himself, it seemed, than to Hap. He turned, still gently working his cud. "Up in back of the shack I expect." Blondell gazed over where Lew was lying. "You must be the reason why they didn't fire the place last night. They told me Thompson had likely killed you. They heard a shot in here last night." Without paying any more attention to Lew the cowman lifted his hat, scratched a thin thatch of curly gray hair, re-settled the hat, and turned to expectorate out the doorway.

For Hap this stranger was something of an enigma. He was tough and evidently fearless. He was also curt and gruff but he still did not appear to be convinced of a course of action. Hap leathered his six-gun and said: "I guess you can go, Mister Blondell. I thought you might be ready to side with Leggett."

Blondell shot a question right back. "What makes you think I'm not fixin' to side with him the minute I walk out of here?"

Hap showed a trace of that rough, humorless small smile again. "If you do, it'll be no worse for me than it was before you showed up. The odds were four to one before. You're not going to make them any worse. Especially since you're not going to take those guns outside the doorway when you walk out of here. Instead, you're going to toss them back inside to me. You ready to go?"

Henry Blondell slowly shook his head. "Nope. I'm not ready, Mister Thompson." Instead of elaborating, he turned and stepped to the doorway, looking out and around as though he was not in any personal danger from a gun behind him and perhaps three other guns somewhere in hiding outside. As he turned and moved away from the opening, he said: "You see, Mister Thompson, a cowman don't ride no thirty miles or whatever it was up here from the range country lookin' for strays, because, if you was a cowman, you'd know damned well cattle don't stray that far up into mountains like these." He walked back where Lew was lying and said: "What's your name, cowboy?"

"Lew."

"There's more to it than that."

"What the hell difference does it make? Take that gun away from him and help me up."

Blondell went on chewing. "I asked your name."

"Lew . . . Lew Burdett. Now take that belt off my ankles and help me up."

Henry Blondell still did not move. "You need some whiskey, cowboy, and that busted arm's too swollen now to put splints on it." He turned toward Hap. "You fellers just rest easy." Blondell

112

turned to cast a critical gaze around the interior of the cabin. "Thompson, you peeled them fir rafters and all, did you?"

Hap was becoming more puzzled each passing minute. "Yes, I did that. I built the whole cabin . . . just never got the front finished. Just what do you have in mind, Mister Blondell?"

The burly man's tough features continued to study the walls, the corners especially where notching showed. He acted as though he had not heard Hap's question. "You're one hell of a carpenter, Mister Thompson," he said, showing admiration in his voice, the first hint of any emotion he had showed. Then he brought his hard eyes back to Hap's face and also said: "But you sure are in a pack of trouble." He stepped to the doorway to expectorate again, more lustily this time, and came back with a loud sigh. "Just set down, gents, and rest your bones. None of us is goin' out of here, it don't look like."

From up in the forest out back a man with a strong voice called out. Hap knew the voice because he had listened to that man before but he did not know the man who owned it.

"Hey, cowman . . . come on out of there!"

Blondell cocked his head slightly, chewing without breaking cadence. "Leggett," he told Hap, hard eyes drawing out narrower. "I'll tell you what I can do, Mister Thompson. I can walk out there and palaver for an hour or so, or I can stay in here and let 'em sweat about that. Which would you figure I'd ought to do?"

Hap's bafflement deepened. "Just what the hell are you up to?" he asked.

Blondell did not take his eyes off Hap or alter the gentle movement of his jaws as he said: "I reckon I'll just set in here. Cooler." He went to the rear door, studied the wooden brace across it, and called out in a bull-bass deep voice: "I'll come out when I'm through in here. I told you that, Leggett!"

Hap expected a retort. So evidently did Henry Blondell, judging from the way he leaned over, listening and waiting. But there was no answer, and, as Blondell turned, Lew was scowling up at him. "Who the hell are you anyway," he growled, "a lawman?"

Blondell shook his head and studied Lew's bad arm. "A cowman. I told you that, cowboy. Just a grassland cowman. And something's got to be done about that arm of yours before too long."

"I'm no damned cowboy," snarled the injured man. "No one in his right mind follows that trade, mister."

Blondell accepted this without losing any of his imperturbability. "The fellers who follow it, mister, don't often end up in the shape you're in." Blondell went back to the front doorway and stood a long while gazing out where the sun was steadily climbing.

# XI

Someone out back let go with a gunshot. The bullet flattened against solid wood and Henry Blondell cocked an eye at Hap Thompson. "I'm supposed to get scairt and rush out of here," he said.

Maybe that was the reason for the gunshot. Hap was not totally convinced, however, so he moved toward the rear wall to listen in case they were closing in for an attack. He heard nothing but then he probably would not have been able to hear anything in any case.

He started to turn toward the cowman when the blue jays began their raucous calling again. This time it was Lew Burdett who said: "Cowman, you're going to wish to hell you'd gone out of there."

Blondell went on gently chewing. He did not even look at the injured manhunter, but he stood a little to one side for a long moment before turning to say: "Looks like maybe we got company, gents."

Hap went over to peer out, also. Blondell was right. There were two men riding directly across the meadow from the east. Hap's bay horse was standing erect, watching, but the pair of horsemen completely ignored the horse and kept facing toward the cabin. Evidently the manhunters had seen these additional newcomers, too, because now the blue jay calls quickened briefly, then stopped completely.

Blondell spat through the doorway, relaxed with thumbs hooked in his shell belt, all his weight on one leg. He seemed close to smiling.

This time when the pair of manhunters started out around the cabin to make an interception, Henry Blondell wagged his head. "Someone's in for a surprise," he murmured while continuing to stand where he could watch.

Hap began to suspect that the grizzled range cattleman beside him was somehow involved in this fresh confrontation, but Blondell did not speak again, not even when he and Hap could see the pair of manhunters aiming to halt the other two riders out yonder. This time the meeting was briefer. The newcomers seemed disinclined to palaver as long as Henry Blondell had. They halted and spoke with the pair of manhunters, then brushed past on their way to the cabin. Slightly to one side and behind them the pair of manhunters remained motionless for a moment. They were probably discussing something, but they were too distant for Hap even to see their lips move. Then they urged their horses after the advancing pair of riders, and finally Henry Blondell spoke. He sounded slightly amused. "That Leggett feller is a tough-acting individual."

From back closer to the rear wall Lew Burdett,

who had been intently listening and looking, made a rough comment: "You got no idea how tough he is, cowman, and, if those fellers are friends of yours, you're goin' to find out about Spade Leggett!"

Blondell acted as though he had not heard Burdett. He continued to stand at ease, gazing out where those four riders were steadily walking their horses in the direction of the cabin.

Hap was now just a spectator. Henry Blondell had usurped the initiative, something Hap did not dwell upon, although if he had, very probably he would have not felt the least bit slighted. Something was occurring of which he could only make a general surmise. As he watched the oncoming horsemen, he saw one of them, a large, bulky man in an old blanket coat despite the morning sunlight, raise a gloved hand and gesture as though to emphasize something he was telling the pair of manhunters, then the same large older man halted his horse and spoke earnestly for a moment before urging the horse onward again. But this time the pair of manhunters was unwilling to be walked away from. One of them called sharply. Hap and Henry Blondell saw the pair of strangers halt and turn back. Blondell made a slight clucking sound as though he did not approve of something. One moment later the lean and younger man riding with the large man snapped out a whiplash sentence, and, although Hap heard it, discerned the coldness and the menace in the voice, he did not hear what had been said. Henry Blondell chuckled. He wagged his head slightly over some private joke.

The pair of manhunters suddenly reined out in front of the pair of newcomers and rode stiffly in the direction of the cabin. From out back, up the hill in the timber, a dog-coyote made a loud coughing bark, repeated it several times, then stopped sounding. Henry Blondell left Hap and strolled out front, picked up his six-gun, wiped it on his trouser leg, and sank it into his holster. He also picked up the Winchester, then stepped back to the wall, and simply leaned there, holding Hap's carbine grounded at his side. He seemed to be smiling but Hap could not be sure without also going outside to expose himself, something he had no intention of doing because, as the four riders came closer, he recognized one bearded man and another who had not shaved recently but who was normally clean-faced, as two of the manhunters from their camp downcountry.

He said: "Is one of them Spade Leggett?"

Blondell answered quietly without taking his eyes off the oncoming horsemen. "Yeah. That feller without the whiskers . . . that's Leggett." Blondell spat. "And that big feller in the old coat . . . that's Charley Dawson. The other feller . . . the tall feller riding with Charley . . . that's Leo Savage, and me, I'm range boss for Charley Dawson."

It was part of the explanation and Hap had to be satisfied with it because now the four riders came up and halted, Leggett glaring from Blondell past to the dimly seen shadow of a man just inside the doorless opening of the house.

Charley Dawson said—"Get down."—to Leggett and the man beside him. Dawson and the dark-eyed lean rider at his side made no move to dismount, not even after the pair of manhunters had swung off and stood bleakly facing Blondell. Leggett said: "You told me you was a cowman huntin' lost critters."

Henry shook his head. "I told you I was a range man and that my job was to look for strays. I never said I was up here huntin' any lost cattle. Leggett, if you knew anything at all, you'd known cattle wouldn't be up here."

That lean rider gestured toward Leggett and the bearded, villainous-looking man beside him. "Shuck those guns, gents!" When this man spoke, his voice had an echoing sharp sound of menace in it.

Leggett turned toward Charley Dawson. "I told you out there, Mister Dawson, we got a perfect right up here. The feller inside the house is an outlaw wanted by the . . ."

"Mister, I said shuck those guns!" the lean rider repeated and looked squarely at Spade Leggett.

Leggett still hung back, glaring at the pair of mounted men, until Henry raised Hap's saddle

119

gun and poked Leggett in the back with it. And cocked it.

Both Spade Leggett and the bearded man promptly lifted out their weapons and dropped them.

Hap came to the doorway and leaned. Leggett stared at him. "Bank robbery and now murder, too!" he exclaimed.

Blondell answered that. "He didn't kill your friend. Just cold-cocked him and busted his wrist. He's lyin' on the floor inside."

Leggett did not act either relieved or pleased. "Then it's criminal assault and Thompson bein' a fugitive makes it just as bad."

Someone walking around from the north side of the cabin attracted everyone's attention. Another bearded man, darker than his look-a-like and not quite as tall but otherwise just as worn and soiled and raffish-looking, stepped into view, very erect and indignant-looking. Behind him was a slim cowboy with taffy-colored hair showing beneath his carelessly worn old hat, who was holding a cocked Colt in his right fist and was broadly smiling.

The taffy-haired rider winked at Henry Blondell. "He was sittin' up there like an old boar bear, scratchin' his rear, watchin' Paw and Leo herd his friends along."

Leggett and the second bearded man exchanged a look. Leggett growled in disgust, and the latest captive, stung by that, said: "You wouldn't have done no better!"

Charley Dawson swung to the ground. He had seemed large when he'd been atop his horse, but, standing beside the animal, one gloved hand still lightly upon the saddle horn, he seemed even larger. He and Henry Blondell resembled each other, not exactly in features or even altogether in their strong, thick builds but in the way they spoke and remained largely expressionless and in the way they seemed to regard things. They should perhaps have shared those affinities. Henry had ramrodded the first herd of Texas cattle Charley Dawson had brought into the Curran Valley countryside thirty years earlier; those two men had shared the identical life and environment for that long and it was bound to shape and mold them in similar ways.

Leggett's resentment had been building until now he was angry enough to say: "Mister Dawson, this feller Thompson is our prisoner. We're actin' for the law in catchin' him and bringin' him in. If you interfere, you'll be . . ."

"Shut up!" the large older man said coldly, and made a gesture. "Take your men and clear out!"

Leggett was clearly not a man who was ordinarily spoken to in this fashion. On the other hand at least one of the men with Charley Dawson had a cocked gun already in his hand and that lanky, dark rider, the one who seemed to be appropriately named Leo Savage, was waiting, right hand loose and relaxed within inches of his holstered Colt.

Leggett's companions seemed more willing to leave than Leggett was. The man who broke the tension was that second bearded manhunter, the one Charley Dawson's taffy-haired son had successfully stalked. He said—"Hell!"—in a monumentally disgusted tone of voice and brushed past Hap to lean and peer inside.

Lew Burdett's voice came forth from the inside. "Hey, John, get this damned belt off my ankles and help me up."

The bearded man went inside and young Dawson walked over to stand in the doorway to keep an eye on both the manhunters in the cabin.

Leggett and Dawson stonily regarded one another. Henry Blondell reached and jabbed Leggett again with the tip of the carbine barrel. "Do what you're told," he said in that same calm, hard-toned manner of speaking he had used since first reaching the cabin. "Git!"

Leggett turned finally, snatched at the reins to his bay horse, and turned away. Dawson's uncompromising look followed him. When the bearded man who had ridden out with Leggett also reached for bridle reins to walk away, Dawson said: "And keep on going . . . all of you!"

The bearded man turned dark eyes upon Charley

Dawson. "You own this land up here?" he enquired, guessing the truth about that.

That lanky man said: "Right now we sure as hell do, mister, and, as long as we're here, we'll boss it. That answer you?"

The bearded man turned to follow Leggett on around the north side of the cabin. He stopped once, just before passing from sight. Another rider was approaching, this time from about the same direction Henry Blondell had first appeared from. The bearded man shook his head and walked away. He may have entertained some notion about guns and equal numbers but now here was another one riding out of the timber and, for all he and Leggett knew, there might be more of them. The obvious thing to do now was rendezvous and palaver.

Dawson looked at Henry. "How bad do they want this feller?"

Blondell answered shortly. "Six thousand dollars' worth."

Even Leo Savage's brows shot up. Young Dawson turned in the doorway. They all stared at Hap, making him distantly uncomfortable. Savage made a low whistle, then said: "For that kind of money they aren't goin' to just ride off, Charley."

Dawson turned to watch the approaching rider as he said: "They damned well better ride off, Leo."

Hap was the last man to turn and concentrate upon the oncoming rider. His attention was distracted when the bearded manhunter emerged from the cabin supporting Lew Burdett. The men looked at the mottled, badly swollen hand, wrist, and arm but said nothing as the healthy manhunter helped Lew walk around the cabin in the wake of the other two. Young Dawson ambled along to watch them depart. He had holstered his six-gun.

The sun was high, the warmth was increasing, and for an autumn day it was downright warm with a promise of genuine summer heat later on.

Henry Blondell handed Hap his Winchester without a word. None of Charley Dawson's men seemed to be very talkative, unless they had something they thought needed saying.

# XII

That distant rider halted, then turned to approach Hap's horse. Over there, after dismounting, the rider stood beside Hap's animal gazing in the direction of the cabin and young Dawson said: "Paw, I think we'd sort of ought to ride after those fellers, make sure they head back down out of here."

Henry Blondell, with an amused look on his face, exchanged a long look with his employer. Charley Dawson twisted to glance out where the rider was standing with Hap's horse, turned back, and grunted: "Maybe, Son, maybe."

Blondell was the last of them to swing up across leather. He was still looking amused about something when he nodded briefly at Hap. The others rode around the north side of the cabin. Blondell waited a moment before following, then he dryly said: "Mister Thompson, for all you know that might be a horse thief out yonder foolin' with your horse. You'd best go look."

Hap stood in sunlight, looking after Blondell and the others. He was still in limbo. Dawson had not impressed him as a man who would condone outlawry of any kind. Hap had ridden for his share of those old mossyback ranchers; they had a very simple rule-of-thumb—people did not steal or kill, but if they did, they were punished for it no matter how long it took armed men to ride them down. Punishment in most cases, while never openly discussed, usually involved a stout tree limb and a hard-twist lariat rope and afterward—silence.

He rolled and lit a smoke, watched that solitary horseman over across the creek a fair distance, then he leaned aside the Winchester, and started walking.

The heat was increasing but a faint mistiness seemed to be forming again, which would, providing it did not dissipate, mitigate the heat somewhat. He halted at the creek for a drink of clear, cold water, splashed some over his head and face, felt the roughness of unshaven cheeks, dumped the hat back on, and resumed walking.

Not until he saw the distant person raise up from a bent position to bridle Hap's horse did he pay very close attention, and, when he was much closer but still too far to speak in a normal tone of voice, he began to have a strange feeling about this other newcomer. Then she turned and smiled, stepping from between the two horses, when he was only about three hundred feet away, and he halted for a second in purest surprise.

"Mary?"

"Are you all right, Hap?"

He wanted to laugh for the first time in days. Instead, he hurried on to where she was waiting.

"I'm sure glad you're back. So help me, I thought I'd never see you again and it sure pestered me to think that," he said, halting close to where she was smiling at him.

"I was coming back, but I wasn't too sure you'd still be here, so my father sent Henry on ahead."

He gazed at her. "Dawson is your father?"

"Yes. And Tige, the light-headed rider, is my brother. Those other men ride for the ranch." She offered him her cool hand, and, as he reached to take it, she said: "What happened to your razor?"

"In the saddlebags along with everything else I own."

He squeezed her hand; she squeezed back and released him. As she turned to lean on her horse and raise up to unbuckle a saddlebag, he stood admiring her. She was very handsome from the front or the rear. As she settled back down and turned, she held something in front, offering it to him.

"Half of a beef roast I stole from the cook shack. And a bottle of beer I stole from under Henry's bunk. And some sourdough bread."

It was a tidy bundle tied securely in a gingham napkin. He could smell the meat. It reminded him how hungry he was and how long he had been without anything to eat.

Her gaze lingered on his. "I was scairt half to death, Hap. I thought they might have caught you. Henry promised to find you, but I was still afraid. Are you sure you're all right?"

He was opening the gingham cloth as he answered. "Need a shave and a bath and some clean clothes . . . and something to eat."

They sat down between the drowsing, hip-shot horses, savoring horse shade with its agreeable aroma. She watched him wolf down the food and refused to share it with him. When he tasted the bottled beer, she said: "They make it in the blacksmith shop at the ranch and it's strong. Stronger than the beer folks sell in town."

It was the truth. He could feel the delicious effect almost immediately and decided that, if he had drunk the beer before eating the bread and meat, he would have been in rare spirits. As it was, he loosened in the shade, finished eating, and smiled over at her.

"You want to know something? I sure missed you, Mary. How's the roan horse?"

She snorted. "How am *I!*"

"Well, yes, you, too."

They laughed. "I'm fine and the cook at the ranch is looking after my horse."

It had been a grueling ride for her, out and back, and, although she had certainly seemed very nearly recovered from her accident a week back, the hardship she had endured for his sake could not have expedited the healing very much, so he said: "I sure do owe you, Mary."

"Then we're even, Hap, except that I got some gray hair worrying whether Paw and the men could get up here in time . . . Hap?"

"Yes'm."

"I had to tell my father about you. I couldn't just say I found a man up here living by himself and he saved my life and there were manhunters after him. I had to explain why they were after you."

He could guess from her expression what Charley Dawson's reaction had been. He'd had plenty of time to study her father. "And he wasn't exactly delighted."

"My father has worked hard against all kind of odds, Hap, including horse thieves and cattle rustlers. He doesn't favor outlaws of any kind."

Hap finished the beer and leaned down in the grass, supporting himself on one elbow while he looked over at her. She had always been handsome, even when he'd first found her covered with mud and blanched and disheveled, but now, cleaned up and slightly flushed from the warmth and looking relieved of her worry about him, she was downright beautiful. At least he thought she was, so he said: "Mary, what do I have to do to be able to follow you back down out of here?"

Her color increased. "You don't even know me, Hap."

"Yes I do. I got so's I could pretty well figure you out, even last week when you'd just lie there and look at me without saying a word."

She gently shook her head. "No you don't. Well, maybe a little, but there's an awful lot you don't know. I got married five years ago."

He had forgot to remember that once he had wondered about this. Right now the words were like a blow. To prevent her from seeing the expression he was unable to hide, he lowered his head and began to roll a smoke. "I guess," he said, speaking slowly, "anyone as nice and pretty as you are would have to be married." He lit up, raised solemn eyes to her face, and forced a smile that did not quite come off. "Well . . ."

"I'm not married now, Hap." He trickled smoke without moving or taking his eyes off her. The silence ran on for a time before she said—"Ride over to the cabin with me."—and jumped up.

He had to saddle his horse, and, while he was doing this, she leaned across her saddle seat, watching him. When he finally turned the horse, then swung up, she also mounted. She was smiling as she said: "I've never seen an Indian summer hang on the way this one has. Have you?"

He hadn't. Nor had he thought much about it lately. Those distant mountains were still a blaze of scarlet, yellow, russet, and near-white where pockets of aspen grew in low places. The softwood though, pines and fir trees, were exactly the same shade of dark green and reddish-brown that they always were, any time of year.

He killed the smoke and studied the solid dappled gelding she was riding. He had to be young to be that dappled and yet he was in the bit. He commented about this. Mary leaned to stroke the neck of her mount. "I started breaking him a couple of months ago. My brother got me to do it. I know why he and my father cooked it up. Anyway, I've never had a colt respond the way this one has. Actually he was in the bit after two months. Only one month in the hackamore. He's not really reined yet, but he will be in another few months . . . Hap?"

"Yes."

"I'll trade him to you for your horse."

He laughed. "I could no more trade this horse off than I could fly over the moon. He and I've been partners too long. But any time you want to ride him, you're plumb welcome."

At the cabin she saw the guns on the ground out

front. He explained that the manhunters had left them there. When they dismounted, she went over to look in from the doorway. "It's not the same, Hap."

He scratched his head and reset his hat before replying. "It sure served me well, though. There are some bullet holes in the walls now that weren't there before . . . Mary? Is your paw going back directly?"

She turned to face him. "Yes. Why?"

"Well . . ." His eyes slid from her face to the cabin. "Well, if those manhunters pull out, maybe I'll stay on here for a spell longer. At least until it gets cold."

She kept staring at him. "Is that truly what you started out to say?"

It wasn't, and he could not quite find the courage to say what he'd meant to ask her—about staying up here with him again. He straightened up, looking around into the golden, magnificent day. "I figured once, before all the trouble started, when you and the roan were up to it, I'd take you over where there's the bluest lake you ever saw west of here a few miles and maybe we could set up a little camp and do some fishing."

She kept looking straight at him in that very honest, very direct way she had of doing, a mannerism he had learned to expect from her right from the first day he'd brought her back to the cabin injured and dispirited.

"But now it's too late?" she softly said. "We couldn't do it now?"

Heat came into his face. He could feel it. Because he was bronzed from years of exposure, however, it did not show up as high color when he answered. "I guess . . . Mary, your paw wouldn't like the idea. Neither would your brother. And maybe those other fellers who ride for your . . ."

"Hap Thompson, I'm a grown woman!"

He never would have disputed that. "Sure, but you got a reputation."

"I had one before, when I was up here with you."

"That was different. You were hurt and all."

"It was no different. Not if folks knew about it and wanted to make something of it." She pointed to her horse. There was a blanket roll behind the cantle above the saddlebags. "I'm willing, Hap, and I guess I'm prepared."

He started automatically to fish around for his makings, something he did instinctively when something came up he had to grapple with in his head. Then he dropped his hands and raised his eyes. "I don't think we'd ought to do it without at least saying something to your folks, Mary."

"They know."

He stared at her. "They . . . know?"

"I rode most of the way up here with them. With my brother and father, with Henry and Leo. They're my family. They're the ones I came back

132

to after. I decided I had to come back. On the ride up, I explained about you. How . . . nice, how decent and gentle and kind you'd been . . . I told my father and Tige that if you weren't hurt . . . and even if you *were* hurt . . . I was going to stay up here and look after you. I said I'd come back, but no matter what we found when we got up here . . . even if they had killed you or had taken you away, I intended to stay for a while because it was a special place to me. *Now* may I go to the lake with you?"

He smiled across the little intervening distances. "You sure can, ma'am."

"Hap? About that money from the bank . . . I think you told me it was hidden up here."

He did not remember telling her that but right now it did not matter. And in fact it *was* hidden up here so he nodded his head.

"Hap? Would you give it all back?"

He would. In fact, he'd ride back and personally deliver it, but when he said that, she faintly frowned. "Would it be all right if my father sent it back with some lawmen from town?"

"He talked with you about this, Mary?"

"Yes. He wasn't going to let those manhunters kill you for the bounty, but he said, if you were alive when we got up here, he was going to take you into Curranville himself. We argued."

Hap, watching her face, decided she probably put up a pretty tough argument. He smiled. "On our way back down out of here, we'll fetch back the money pouch and give it to him."

She loosened all over, briefly leaned in the cabin doorway, then pulled herself upright, and went over to her horse. "Show me the blue lake, Hap."

# XIII

It wasn't much of a ride really, particularly under a misty sky that prevented real heat from reaching them and also through forested country for about two-thirds of the way. Nor did they see any tracks except for a few made by cloven, pointed hoofs, but occasionally they found a rubbing-tree where big high-country bucks had rubbed their horns off after the rutting season was past. In fact, when they came out of the last curve of trees to the pale emerald meadow the feeling in them both was of being in a place where people had never been before. Then they rode across the lush meadow to the blue lake's edge and found some ancient stone benches where the *anasazi*, the Old People as the Indians called their ancestors, had fitted stones with painstaking care so that they were perfectly niched, but there was little now to show that once there had been a pit between the stone benches and across the pit from one stone bench to the other bench had been placed green poles. This had been where the Old People had made meat, had smoke-cured fish and game for winter supplies. There had no doubt at one time been many brush shelters up here, too, perhaps a fairly large community, but there was no sign of that now, either.

The lake was not large, perhaps a mile across and about two-thirds of that distance wide, but where those black-rock barrancas had been gradually yielding to a bluish-veined series of granite cliffs for about a mile before Hap and Mary Dawson had got here, the reflection was different from that of many other high-country, volcanic lakes. And the moods of the flawless sky, normally an even darker blue, helped make the water seem almost violet in its blueness.

They off-saddled and let the horses graze back into the meadow. Her gray was young and might therefore have gone exploring but it had formed one of those quick attachments to his horse young horses frequently achieve and his horse, older, wiser in the ways of horse/human companionship, would not go very far from the scent of his owner.

She watched Hap make their camp and pitched in to help. She helped him gather deadfall firewood, which was smokeless, and even laughed when he told her she didn't know how to build a stone ring for their cooking fire, although she had forgot more about cooking than he would ever know.

Then they sat in the warm afternoon, occasionally swatting at flights of incoming gnats, until he said he had to go on around the lake and bathe. She said: "Please take your razor."

He walked a mile on around through the trees and came upon a half-grown cinnamon bear up a fairly large aspen tree. The little bear was so stunned at the appearance of the two-legged creature, he clung to the tree without moving for a long while. He had climbed up there because some blueberry vines had entwined the little tree. His mouth and nose were stained bright blue. Hap laughed at him and immediately the little bear began to groan and whimper, to growl garrulously and whine and look around as though either for a way to escape or for help in this sudden and terrifying confrontation.

Hap left him, found some red cinnabar rocks jutting into the water, and shucked his shell belt, boots, hat, and finally all his clothing, then he stepped into the water clutching his chunk of lye soap. It was like encountering an iceberg. This lake was probably spring fed from below, as were many mountain lakes, but it also was fed by snow water run-off from the eternally snow-covered highest peaks.

He worked his way out, ducked down, jumped back out to lather all over, then went gingerly back to rinse off. Then he sat on the cinnabar rocks to let the sun dry him. The last thing he did was shave, and finally, refreshed, he started back.

The cinnamon bear was gone, no doubt still grumbling and moaning and whining the way most bears did, talking to himself as he fled. There was a thin wisp of pale smoke rising on around the lake where Mary had a fire started. Hap walked the last hundred yards watching her there, kneeling at their fire, her head bare, slanting sunlight on the meadow beyond as a beautiful background. He halted for a time, watching, admiring her when she arose to move about their camp. She was lithe in her movements, and yet she was sturdy rather than lean. He wondered how much he ought to tell her about how he felt toward her, deciding—wisely—to allow the situation to develop by itself. He had seen that sudden expression on her face that he had seen many times among those he had abruptly encountered in the mountains, the look of fear and a willingness to flee. As he continued on around the lake, his mood changed to one of contentment. A deeper feeling of it than he had ever felt before.

Of course she was the reason for this, and yet he had known women in his lifetime, not a lot of them, nor had he ever been inclined to linger very long in the towns and around the big ranches where they were, but he had known several and not one of them had ever made him feel as he felt now, coming around the final turn of lake shore where she saw him and rocked back on her heels to study him critically and to smile as she said: "Now, that is much better. Don't ever grow a beard, will you?"

He sank down beside her, tossed his hat upon spongy pine needles, and said: "Is there such a thing as a female hermit?"

She blinked. "A what? I don't know. I never heard of one. Why?"

He lay back in the warm late day. "Since I've been in the Dogwoods, I've sort of thought maybe I'd become a hermit. Trap in winter, hunt and fish in summer." He grinned. "Just loaf and maybe turn into a hermit. Thing is . . . doing it alone wouldn't be as great as . . ."

"You can't be a successful hermit unless you *are* alone," she told him very seriously. "That's what a hermit is . . . isn't it? A man who lives apart from everything all by himself?"

He'd never known a hermit. "Darned if I know. Anyway, maybe I won't be one." He rolled up on his side, propped his head on a palm, and watched her. "I guess I don't want to be that lonely. Not now anyway."

She had emptied her saddlebags and had also emptied his. Now, looking quickly away, she said: "I've figured it out." She pointed to their provisions. "We can stay up here for about three days."

He gestured toward the lake. "What about the fish we'll catch?"

She laughed at him. "I used to go fishing with Henry and Tige and my father. If we'd ever caught all the fish they *talked* of catching, we could have lived for a year. But it never worked out that way."

"Maybe they aren't good fishermen, Mary."

She was still smiling when she said: "Are you?"

He hung fire over his answer, then finally told the truth: "No."

They laughed, and, as feeding time arrived out over the blue lake, as gnats skimmed low in the cooling afternoon, trout leaped and splashed. Mary turned to watch the fish and Hap turned to watch Mary.

She was muscular and very handsome even in profile. He sighed and raised up a little more also to look out where the fish were feeding. The lake teemed with trout. He told her that only once had he been skunked over here and that was the first time he'd seen the lake and tried his luck with an Indian fish trap made of green willows, because he hadn't had any line or hooks with him. But every other trip over here he had caught a fair limit, about twenty fat trout, even a few lunkers, those big, fat, older trout that spent most of the day lying in dark places along the steep shore.

She settled down beside him, knees up, arms encircling them, looking gravely out where the fish jumped. The sun was leaving gradually; its red-saffron rays came on a slanting angle, burnishing the lake to a shade of coppery blue rarely found anywhere but in the high country at autumn.

He reached over to pitch a twig on the dying fire, not because they needed warmth but to keep the fire burning until they were ready to use it, then he said: "I'll sleep over yonder. Near the trees where I can see out where the horses are. Got to sort of keep an eye on them."

She turned. "They won't go away, Hap. And even if they did . . . this is a perfect place, isn't it?"

He had always thought it was. "Maybe as close to heaven as I'll ever get."

"May I ask you something, Hap?"

"Sure."

"Did you ever kill anyone?"

He had expected something personal but nothing like this. He turned to look out where the fish were still feeding. "I've had a few fights. Twice I've leaned on hang ropes when I was riding for outfits and we ran down cattle thieves." He looked up. "Is that enough of an answer?"

She nodded. "I asked because . . . well, robbing a bank . . ."

He slowly wagged his head at her. "I wasn't a professional outlaw, Mary. I . . . just did it. Like a damned fool youngster does risky things . . . for the excitement of it . . . only I wasn't a youngster, I was a fool. A plain out-and-out darned fool. Before that I'd done a lot of things . . . cowboying, freighting, driving stages, even some mining and mustanging. I was only an outlaw once, but I sure did a fine job of it that one time, and, if those manhunters had got me, I'd have spent a lot of years repenting. And . . . I was restless. I guess I was looking for something and thought it was more excitement." He looked steadily at her. "It wasn't that. It was something else, and I never figured it out until just lately."

"What was it?"

He felt heat rising to his face again and looked out over the water. "It'd make you uncomfortable if I told you, Mary. Well, maybe in a day or two."

She continued to gaze at him. After an interval of silence she said: "Hap, my husband was . . . he robbed a bank."

A big trout jumped not ten feet off shore and Hap ignored it to look up at her.

She almost smiled. "But not with a gun. He worked there. It was back in Independence where he had grown up. In Missouri. He managed the bank. He stole money for two years before people found out about it."

"And he got away?"

"No. But he almost did. And he made me ride with him. He said we'd find the James brothers and the Daltons and join them. I tried to get him to go back. I guess I tried too hard."

"What do you mean?"

"Once too often, I guess, Hap. He broke my arm

and beat me senseless." She shrugged her knees up closer, lowered her chin to the encircling arms, and looked out over the lake. "I lost our baby. Some farm people found me and took me to their town. I almost died. I really *wanted* to die. My husband wasn't at all what I'd thought he was when we were courting. He . . . well . . . he was very cruel, but it never showed until after we'd been married a year. That was not the first time he knocked me senseless." She paused to avert her face, and Hap groped for something to say, but he was far from being knowledgeable about the kind of situation so he simply leaned there until she straightened up, saying: "I wanted to say something to you about this when you first found me, when I asked you to go away and leave me up there, leaning against that tree. I wanted to try and explain why I didn't want ever to go back."

He watched the light turn soft, turn shades darker as daylight continued to fade. "You don't have to tell me any of this, Mary."

"Hap . . . I *wanted* to tell you. You . . . turned out to be such a different kind of man. At first I didn't believe it, then I knew you were completely different. And, anyway, you had a right to know because I knew you wondered."

". . . Mary, what happened to him? Did he find the James boys and the Daltons?"

"Yes. Do you remember reading about the Northfield raid?"

He remembered. It had made the headlines of every newspaper in the country. "Where the law and a posse rode them down and nearly wiped them."

"My husband wasn't in the raid on the town. They said in the newspapers the survivors said he and another man who hadn't proved themselves yet were left to mind the horses. But when the band was ridden down and cornered, my husband and the other man were killed."

Hap let go a big ragged breath. "Outlaws," he murmured. "Damned fools from start to finish." He pitched a pebble into the nearby shallows and looked around, then hauled himself up to sit straighter beside her. "You knew I was one."

"Yes. I cried all the way down from the meadow to the home place. I guess I looked pretty terrible, puffy-eyed, scratched face, torn clothes. Tige and my father had been worried sick. They told me they had sent men out looking for me but they had never thought I'd go that far into the mountains. . . . Then, when I told them about you, my father just sat down and stared at me. 'Another one?' he said. 'Mary, not another one, for heaven's sake.' I had to talk myself hoarse on the ride back. *I* knew you were different, Hap."

He remembered the hard way her father had looked at him, at the gruff, icy manner he had exhibited out front of the cabin, and decided Charles Dawson's attitude toward Spade Leggett had not been entirely because he disliked bounty hunters. "He'll never like me, Mary."

She passed that off easily. "If you knew him as well as I do, you wouldn't say that. Hap? Will you give him the chance? Will you make me a little promise?"

"Sure."

"Don't ride off. Don't ever ride off without me?"

He looked at her. "Mary, you don't know . . . you might be making the mistake of your life."

She smiled faintly and ruefully. "No. I've already done that. You can't do it twice. Not the biggest mistake. Promise me?"

"All right."

She sat a moment, then leaned slightly until their shoulders brushed and sniffled. "Isn't it time to start supper? Are you hungry?"

He should have been. He had every right to be hungry but he wasn't. "Not really hungry."

She pulled away and turned to the fire, her mood different, her voice normal as she said: "But you've got to eat anyway. What will it be, sardines and biscuits or tinned beef and biscuits?" She turned. "Or fish?"

They smiled at each other. They'd had plenty of opportunities to catch fish but now with fading daylight and approaching night the trout were through feeding and would not rise to bait until tomorrow.

# XIV

A man had been tracking them but he did not get close to the blue-lake meadow until early dusk, and even though he found their horses, he was a long time picking up the scent of their cooking fire. Hap was thinking pleasant, private thoughts when Mary's gray horse nickered. Without a word to her he unwound out of his sitting position and stood, gazing across the slight rise of land that sloped upward from the lake side where they had established their camp.

He could see the horses but he could not see what had interested them. He could make out that his horse was also interested in something over toward the forest fringe to the east. The gray, being young, was more likely to whinny, to show coltish interest, while his horse, being older and infinitely more experienced, would not stand as he was doing now, head up, motionless, ears pointing at something that intrigued him, if it were simply a deer, one of the natural denizens of the mountains, because after a year in this area those creatures—excluding bears or wolves or catamounts—were totally familiar to him.

Hap waited a moment to watch, to make certain from the way the horses were watching that whatever it was had to be moving on around in the direction of the lake without leaving the forest. Mary was over by their supper fire as still as a stone, one hand gently pressed to her lips while she, too, watched and listened.

When Hap moved away from her, she seemed about to call him back but she did not do it, and within moments he, too, was hidden by the late-day darkening gloom of the timber. He had the horses out in the meadow to help him. At least in a general way to point in the direction of whatever it was that had interested them—and Hap was certain it was another human being. The gray would not have nickered like that unless whatever Hap was stalking was either another horse or someone riding another horse.

He was right, but it was so dark in among the huge trees that by the time he was able to ascertain it was a horseman, he could make out almost nothing more than movement even though he was well within pistol range when he made the discovery. The stranger acted as though he thought he had not been discovered. He was slouching along on a stout sorrel horse as relaxed as a rider could be. He did not keep his head moving or he probably would have seen the shadow moving to make an interception. Even when Hap moved finally to block the horseman's onward progress and the rider reined up, dropping both hands to the saddle horn as he peered ahead, there was no recognition right away.

The horseman said: "Good evenin'. Sure hope you folks got some trout for supper."

It was Henry Blondell, range boss for Mary Dawson's father, but Hap did not immediately holster his Colt. "You must be good at tracking," he told the enigmatic range boss, "to find us in the dark."

"Well, no, not exactly. I found the trail long before sunset, and, after bein' on it for a mile or such a matter, the horse sort of took over and kept on the big game trail leadin' in here. But I'll sure admit for a while now I been wonderin' where I was goin' to get supper."

Hap's feeling toward this man was ambiguous. Henry had been his ally but he had never acted as though he wanted to be Hap's friend. Of course in the light of what Mary had recently told him, it was not hard to guess about Blondell's feelings toward Hap Thompson, but that changed nothing about Hap's sentiments as he said: "Why are you here?"

Henry Blondell was silent for a long time before he said: "You see, I've been around the Dawsons since the kids were buttons. I taught 'em some of what they know about riding and roping and reading sign and knowing cattle and such like." Henry's tough features even in the bad light showed an almost paternal little smile. It was an easy, fearless expression; he had not once looked directly at the six-gun aimed at his middle. "I knew their maw before she died, and I guess you might say I've always figured I was a sort of uncle to 'em . . . especially Mary and particularly after all she went through with that worthless bastard she married. Mister, she's not going through anything like that again . . . and you can put that gun away because it wouldn't stop me."

Hap believed the range boss. He had got to know something about him. There was a lot he did *not* know but the basic convictions of Henry Blondell and many men of his kind Hap had known were fairly rudimentary. Hap said: "Where are the rest of them? How far back?"

Henry shook his head. "They didn't come. I'm alone. Her paw and the others got in behind Leggett's crew, and the last I saw they was herdin' them like a quartet of old gummer boar bears on ahead of them down out of the mountains." Henry shifted in the saddle. "Where's camp? I don't figure to set out here all night palavering."

But Hap was not quite ready yet. He said: "You figure to take her back with you?"

Henry, who had been unable to reach a conclusion about this in all the miles he had recently ridden, raised a hand to scratch his cheek gently. "I guess you could say I'm sort of her uncle, Thompson, but I don't figure I'm her keeper. I don't aim to see a man ever do anything like that to her again, but she's a grown woman an' about all any of us can do is sort of set back and watch developments. That's not much of an answer, but I can't give you a better one." Henry moved again in the saddle, showing increasing impatience. "I'll tell you one thing. I told her paw and her brother you didn't strike me as a feller who'd be that underhanded . . . like her husband was . . . or that cruel." Henry's gaze hardened. "And, mister, you better not make me out wrong. I sure wouldn't take kindly to that. Now put up that damned gun and let's move along. It's gettin' dark."

The last remark was right enough. Hap holstered his Colt and turned to lead the way. They had a fair distance to traverse, and, although Henry Blondell said nothing for the first part of it, when they had the glowing, low fire in sight, he made a comment that Hap nodded over. He said: "If I was a man who had found a woman to be with, this here is about the best place I could find to be with her in . . . Thompson?"

"Yeah."

"How is she?"

"Fine, except the scratches on her face still. . . ."

"Oh, hell, I didn't mean that. Scratches heal. The things which *don't* heal aren't on the *outside*."

Hap stalked along in silence for a few yards before saying: "Why ask me, Henry, yonder's camp. You can ask her."

She saw them crossing, and despite the dimming

visibility she recognized the range boss at once. Maybe it was simply relief, maybe it was something different, but she ran over, and, as Blondell swung down a trifle stiffly, she flung herself in his arms. Hap watched briefly, then took the foreman's horse over to free it and turn it loose out where the other horses were. He took a lot of time doing this because he wanted Mary and Henry Blondell to use as much time as they might need together, alone.

He even walked out with Henry's animal to where his horse and the gray colt were, something that turned out to be unnecessary. None of these geldings was a fighter. Rarely did geldings actually fight. He lingered a moment in the night, then turned back, wondering how long Henry Blondell was going to remain at the lake. He liked Henry the way one man who shared an identical set of rangeland convictions would like another man he did not know very well, but this was different; he mildly resented Henry's being here and not entirely because of the range boss's protective feelings.

When he saw them, they were together at the fire. Mary looked up, watched Hap approaching, sat perfectly still for a moment, then stood up and went over to him with a tin plate of food, and, while they were out there, she said: "He . . . he'll leave in the morning. I'm sorry he came, Hap."

It was impossible to be annoyed with her. In

the first place this threesome was not her fault, so Hap grinned. He held out a hand that she met halfway, her palm cool against his palm. Then they turned slowly back and she seemed lost in thought until they reached the fire.

Henry was comfortable with his spurs, his gun belt, and hat in the grass nearby, his contrasting stark white forehead particularly noticeable in the gloom, as opposed to his cheeks and lower face that were sun- and wind-weathered. He smiled and gestured for Hap to drop down, then as though they were old friends he said: "Can you hear those trout out yonder?"

The lake was as silent as a tomb.

Henry chuckled. "They're down deep figurin' on how to get your bait tomorrow without gettin' hooked. You got some line and hooks?"

Hap nodded. "Always carry a roll of line. You like to fish, Henry?"

"Sure do. You?"

"Yeah." Hap studied the older man. Henry Blondell was a man who would be a generous, good-natured friend exactly the way, as an enemy, he would be a man to be reckoned with. Hap said: "You could hang around tomorrow and use my line if you wanted to."

Mary slowly raised her head. Hap didn't notice this but the range boss did, and he cleared his throat a little. "Well, I'd sure admire to, but I got to meet the crew back at the home place and we got to move cattle before this here good weather ends." Henry finished his meal and groped for his chewing cud. He offered it first to Hap who declined with a grin. "Never was man enough," Hap told the range boss, and Henry smiled. "Well now, me, I never could stand cigarettes. They make me cough somethin' fearful. Make m' eyes water and all."

Mary got busy at the fire ring, taking no part in the talk, not even when Henry said: "We sure got a lot of work to do, down home. Got to use every rider we can find." He looked straight at Hap. "Had a feller get sick on us last month and quit and by golly you know this late in the season it's impossible to find a replacement."

Hap sipped coffee trying to decide whether or not he had just been offered a riding job. He decided to take a chance and said: "I'd be right glad to lend a hand. When we come down from here, Henry."

Blondell accepted that as though he had expected no other reply. "Fine . . . uh . . . when do you folks figure to be down . . . if I'm not buttin' my beak in where it don't belong?"

Hap felt color rising into his cheeks again, so he peered intently into his coffee cup looking for floating grounds, of which there was none.

Mary answered from over closer to the dying fire. "Two or three days."

She said it almost as though it were a challenge. Henry Blondell also became busy examining the contents of his tin cup. "That'll be just fine," he told them, then tossed down the last of the coffee, flung away the dregs, and reached for his hat. "I been up and stirrin' since 'way before sunup today and I'm ready to bed down."

They said nothing although they watched as he went over to his saddle, and moments later, when he tossed them a little wave and went hiking out into the darkness, they waved back.

For a while neither of them spoke. Mary offered Hap what remained of their supper. He said— "Save it for breakfast."—and in the same breath also said: "I hope he's an early riser."

She grinned. "He is. Did he mention the bank money to you?"

"No."

"He did to me and I told him what you'd said about bringing it down with us and giving it to them to take back to the bank." She settled closer to where Hap was sitting, so close in fact that he could detect the very faint lilac scent of her hair. "Hap? Should we be . . . doing this?"

He considered scuffed boot toes when he answered. "*I* sure believe we should. But then, I'm a man and that's different."

She looked a trifle shyly at him. "I'm glad there's that difference."

He raised his eyes. "Should we?"

"I want to, Hap . . . but afterward?"

He had considered this before and had decided

not to bring it up for another day or two but time appeared to have got telescoped for them some way; they were not new acquaintances, not in terms of danger and co-operation and appreciation of one another; not in the ways in which most people had to be together for a couple of years at the very least to learn about each other.

"Afterward," he told her quietly, "I guess you could put a ring in my nose and lead me back." He grinned. "But you could have done that any time, I guess. Maybe even back when I first brought you to the hide-out and you'd just lie there, staring at me."

"Back then . . . really?"

"I think so. Thing is, Mary, it happens when a man don't really know it's happening. I didn't really know it *had* happened until I rolled out that morning and you were gone. . . . That was sort of like the bottom had dropped out of everything." He blushed in the darkness. "Worse than a young buck. You got any idea how much older I am than you are?"

"What does that have to do with anything, Hap? Do you know how old *I* am in . . . learning things, in anguish and pain, and . . . a lot of other things? About a hundred."

He did not want her to go back into her memories. He had learned how to prevent that and he moved to prevent it now by saying: "You're sure hangin' together well for an older woman. I once had a horse like that. To look at him you'd never . . ."

She swung. He caught her wrists swiftly but gently and both fell back laughing. "I don't know why you get upset over bein' compared to a horse. This was a real *good* horse." He held her back. Gradually she ceased resisting, loosened in his grip, and looked directly up into his eyes. "I might have a terrible temper, Hap, for all you know. And nag a lot. And be fiercely jealous. And . . ."

"All right. I might be a drunk and mean to horses and maybe I'll get fat and bald and cranky and . . ."

"You're not mean to horses, I know that. And if you get fat, I'll cut back until you're lean again. As for being cranky . . . you're not that disposition at all. You never will be."

For a moment they were softly silent, close and instinctively troubled and a little fearful. Out across the meadow Henry coughed, cleared his throat, and lustily spat.

Mary sighed. "I love him. He's been a second father to me. But right now . . . why does he have to be here?"

"That's easy, Mary. Because he also loves you."

". . . Hap?"

He nodded down into her eyes instead of answering. Not right then anyway but a moment later he answered her. "I do, too."

She moved slightly against him, held her heavy

lower lip between her teeth, and burrowed her face against his forest-scented shirt front. The moon had come, arriving unnoticed unless out where the range boss was lying he saw it. Neither Mary nor Hap saw it.

Distantly two roving coyotes passed along and sounded to the heavens before faintly detecting human scent, after which they stopped being noisy and instinctively fled. Otherwise the night was warm and hushed. The moon climbed, changing color as it ascended until it was the color of ancient rust. The blue lake had turned black. It did not have a single ripple across its steely surface and against the grassy shoreline it was motionless, too.

She stirred in his arms and whispered. "If someone had told me last week I'd want to live . . . I wouldn't have believed them." She rolled free and gazed up at him, saw the moon, and said: "Look up there."

He did, then he looked down at her again. She smiled softly. "I'm glad you shaved. Do you know what I did while you were gone this afternoon?"

He shook his head. He was sure he knew but he shook his head anyway.

"The same thing you did . . . bathed in the lake."

He teased her. "Yeah, I saw you." He could feel her suddenly stiffen and softly laughed. "Naw, I was only joshin' you."

But she continued to be unsmiling. "Are you sure?"

"Cross my heart. Anyway, I was too far off even if I'd been able to see you."

She sighed. "Do you like to tease people?"

"Only you, Mary. All right?"

"Yes, all right. Hap? It's just impossible that this can happen to me again. And so soon afterward."

He felt instinctively that she was pleading for time. He raised a hand to lift away a heavy dark coil of hair. "We'll fish and laugh and explore for a couple of days, then we'll go down and work cattle at the ranch and maybe, if the weather holds, we might be able to slip away and come back to the hide-out again."

She shook her head. "The weather won't last. Winter is close . . . and I don't think I really want to put it off like that."

He eased down beside her. It was warm but it was not going to remain that way much longer. "Take your time, Mary. I'll wait. I've waited all my life, so another few weeks isn't going to kill me."

She raised up and leaned, looking down at him. Then she kissed him with a full and gentle pressure, moving her lips across his mouth until the sudden explosion of banked fire deep down made him respond with a surge of need and want that was almost overpowering, and the rusty old moon was the only witness.

# SHERIFF OF HANGTOWN

Russian Gulch, Murderer's Bar, Missouri Gulch, Dead Indian—and Hangtown—all got their names through obvious association. The list didn't end there: Nigger Beach, Horse Thief Cañon, Hold-Up Bend, Spanish Spur, the names went on and on, each with its singular meaning for a town or a settlement, or just where a few old rotting log houses, windowless and haunted, abandoned by all but wood rats, lingered to mark the site of some flash-in-the-pan gold strike, trail town, or trapper village. But Hangtown got its name justifiably and it didn't wither; instead, it prospered right from the start. It lay in California not far from the Sierras, the great Central Valley, or, for that matter, the majestic Pacific Ocean. The early-day miners hung that name on it. Some said Hangtown's justice was more abrupt, its supply of hemp rope inexhaustible, and the temper of its citizens less susceptible to maudlin mercy than anywhere else along the Pacific slope. One thing was demonstrably certain: Hangtown took no guff. Thieves of any kind, horse, cattle, land, or placer thieves, were anathema.

Such a philosophy paid dividends. Long after the last 'Forty-Niner had passed from the scene, the precedent remained; crime in Hangtown was actually less than elsewhere, and even when this was debatable, two things stood out. One, if outlaws came to Hangtown, they did not linger. Two, whether the mawkish, the weak and maudlin believed in swift execution or not, when a renegade was hanged in Hangtown, he certainly never went anywhere else to commit further crimes, for hanging, like shooting, had an alarmingly high mortality rate. But there was opposition. Not only to the short shrift given convicted outlaws, but also to the method they were subjected to in their punishment, and even, as time rolled past, to the name of the town.

"Hangtown," sniffed Parker Malone's wife, Ellie, "is like the brand of Cain. Even our children have to carry it wherever they go all their lives."

To Claude Lucas who operated the local livery barn this seemed like an unnecessary over-statement. "Why all their lives?" he'd wanted to know. "A feller can be born in Hangtown and move somewhere else, Ellie."

Parker Malone's wife had pounced. "Certainly, Claude, and forever after when anyone asks where were you born, or where did you grow up . . . you must say Hangtown!"

Claude subsided to consider the possibilities this fresh view put upon things. He did not personally much care one way or another. In fact, Claude had lent a hand upon a rope or two in his time. He knew from grim experience that outlawry diminished in a town in direct proportion to the toughness of the punishment meted out. But—times change, people turn soft, and, as security and reasonable affluence continued, the lily-livered come more and more to speak for the community. They are the same lily-livered souls who cry for the sheriff to shoot a frothing dog or a rabid skunk, or even, sometimes, a rebellious horse—which is termed an "outlaw" when in nine cases out of ten he simply has his bluff in on a bunch of physical cowards who possess two legs instead of four. And it can go further.

Dick Ruffin sold Vernon Florin a big blood bay that mouthed five years of age and had a tough, wise, little shoe-button black eye on him. He was one of those big, strong critters that could stand across the corral from a man and look down his long snout, bringing definite qualms to the man although a hundred and fifty feet of open ground separated them. Dick had sworn up and down the horse was gentle. "But spirited," he'd said. "He ain't no kid's pony. He'll take you where you got to go and he'll fetch you back, but you can't molly-coddle him with apples and sugar. What he wants is for you to get about your business, slap the saddle on, screw it down, knock back the bit, climb up, and do your work. He ain't lazy nor mean, but he won't stand no foolishness."

In short, Dick was describing a man's horse. The

trouble was that basically Vernon Florin was masculine in appearance only. Oh, he wore britches, boots, a wide-brimmed hat, and his six-shooter, but so did everyone else in the Hangtown country whether they mined, felled timber, or punched cows. The trouble was, like always, it was generally impossible to tell what was inside the package by looking at the outside of it. That blood bay put the Indian sign on Vernon the first time he went into the corral with his saddle. The horse went over in a corner, rolled his eyes, snorted, and stood as stiff-legged as a bronco. He wasn't exactly afraid of Vern, just doubtful; they were both strange to each other. But he was a powerful animal and Vern's fortitude just naturally oozed out through his boot soles. He'd taken his rigging back out of the corral, put it on another horse, and did not go into the blood bay's pen again. When he saw Deputy Sheriff Wesley Potter in town, he darkly hinted that Dick Ruffin had flim-flammed him.

Wes was something rare among deputies; he knew as much law as most prosecuting attorneys, and the way it read on horse trades was quite plain. If a man sold you a horse and deliberately lied about the beast, you had ready recourse, but if it was a horse trade, then the law wisely and correctly assumed each man was out to bamboozle the other, and, when one of them actually got bamboozled, it was just his tough luck.

Wes explained that to Vernon. But he went even further because Hangtown wasn't a large place, folks pretty well knew other folks' business, and the tale of that trade was common knowledge. "That old mare you traded to Dick's been lame in front for a couple of years, Vern. When you said she was just tender-footed, you knew a darned sight better."

Vernon didn't deny this, he simply side-stepped it by saying: "But I give him thirty dollars to boot, Wes, an' that's what I'm gripin' about."

It was a poor argument, Wes tired of it, and said: "Vern, you set out to beat Dick and instead you got beat. Stand up to it like a man. It happens to all of us sooner or later in horse trades."

"But, Wes, that danged horse'll kill me. He's got a real mean little eye on him."

"Not if you don't get on him, he won't," stated the deputy, and turned to walk away.

But Vern wasn't finished. "Hey," he said, sounding aggrieved, "I want to trade back, Wes. How about you goin' out to the ranch and talkin' to Dick?"

The deputy's reaction to this was to feel ashamed for Vernon; it just wasn't done. A man took his licking and he kept quiet about it. He looked back and said: "If you want to do that, go do it yourself." Then he walked away, leaving Vern standing up near the livery barn looking spitefully after him.

Vernon Florin wasn't a likeable man. He had a long, weasel-thin face and crafty eyes. He was a man without ethics or scruples, but more than that he was a coward; he'd lie sometimes when the truth would have fit better. He didn't drink a whole lot, but he schemed, and as Wes had once said about him: "If there were only two ways to make a living, the right and wrong way, Vern would take the wrong way just naturally."

Dick Ruffin, on the other hand, wasn't a liar or a coward, but he was noted for his sharpness. He raised good horses on his ranch over against the hills, and like Vernon had never married. Rumor had it that once he'd packed into the Sierras, didn't return for two years, and, when he came back out of the mountains to his ranch that time, he brought a handsome Shoshone squaw. Well, in the early days before cattle had replaced placer mining, that was how things often worked out. The hide sides of a teepee frequently replaced the more decorous wood walls of a church when the mountain men, trappers, hunters, miners, and cattlemen got swelled necks like rutting bucks in the springtime. But if there was any truth to that yarn no evidence remained to support it. Dick lived alone on his horse ranch now, and although he wasn't exactly an old man—being, so he calculated, somewhere in his early fifties—he'd never made any overt advances to the eligible spinsters or widows in town.

Then he turned up dead.

An Anchor cowboy passing through stopped at the old log house in its peaceful forested setting to see whether Dick wanted anything fetched back from town, and found him flat out on his back with a bullet hole smack dab between his eyes. The cowboy's name was Stan Darcy; he'd been working for Anchor six years and was known on the range as well as in Hangtown as a good hand. In fact, each fall he and Wes Potter packed into the high country for the hunting and fishing.

"It's just like I said," he told Wes in town. "Someone let the old boy have it from no farther than maybe five, six feet. His shirt was scorched and the hole in his old blanket coat was big enough to drive a team through. But he hasn't been dead long. I'd judge maybe only one or two days."

Wes was interested. He was also mystified. Dick Ruffin had his enemies, just like every other positive thinker since the beginning of time. "But who," he mused aloud, "would shoot him?"

Stan didn't know, although he conceded that Dick'd had his share of detractors. "The old cuss staked out a hide or two now and then. We never caught him at it, of course, or he'd have quit breathin' a long time back, but we missed a yearling every now an' then. Usually in the fall, which is when those old half-Injun fellers jerked their winter meat. But like Mister Harriman said, it's sometimes a sight cheaper to feed 'em than to fight 'em. Besides, Anchor's got two thousand head. What's one yearling a year?"

The way Stan referred to Dick as half-Injun did not mean Ruffin had been a half-breed; it meant that, like many old-timers, Ruffin had lived around Indians so long he sometimes lived and acted like one. White Indians they were called a half century earlier, but there were very few left any more, and those few, like Dick Ruffin had been, were mostly live-alones who bothered no one. At least, as Stan had implied, they never got *caught* bothering anyone.

Wes made the trek that same day, taking with him a flat-bed wagon and a dirty old length of canvas, some tools, and his old Bible. Just before he got near the hills, he was intercepted by Mosely Crawford, Anchor Ranch's range boss and general manager. Mosely was a burly, swarthy man whose dark, tough looks gave a deceptive first impression, for although Mosley was tough and willing any time, anywhere, if the challenge was offered, he actually was a good-natured, easy-going, and likeable man who laughed easily and smiled often. Now, though, he was not smiling.

"You goin' up to bury Dick?" he asked, and, when Wes quietly nodded, Mosley said: "What the hell kind of a feller would shoot him?"

Wes didn't know. Since he hadn't even reached the cabin yet, he couldn't even make a good guess. "Maybe someone who wanted his horses," he murmured.

"Naw," contradicted burly Mosley Crawford. "I just come from his range. The horses are all there. I ought to know. Every spring an' every fall I got to go out and chase them back through the fence."

Wes nodded. It was common knowledge how Dick would slyly open the drift fence between his short-grass range and the more lush pastures of Anchor Ranch, and ease his horses through to catch maybe five or six days of good grazing before the Anchor riders saw them and pushed them back where they belonged.

"An' he had no money," stated Mosely Crawford. "Hell, I doubt if the old coot had ten dollars to his name."

"It doesn't have to be horses or money," said Wes, raising his lines to drive on. "You'd be amazed at some of the fool reasons folks use to shoot other folks over. Well, I got to get this done and get back to town, Mosley. See you again."

It was exactly as Stan Darcy had said. Dick Ruffin was lying on his cabin floor as dead as a stone with that bullet hole in his brisket, his faded and sightless eyes staring straight up at the ceiling. He didn't look angry or surprised or even regretful; he just looked dead.

Before he set out to plant old Dick, Deputy Potter made a slow and very thorough search of the cabin, the corrals, the log barn, and even out and around through the nearby trees. He found horse tracks all over the place. Some were shod horse marks, but mostly they were imprints left by unshod animals. Dick only shod one or two horses—the animals he used most frequently. Otherwise there was nothing. Not even any boot tracks that could have belonged to strangers, and that wasn't hard to determine, either, because Dick had done his own re-soling; the result was an easily identifiable track.

He went back inside and drew out a handmade chair to sit and gaze at the dead man, and think. Dick's six-shooter was hanging from a wall peg in its scuffed old holster. It was fully loaded. He had several shoulder guns including a long-barreled old single-shot musket and two Winchester short-barreled saddle carbines. They, too, were loaded, hadn't been fired, and rested in place upon their pegs over the mud-chinked wood fireplace.

Obviously whoever had walked in and shot Dick had either known him well enough to get that close before firing, or had slipped up without him hearing them. Wes strongly doubted that anyone could do that; for one thing Dick Ruffin had lived as long as he had partly because he could hear a pin drop at a hundred feet. For another thing, just naturally, an old Indian-lover like Ruffin was never wholly relaxed. Living with peril for a half century made a man different from other men. So—it had to have been someone Dick knew. But who? He thought of Vern Florin, but put Vernon out of his mind because he just wasn't the murdering kind. He might steal a man blind or cheat him, or lie him into getting skinned, but he wasn't a killer. In fact, sometimes Vernon went a week at a time without even wearing a gun. There was the resentment over Dick's beating him in that horse trade, but, hell, if everyone old Dick had shaved a mite trading horses had taken out after him with a .45, Ruffin would have been dead and buried forty years earlier.

Wes arose, went out, and pulled the shovel from his livery rig. He'd already selected the site; it was in the shade of a giant old red-barked fir tree near the creek where the earth would be soft for digging. He hung his vest and hat on a low limb and went to work, digging and sweating, and trying to imagine not so much *who* had shot old Dick, but *why* they'd shot him.

When he was waist deep and aching, he paused to discard women, horse trades, range disputes, some old feud, and robbery, the usual causes for murder. He leaned on the shovel, taking a breather, exasperated over his inability to come up with a single reason why Dick was lying in there, murdered. Unless a lawman could figure some *reason* for a crime of passion, he could make no headway at all toward solving it.

He dug a little deeper, climbed out, got an old piece of canvas, and went inside to roll Ruffin into it. The old cuss was heavier than he looked. When he got him back out to the grave, he knelt and went through Dick's pockets. There was an elaborately engraved gold pocket watch—with someone else's initials on it—some wadded-up paper money, a tobacco sack and papers, a Barlow clasp knife with a chipped bone handle, and a soiled old blue bandanna handkerchief. Aside from that, there was only a little ball of catgut, used for mending everything from harness to trousers, and a honing stone for keeping the knife razor-sharp.

Wes rolled the gold watch along with everything else into the bandanna, lowered Dick, arranged him comfortably, then started filling in the hole. To Wes's knowledge, Dick'd had no heirs or relatives. He'd spent many an evening in late summer up here where it was blessedly cool, sitting out on the porch facing the mountains, talking with Ruffin. Never once had the old cuss ever mentioned a kinsman, although he'd talked freely and openly of his escapades among the Indians as a youth, of his old-time friends, and of the places he'd been and the things he'd seen. But there was nothing particularly unusual about that.

Not, Wes told himself as he mounded the grave, that it mattered; aside from his horse herd Dick hadn't left anything behind folks would contend over. John Harriman, the owner of Anchor Ranch, would probably wait until Ruffin's two sections of land came up for taxes, and bid them in. No one else would want or need the land because it was more forest than grass, sometimes steep and rocky, sometimes so layered over with resin and needles that even if the trees were cut down it still wouldn't grow grass. The buildings weren't much—the cabin, one large room, the log barn, with a definite list to southward, and a shoeing shed with three sides and a roof that leaked like a sieve.

Wes finished, took the shovel back, tossed it into the wagon, got his Bible off the seat, and went back to put on his hat and vest before he thumbed through the book for something he thought might be appropriate, then read in a clear, even voice Dick Ruffin's last rites.

It was by then close to sundown; red sunlight slanted down through the stiff treetops like the glow through cathedral windows bringing on a depth of hushed stillness fitting for the scene. Wes closed his Bible and stood a moment letting his thoughts drift from the murder to other things. The time he and Dick had gone to a secret pool in the mountains for fat trout. The times they'd sat on the rotting old porch, talking away bland summertime evenings. The day old Dick showed Wes how to make a squaw bridle out of a length of rope, and also how to make hobbles from an old piece of rag. That day old Dick had grinned, saying: "Wes, if a man could live long enough, he'd know just about everything there is to know. But maybe it's like the Injuns say. If a man learnt it all, there'd be no point in him goin' on to the next life. He'd just as well stay right here . . . and, hell . . . who'd want to think there was nothin' ahead but more of the eternal same?" Well, now Dick knew something no one else knew. If there really was an unearthly *paha sapa*, he'd be there about now, ready to learn whatever came next. Give him a year or so and he'd have a horse herd going; give him five years and he'd have his claim staked out and his cabin built.

Wes walked slowly back to the wagon, climbed up, lifted the lines, and kicked off the foot brake. There wasn't a sound in the cabin clearing; only that soft red light coming down in a filigree pattern through pine and fir limbs to touch the moist earth mound. He turned around and headed back the way he'd come.

He wanted to drift up through Dick's range and look at the horses, but it was too late in the day, so instead he drove unhurriedly back to Hangtown, put up the outfit at Claude's barn, and went down to his jailhouse to lock up. He had no prisoners to feed, and he'd already read his mail, so what he now did, he undertook because it was strong habit. He went to the bathhouse out behind the rooming house where he stayed, cleaned up, put on fresh clothes, and ambled around to Stub Pearson's hole-in-the-wall café. Digging graves might be solemn, sad work, but there was no denying that it also encouraged a man's appetite.

Stub was a stocky man of slightly less than average height who invariably had a cud of tobacco pouched into the right side of his face, giving him the look of a man perpetually afflicted with a toothache. He'd been a range cook, cowboy, freighter, even a placer miner, but rheumatism had driven him to more sedentary pastimes. He wasn't the best cook in the country, but in Hangtown at least he was the most popular. No sooner had Wes eased down at his counter than Stub went to work at his stove without bothering to ask for Wes's order. The reason for this was quite simple; Stub cooked something different every day, but for each twenty-four hours, at dawn or after midnight, his diners got whatever it was he'd hatched that particular day. There were no short orders and no selection. Stub's years as a chuck-wagon cook were carried over into his public trade. You ate what he piled on your plate, or you damned well went somewhere else. He didn't care which.

As he now worked, he said: "Too bad about Dick Ruffin. I heard some Anchor men talkin' about it this noon. I been tryin' to puzzle out why anyone'd do that to him."

Wes said indifferently: "What did you come up with?"

"Nothin'. How about you?"

"The same. Nothing."

"You bury him?"

"Yeah. Under a big fir tree near the creek."

"Find anythin' up there?"

"No."

"The hell you say. It don't seem to me, Wes, a feller could ride in, murder Dick, an' ride out without leavin' *some* kind of a mark behind."

"Well, this one did. What're you puttin' on that plate?"

Stub paused in his dishing up to look. "Seems sort of like catch-as-catch-can stew." He glanced around. "Why, don't you like catch-as-catch-can stew?"

Wes sighed. "Love it, Stub," he softly said. "That was hard work up there. Just get it over here on the counter."

Stub obeyed because he was about to serve it up anyway. He went back for the coffee and glass of water that accompanied every meal he served, then he drew out a stool behind his counter, sat down upon it, and masticated his cud very gently as he soberly gazed out through his solitary, fly-specked window into the darkening roadway.

"Would Vernon do it?" he asked. "He's been

bellyachin' about a horse trade he made with Dick."

Wes chewed, swallowed, then said: "Naw. Vern just naturally bellyaches. But I can't picture him walkin' up to within a few feet of someone and pulling a trigger."

Stub thought on that a moment, then said: "That close, huh? Well, whoever he was, I'd reckon he'd have to be almighty cold-blooded to kill a man like that."

Wes had long since arrived at that same conclusion, so he just continued eating without any comment. He knew Stub well enough to anticipate his next question, and answered it in advance. "It wasn't over his horses. Mosley Crawford said they're still all up there."

Stub swallowed, sought for something to anchor his speculations to, failed, and waggled his head dolefully back and forth. "It just don't make sense," he muttered, and peered into Wes's coffee cup. "I'll fetch you a refill," he said, and ambled over to the stove. "But there's got to be a reason."

Wes finished eating, paid up, and left the café. Darkness was settling over town. It came in heavy layers down from the rearward peaks and slopes, bearing with it the soft, seductive fragrance of forests and flowering meadows. Springtime within a hundred miles of the Sierras was a blessing rarely matched anywhere else on earth.

Stan Darcy and Mosely Crawford entered town

from the east, riding leisurely. They weren't the only Anchor riders up along saloon row, but they were the first ones Wes saw ride in, and, when he strolled up toward the tie rack where they were getting down, they also saw him, finished securing their animals, ducked under the rack, and walked up onto the plank walk.

"Well," Crawford said, "you got it done, we saw. It's about where I expect Dick'd want to be planted, too. Right nice spot."

"You rode by, up there?" asked Wes.

Mosley nodded and Stan Darcy fell to making a cigarette that he licked closed, popped between his lips, and lit.

"Yeah, we rode through on our way down here," the range boss replied, then gave his shoulders a little hitch. "I used to get mad enough at Dick to scorch his hair, for easin' the horses over onto us. But dog-gone it, he was a good cuss. Aren't too many of us real good anyway."

Darcy gazed up and down the roadway, then back again at Wes. "Get anythin' to go on up there?" he inquired, and Wes gave Stan the same answer he'd given Stub Pearson at the café. "Nothing. No rhyme or reason for it."

Stan was realistically philosophical about it. "It's not like the world's goin' to end for that matter," he said, inhaling and exhaling. "I sort of liked the old cuss, too, but those things happen . . . and life keeps right on going."

Wes nodded, hiding the annoyance that was rising up in him. Stan hadn't really known Dick Ruffin. Mosley had, but Mosley hadn't made that callous remark, either. It was true, of course. The passing of one old has-been wasn't going to affect life along the southern slope of the Sierras, or the west slope, either. Still and all . . . Wes changed the subject. "I expect we'll fetch in the horses and have an auction. But what we'll do with the money afterward I'm damned if I know. He didn't have any kin. At least he never mentioned any."

Mosley said, twisting to glance up where the noise and lights were: "Come along, Wes. We'll buy you a drink."

"Maybe later," the deputy murmured. "I got to go write up the report for the sheriff over at county seat. If I don't do it tonight, I'll likely forget to do it at all. I hate those lousy reports. See you fellers later."

He left them, strolling at an angle across the dusty roadway toward his jailhouse. Being the only lawman in a town had its advantages, and its pure disadvantages, too. Having to file reports all the time was the biggest disadvantage. Being able to have a few drinks on county time was one of the better advantages.

179

Silas Houseman who ran the most patronized general store in town was a short, wiry man with thick, lank black hair and watery brown eyes. He was in his fifties and a widower. Silas had only one genuine interest in life—money. He'd work as hard to make a small profit as to make a large one, but in neither case would he allow himself more than a certain length of time to make a deal. He worked hard; no one ever denied that. Along with his regular mercantile business Silas had his finger in a number of other enterprises. He'd loan money—when the security was ample, of course—or buy and sell grain, hay, harness, even wagons and buggies. He owned the building in which his store was located, and had built another building uptown that he'd rented for several years and had then sold. He had three employees in the general store and a warehouse-man out back where he bought and sold or traded such other things as household goods. It was half enviously said of Silas that if he died and went to heaven—*if*—he'd appraise the Pearly Gates while awaiting admittance, and make a deal on the spot with St. Peter.

You couldn't get anything out of Silas

Houseman during the day but business. His mind had trained itself to think only about trade from dawn until dusk. But after the store was closed, Silas was a different man. He liked an occasional drink, played poker now and then, and would discuss politics, social events, the weather, anything under the sun with you without even mentioning business.

But the first time Wes Potter ever knew Silas to combine both business and pleasure after work was the evening he returned to town after burying Dick Ruffin. He was back in his office going over that stuff he'd wrapped in Dick's blue handkerchief, when Silas came in, his glasses half down his nose, his watery brown eyes round and solemn. He saw the gold watch and other stuff and looked over the top of his spectacles.

"What you got?" he inquired, moving for a closer look. "Pawn stuff?"

Wes said it was the effects from Dick Ruffin's body and Silas turned away and sat down. "I was up at the saloon where those Anchor men are tonight," he stated, "listening to the talk. It's a real mystery, but everyone has some notion about why Ruffin was killed."

Wes leaned back. "It always works out this way," he retorted. "Folks have more fun when they don't know the facts. It's pretty hard to embroider facts, but as for gossip . . . it's got the sky as its limit."

"Well," said Silas, removing his glasses and sighting through them, "I just listened."

"What else could you've done?" asked Wes, and Silas dropped his bombshell.

"Oh, I could've told them a feller offered me Dick's guns this evening just at closin' time."

Wes looked straight at the older man. Silas took out a handkerchief and went to work polishing his glasses. He'd blow on them, polish, and repeat the process. When he finished, he raised his eyes to Wes. "Well, aren't you interested?"

"I'm interested. When you're through meddlin' with those damned glasses, you'll talk."

Silas softly smiled. "He wasn't more'n twenty-two or -three, tall, slight-built, hair as black as mine and eyes like wet obsidian. I'd say he was a 'breed, but he talked as good as any cowboy and he looked the part . . . except for the way he wore his gun."

"How was that?"

"Belted high, Wes, with the grip on the left side, butt facing to the right."

"Border cross," Wes murmured, and Silas, not able to quite make out the words, squinted quizzically. "Border cross," Wes repeated. "It's a particular kind of fast draw, Silas. You don't see many of them. They reach across with their right hand and yank the gun from left to right."

"Fast, is it?"

Wes nodded. "It's fast. But I never knew a

cowboy to use it, and you said this feller was a range rider."

"I said he *looked* the part. I didn't say he actually was a range rider. How would I know about that? I never saw the feller before in my life until he walked in this evening just at closin' time offerin' to peddle me those guns."

"Did you buy them?"

Silas's droll expression turned sly. "No. I told him it was closin' time and I'd already locked up the cash, but, if he'd come around in the morning, I'd make him an offer."

"Good thinking," Wes murmured.

Silas nodded. "I figured you'd want to look him over. He's up there at the Quaking Aspen Saloon, sitting at a wall table back by the door that leads into the card room. You can't miss him. He's got that funny way of wearing his gun."

Wes grimaced. There was nothing funny about a border cross draw; in fact, of all the unfunny things in Wes's world, that was just about the least unfunny. "Tell me, Silas, what did he say about the guns? I mean . . ."

"I know what you mean. He didn't say a word. Just laid them out on my gun counter, a couple of old Winchesters and an old long-barreled muzzle-loader with the most beautiful bird's-eye maple stock you ever saw, and asked me what I'd give him for them. I recognized the guns, especially that musket, and stalled him until tomorrow. I'd never seen him before, Wes. I know most of the riders hereabouts, but this one . . . no."

Wes stood up. It was late, his back ached, and he was tired, but all that seemed forgotten now. What he wanted to know was not so much how or why this cowboy had stolen those guns, as where he'd been while Wes had been burying old Dick, because it was a fair ride to Hangtown from Ruffin's horse ranch in the foothills, and, if he'd showed up here in town only a little while after Wes himself had returned, then he'd have to had been up there at about the same time Wes was there, doing all that digging. And that offered some very interesting possibilities. Unless he'd been watching from back in the forest, or had actually killed old Dick, how had he managed not to see the lawman, or be seen by him?

"That's all for now," he told Silas, and left the merchant sitting in his jailhouse office.

The night was well advanced and turning cool. There was the usual breeze coming in from the mountains. Along toward morning it got downright cold this time of year—early spring—and it wasn't unusual for a rind of frost to form on water troughs right up into June.

Saloon row was at the northeast end of town. Everywhere else lay darkness or only an occasional light, but up there where the noise and music came from it was as bright as day inside, and nearly as bright outside, where carriage lamps glowed on each side of the doorways to light the way for the thirsty or the adventurous.

The Quaking Aspen Saloon was a popular hangout for range men. It always had liquor and, in a separate room, the card and dice games. Sometimes—but not often—when an itinerant dancer passed through, it also had female entertainment. But usually it was an entirely masculine world. The range men seemed to prefer it that way, too. Not that they were the least bit averse to twinkling heels and a tight bodice—far from it—but in a place where there were only men, a cowboy didn't have to watch either his deportment or his language.

When Wes Potter strolled in the smoke was thick enough to sweep with a broom and the noise was at its height. He spotted Stan Darcy and Mosely Crawford bellied up at the bar along with other men he knew were also Anchor Ranch men, but since they didn't see him, he didn't seek them, either. Instead, he ambled over by the stove, which was unlit, and took a stand where he could see the gloomy shadowy corner tables. He spotted the stranger immediately. He had a bottle, a glass, and was alone. The noise and movement seemed not to touch him at all. He sat back there, long legs pushed out under the table, hat tilted back, dark, large eyes watching all that happened in the tumultuous, big room. Wes couldn't see the man's gun, but he didn't have to; he knew he was gazing at the right man.

A cowboy ambled past wearing a vacuous grin, saw Wes, and smiled. "Howdy, Deputy," he threw outward, and went weaving and listing on past without waiting for a greeting in return. The dark-looking, lanky cowboy saw Wes standing there by the stove, too, and looked straight at him without any expression one way or another on his darkly tanned face.

Wes started over. When he reached the table, the cowboy was eyeing him with a steady, solemn intentness. Wes didn't ask about sitting down; he drew out a chair and dropped down upon it. The stranger showed nothing at all on his face except that bright and assessing close interest.

"Welcome to Hangtown," Wes murmured. "You're new hereabouts."

The cowboy turned that over in his mind a moment, then slowly reached for his bottle, slowly filled his glass, and put the bottle aside. He was a hard one to appraise; there was neither good nor bad in his face. He was young, as Silas had observed, and he did wear his six-shooter in that unusual style, but so far he'd said nothing, so that was all Wes had to go on in his assessment. The cowboy threw back his head and dropped the slug of whiskey straight down, put the glass down, and brought his black gaze back to the lawman again, still as impassively silent as before.

Wes drummed on the tabletop. There was no friendliness in the face opposite him, which made it easier, so he said with all the warmth gone out of his voice: "Mister, you could be in serious trouble." Still the dark, lean man sat and stared and said nothing. "When folks ride into Hangtown wanting to sell the guns of a murdered man, it raises some tough questions."

A dark shadow swiftly passed across the cowboy's dark features, then was gone. He pushed the bottle and glass across the table. "Have a drink," he said in an inflectionless flat voice.

"No thanks."

"I don't blame you. It's lousy whiskey. In fact, it's a lousy night and a lousy town."

"Where you from?"

"You name it, Deputy, an' I've been there."

"What's your name?"

The dark eyes turned sardonic, the long-lipped mouth drooped a little. The cowboy did not reply. He was slipping back into his silences again. He had a disconcerting way of looking straight at a man without blinking or moving, leaving an uncomfortable and very awkward awareness in whoever he stared at. One thing Wes could now sense; this stranger was dangerous. He wasn't just an ordinary range rider; there was something more to him than horses and cattle and cow camps.

"What's yours?" he asked finally.

"Wes Potter, local deputy."

"Yeah. I saw the badge when you first walked in. That storekeeper ran to you." The lean shoulders rose and fell. "It was his civic duty, wasn't it, Deputy?"

"Maybe. We try to avoid trouble around here. As for the guns . . . unless you've got a real good reason for having them, mister, you're goin' to jail."

That blunt statement didn't seem to faze the cowboy. "If you don't like the whiskey," he said quietly, "how about some beer or ale?"

"No, thanks," replied Wes, beginning to tire of this. "You want to talk about the guns here, or over at the jailhouse?"

"Here'll do," murmured the stranger, evidently having come to his decision about this topic. "Those guns belong to me. I offered to sell them because I'm near broke. Bein' broke might be a crime but sellin' a man's own property surely isn't . . . not even in a town with a name like Hangtown."

"Those guns," stated Wes, "belonged to an old feller named Dick Ruffin. He was a friend of mine, but aside from that someone murdered him yesterday or the day before."

"I know," said the cowboy. "I was up there too, Deputy. In fact, I spent a couple of hours this afternoon watchin' you bury the old man." The dark eyes grew briefly shadowed, then that, too, passed and the stranger said: "What a man does when he figures he's plumb alone sometimes gives a feller some insight into the kind of man he is. Now you . . . I watched the way you laid him out in the hole you dug. And afterward how you looked away as you rattled those first few shovel loads of dirt down atop him. Then you read from the Book over his grave. You didn't know anyone was watchin', Deputy. You thought you were plumb alone. You know what I mean?"

Wes knew, but all he said was: "Old Dick was a friend. I told you that. Now then, stranger, I want two things. Your excuse for havin' those guns, and your name."

The dark eyes turned sardonic. Wes was talking tough now, but the stranger's reaction wasn't uneasiness; it was rather a sort of half irony and half willingness also to be tough. No one, making much of a study of the stranger, ever would have doubted his ability. He looked perfectly capable and he acted it. If trouble came, he would be ready and handy.

"I'm waiting," Wes said, leaning back from the table.

"No need for that," said the cowboy, nodding gently toward Wes's right arm, which was beneath the table now. "You're not going to have to draw on me, Deputy."

Wes said: "I'm not as sure of that as you are, but it's up to you."

"The guns are mine. So are the horses up there and the buildings and the land." The cowboy reached slowly into a shirt pocket, drew forth a crumpled, soiled envelope, and tossed it over in front of Wes. "That's my name on the envelope, Deputy. Tom Ruffin. That old man up there was my father." At Wes's slow look of doubt, the cowboy nodded his head. "Read the letter, Deputy."

# IV

It was an old letter and written in the cramped, painfully laborious hand of Dick Ruffin that Wes recognized as soon as he looked at it. By reading the letter, Wes was given adequate time to recover from his surprise—and also from his powerful doubt that this man who said his name was Tom Ruffin was telling the truth. The letter was awkwardly composed but full of a quiet wistfulness. It was dated almost two years earlier and said old Dick would like to see his son. Then it told of his horses and ended with the wish that someday, before it was too late, Tom might come and visit the Hangtown country.

As Wes put the paper down, Ruffin said: "Well, Deputy, I came. I've been sitting in here tonight wondering what kind of a fate it is that does something like this to a man. Waits until the day before he arrives to see a father he doesn't even remember . . . then kills him."

Wes carefully refolded the paper, stuffed in into the worn envelope, and put it gently over in front of Ruffin. "I was wondering this afternoon while I was burying him, how it was that a man who'd lived as long and hard as old Dick did had no kin. I used to ride up and sit with him on the porch in the hot summer nights, listening to him spin his tales. He never once mentioned having any kin. Never even hinted about it."

"Is that so strange?" asked the dark-eyed, swarthy cowboy. "In his day it was nothin' to be proud of, Deputy."

"What wasn't?"

"Taking a squaw."

Wes drummed on the tabletop for a moment. He'd pegged the stranger for a half-breed the minute he'd seen him, exactly as Silas Houseman had also done. He was thinking that, in fact, what Tom Ruffin had just said was the truth; even now, so many years later, while there wasn't open discrimination, folks still eyed half-bloods differently than they did other people.

"Aren't you going to preach a sermon?" Ruffin dryly asked.

Wes stopped drumming and shook his head. He wasn't a complex man; he knew how life should be and he also knew how it was. "No sermon," he muttered. "What good would it do?"

"None, Deputy. None at all. I went to the Indian school over in Nevada. I graduated with honors.

You know why? Because I debated, and one time our debating team took on the tribal council, and I said this world was a changing place, Deputy, that when each generation passed on, it took most of its prejudices with it, that a man is a man . . . red or white. That I didn't hate whites. All I had to do was live long enough an' the whites who hated me would die. The next generation wouldn't have those same prejudices. Well, Deputy, tell me, have I lived long enough yet?"

Wes pondered. There was something about this man that was a lot like old Dick. But there was a wide difference, too. It was this difference Wes wondered about now. He said: "Was your mother Shoshone?"

The cowboy nodded. "Northern Shoshone, not southern Paiute, Deputy. Northern Shoshone. Her mother was a captive Sioux."

That, Wes speculated, accounted for this man's height and obvious intelligence. "A great people, the Sioux," he said. Then he reached for the glass and the bottle. "I'll have that drink with you now."

Ruffin's dark gaze softened. "You'll need a clean glass," he said quietly. "You wouldn't want to drink after a 'breed."

Wes looked up, his blue gaze hardening. "You like to talk that way?" he asked. "Because if you do, Ruffin, you don't believe that stuff you just told me about prejudice dying out."

They regarded one another for a long moment,

then Ruffin smiled with his eyes only. "You're right," he said. "But I'll fetch another glass anyway. You might be a man I'd want to drink with, Deputy."

They had their drink. In fact, they had two drinks. Then Wes suggested that they leave the saloon, and they departed together. Outside, the night was a soft blaze of star shine across a firmament of deepest, enameled purple. Off where the mountains lay, there was a darker blackness, and a timeless fragrance.

Wes led the way down in front of Houseman's store where there was a wall bench. There, he sat down, dug around for his tobacco sack, and went to work manufacturing a brown-paper smoke. When he offered the makings to Ruffin, he got a shake of the head. He lit up, exhaled, and leaned back.

"It's got me stumped," he said. "Dick's murder."

"Enemies?" murmured the lanky half-breed.

"Naw. Not *that* kind anyway. He traded horses now and then and maybe skinned a feller or two, but it takes a special kind of enemy to stand less than ten feet from you and pull a trigger with his gun practically against your chest." Wes turned. "What were you doing up there before I arrived?"

"The same thing you did after you arrived. Looking for something. But I didn't find it. There were plenty of tracks, but none of them was right. Tell me about him, Deputy. It took me a long time to make up my mind to come see him. I had my personal reasons for not being in any hurry about that."

"Sure," Wes murmured, half understanding. "Well, Dick was like all the rest of us. Both good and bad. But I always found the good far outweighed the bad. He used to tell me stories. We went fishing a few times, did a little hunting, too."

As Wes talked, his companion leaned his head back and shoved his legs out, quietly listening, and yet, in some way, he did not seem entirely to turn loose. It was almost as though he either had never known how to relax completely, or had forgotten how. He was, Wes thought to himself, like a coiled spring, and a man had to have a very good reason to become like that. The only reason Wes was familiar with that often kept a man from relaxing was the leashed violence inside him.

He thought of something else, while he talked of old Dick Ruffin. The way old Dick's boy wore his .45 spelled gunfighter. There was a slight chance this was not precisely true. Wes had been around long enough to know a few range men who made a hobby of gunmanship, and wore their weapons the same way professionals did. But generally this was not so; when a man came along wearing his gun tied low or with the trigger filed or the front sight missing—or wore it in the position of the border cross draw—he wasn't just a cowboy. But the paradox wasn't so easy to unravel either, for the man sitting next to him had feeling and

194

sentiment, and even a little humor in him, for Wes had seen those tawny dark eyes ironically glow once, back there at the saloon. If he was a gunfighter, he wasn't the common variety of coldly venomous, totally dedicated killer that was fairly common in the West.

When he ran out of anecdotes, Ruffin said: "Well, I'll never know, will I, whether I shouldn't have come at all, or whether I should have come a couple of years sooner?"

"No," Wes agreed. "You'll never know now."

"It's good to hear someone talk of him who liked him, Deputy. I never did. I never had any reason to. My mother died of lung fever when I was sixteen years old. Uncle Sam put me in the school full time after that. I got an education, but when I wanted to leave in the summers to go find him, they told me it would be better if I didn't. They said white fathers didn't want to be embarrassed by their 'breed kids."

"Hell," exclaimed Wes irritably, "what a lousy thing to tell a kid! Dick wasn't like that."

"I didn't think he was, either, after I got that letter. Only a man wonders, Deputy, why did he take my mother back to her people, then come back here to his ranch alone?"

Wes had no ready answer so he said nothing. He could think of several reasons but they weren't very charitable to the memory of a dead friend, so he refrained from suggesting them.

Ruffin turned and gazed at him. "Kind of hard to come up with a decent answer, isn't it?" he said.

"Yeah, it is. But Dick's not here."

"Would he tell us the truth if he was here, Deputy?"

Wes wasn't sure about that, either. Sometimes you knew people—and at the same time you didn't know them. He said: "Who can say? If you were his friend, you'd say he'd tell the truth. If you were his enemy, you'd say he wouldn't tell the truth."

The cowboy stood up, turned, and soberly gazed back downward. "Odd how things stack up sometimes, Deputy. I knew, when you walked into that saloon tonight, you and I'd have words before this night ended. But I sure as hell had no idea I'd end up liking you." He stuck out his hand. Wes got up, shook, and, as he dropped Ruffin's hand, he gave his head a little rueful wag.

"Come by my office tomorrow and we'll start the process for naming you Dick's heir."

Tom gently shook his head. "No thanks," he said. "Deputy, the surest way for a stranger to get hurt in a new place is to start right in heaving his weight around. I'd just as soon folks didn't even know I was his son. But I expect by now that can't be helped. Still, I don't want whoever plugged him to get me, too. So for a while at least, I'll just sort of keep out of sight."

Wes listened and made a little deprecatory

gesture about this. "I don't see where there could be any connection. You didn't even know him. You weren't involved in whatever it is he got shot over."

"Still," persisted Ruffin, "I'll just stand back for a while. When you find out why he was killed, maybe I'll feel different." Ruffin smiled. "See you again, Deputy." He turned and walked back up toward the hitch rack out front of the Quaking Aspen Saloon.

Wes watched him go, thinking that Tom Ruffin was a likeable man, tall and capable and predictable, not like some half-breeds, who acquired all the vices of both races and blessed few of the virtues. Then he ambled on down to the rooming house where he lived and went on up to his room, which overlooked both the front roadway and his jailhouse. He was asleep ten minutes after he lay back.

It seemed, when he awakened, he had only closed his eyes. That backache was still there, too, but by the time he got down to Stub's place for breakfast, it was less noticeable.

He didn't see Tom Ruffin in town that day, but when Silas Houseman came hopping over full of avid curiosity, he told him it would be all right to buy the guns if they were brought to him again. When Silas persisted in asking the obvious questions, Wes finally told him.

"He's old Dick's son."

Silas was nonplussed. "His son? I never heard he had a son. I never even heard . . . are you plumb sure, Wes? Did he have proof?"

"He did."

Silas sat down. "Well, I'll be damned," he mumbled. "That's one for the book. Wait until Mister Harriman hears that. Old Dick had a son."

Wes looked up. "What's John Harriman got to do with it? Why should he care whether Dick had a son or not?"

"Because he's already got that lawyer feller down the road filing papers on Dick's land."

Wes's face slowly creased into a puzzled frown. "Who told you that?" he eventually demanded.

"The lawyer himself told me. Last night in the card room," replied Silas.

Wes went across to his open office doorway and leaned there, looking up and down the morning-lighted dusty roadway. He knew the lawyer; they'd crossed horns a time or two over some of Wes's prisoners. The man's name was Ben Hedges. He'd put out his shingle three years before. He was a cynical, tough operator from somewhere in the East. When he'd first arrived in Hangtown, he'd had a lovely wife, but she'd left him a year later. By now, though, most of the gossip about that unusual event was worn thin and folks hardly even remembered her. Wes remembered because he didn't think he'd ever seen such a beautiful woman in his life as Mrs.

Hedges had been. She'd had red-copper hair, green eyes, and flesh as solid and handsome as fresh-churned butter.

"Well," said Silas, barging past to reach the outside plank walk. "What're you daydreaming about?"

"You wouldn't believe me if I told you," said Wes, pulling himself back from the past with an effort.

"What about this son of old Dick's?"

"What about him? He's the heir and that's that. Mister Harriman'll find it out in time."

"He won't like it."

"He doesn't have to like it, Silas. What I'm wondering is why he'd bother with that land anyway."

"It adjoins him."

"Well, hell, so do the mountains, and he hasn't filed on them."

Silas said no more for obviously Wes had something on his mind that was making him stubborn and argumentative. Even after Silas started back across toward his store, Wes continued to stand there, in his doorway, gazing southward across the road where Hedge's law office was sandwiched between the saddle and harness shop and a Chinese laundry.

He had no very great esteem for the lawyer, although he did not actually dislike him. It was Hedges's job to try and obtain releases for those who hired him to get them out of Wes's jailhouse. Wes understood that perfectly because he, too, knew a little law. But all the same that didn't make him feel any warmth toward the lawyer. But actually it went deeper than that. Ben Hedges was cynical, sarcastic, and smilingly supercilious; each of those things had rubbed Wes the wrong way one time or another when he and Hedges had come together. He didn't trust the lawyer, either. He couldn't put his finger on the source for that feeling, but it was there inside him, strong and abiding. Hedges impressed Wes as the kind of a man who would do anything or say anything, if he thought it would advance some interest of his, personal or otherwise.

It bothered Wes that wealthy John Harriman who already owned so much of the foothill range would try to get title to Dick Ruffin's two sections. He knew for a fact that Ruffin's land wouldn't increase the carrying capacity of Harriman's range ten head. He also knew Harriman wouldn't care a bit about the timber or the buildings. Then why, he kept asking himself, the big rush to file for possession and ownership?

He ate dinner over at Stub's place, avoided a lot

of questions from Pearson, and got back outside as the sun was just beginning to slide off toward the western rims. Claude Lucas, from the livery barn, came walking along from the direction of the harness shop with several freshly stitched leather halters in his hand. Without any preliminary Claude mumbled that it was a dirty shame, the price saddlers charged nowadays just for stitching up a few old halters.

Wes agreed. Not that he actually felt Claude had been put upon, but because with men like Silas and Claude it was usually easier to agree than disagree because both were sometimes garrulously argumentative.

Claude then forgot about his halters. "Say, I heard something a little while ago. Dick Ruffin had a son."

"Folks have 'em every now and then," Wes murmured, turning to intercept that coated, hatted man coming toward them up the sidewalk. "You better go saddle my horse," he said to Claude. "I got a little ridin' to do this afternoon."

Claude nodded and walked away, beginning to scowl darkly again as he reverted to his earlier unpleasant thoughts. Wes waited until the oncoming man was close, then barred his onward progress and offered a cool little greeting. The other man, nearly the same height and build as Wes, stopped and raised his eyebrows, looking saturnine.

"You arresting me, Deputy?" he asked.

"Can't say I haven't thought about it a time or two, Mister Hedges. But not today. All I'd like from you right now is an answer to why John Harriman wants those two sections of Ruffin's land?"

Hedges's sharp, observant blue eyes stopped moving and lingered upon Wes Potter. "You could go out to the ranch and ask Mister Harriman," he replied. "But I couldn't tell you because that's privileged information. As his attorney . . ."

"As anyone's attorney," stated Wes, interrupting, "you'd feel obligated to keep everything in fullest confidence. Yeah, I've heard that before. It's only a passing interest anyway. But suppose Ruffin had heirs?"

Hedges scoffed. "What heirs? That unwashed old devil lived up there all alone. You find me one person around here who can prove otherwise, and I'll eat my hat."

Wes gazed at the soft headpiece Ben Hedges was wearing. "That'd be worth seeing," he said softly. "With salt or without salt?"

Hedges started to push past. "It's too early in the day for jokes," he growled. "I've got business to tend to."

Wes didn't move aside. Instead, he braced into the impending collision, but Hedges stopped just short, throwing a testy look at the deputy.

"What are you trying to do?" he demanded,

stiffening, turning suddenly angry and outraged.

"Get an answer to a simple question," stated Wes, giving the attorney glare for glare.

"I can't tell you, and I'm not even sure I would tell you if it wasn't a confidence, the way you're acting today, Deputy."

"It's early," said Wes, settling flat down in his boots. "I've got all day."

Hedges could have stepped off the sidewalk and walked around out in the roadway, but he didn't. He slowly reddened and said: "Get out of the way."

Wes didn't move an inch. He hooked both thumbs in his shell belt and grinned. He enjoyed seeing Hedges get angry. "With or without salt?" he said, still grinning.

Suddenly Hedges's face swiftly altered. His anger seemed just as swiftly to dissolve. He peered intently at Wes. "Are you saying that old man Ruffin has an heir?" he demanded.

Wes slouched. "Tell you what I'll do, Mister Hedges. I'll trade you a little privileged information for a little of the same from you."

Hedges stood, silent and intent for a moment, then inclined his head. "It better be factual," he grumbled. "All right, Wesley. Mister Harriman wants those two sections of land because he's undertaking a general policy of range expansion."

"But they're no good for cattle," retorted Wes. "There's nothing on them but trees and rocks, a couple of worthless little snow water creeks, and precious little worthwhile grazing."

"Deputy," exclaimed the lawyer, "I don't make those decisions! John Harriman does. All I do is what he pays me for. He wants that land and I've started suit to quiet title so that he can have it. Now, about this heir . . ."

"Dick Ruffin has a son, Mister Hedges."

"I don't believe it."

"You don't have to believe it. I've seen him, talked to him, and seen his proof. You can file all the quiet title papers you want to. Mister Harriman'll have to buy that land from old Dick's son if he aims to get clear title to it. That's the law."

Hedges sputtered: "But, why hasn't his son shown up before? Why didn't the old man ever tell folks he had a son? I can't just accept some saddle tramp's will-o'-the-wisp claim to being Ruffin's executor without more proof than this."

Wes was still grinning; he enjoyed the older man's obvious consternation. "You," he told Hedges, "don't have to accept anything. You don't have to believe anything. Dick had a son an' he's here now, in Hangtown. Or at least he was last night. So if Mister Harriman wants that land, he'll have to deal with Tom Ruffin. You don't even enter into it, unless Harriman hires you to represent him, and from what I've seen of John Harriman, he'll make his own offers."

Hedges moved over against the building and leaned upon it. He watched Wes's face very closely. Then he flopped his hands up and down in a gesture of resignation. "All right, where can I meet this Tom Ruffin?"

"Damned if I know. But he'll be around. I'll tell him Mister Harriman wants to see him. Only I still can't see what possible reason Anchor Ranch would have for wanting to get those two sections."

"Because of adjacency," snapped the lawyer. "Haven't you ever seen cowmen snap up adjacencies before?"

"Not that kind, Mister Hedges, and neither have you. Unless they've got some reason for wanting them that has nothing to do with ranching."

For a second the lawyer's lips flattened and his sly eyes blanked over. Then that odd expression passed and he said: "Mister Harriman's coming to town this evening. I'll send him over to see you. Let me give you a little advice, too. Produce this Tom Ruffin. Mister Harriman isn't the kind of a man to play jokes on, Wesley, and you can take my word for that. It won't be like arresting some common drunk or some obnoxious cowboy."

Wes stepped aside and jerked his head. He wasn't smiling now at all. Hedges had spoken down to him and it stung a little. As the lawyer stumped on past, Wes turned to watch him go. Someday, he thought, they'd really tangle; Hedges was one of those men who made a career out of antagonizing people who he considered less swollen with importance and prestige than he was. Well, Wes was a very hard man to impress. As for prestige, he didn't give a damn for it one way or another, although, with a man like John Harriman, he understood that it was almost like breath.

Harriman was a large man in more ways than one. He was also a plunger and a gambler. Rumor around town had it that he'd recently lost a fortune in some railroad scheme. Wes knew nothing about that; he didn't delude himself at all. He was a small-town deputy sheriff and John Harriman was a big planner and schemer. He'd come out of the East many years earlier, had bought the Anchor outfit, and had, over the years, steadily expanded it. But Wes knew for a fact that Harriman was far from a fool; he never bought any land that would not bring him a quick return the same year he bought it through an allowable increase in the size of his cattle herds. In a nutshell that was exactly what stuck in his craw at this time. Harriman'd had plenty of opportunities to expand into the mountains, and had never once done it. Yet now, here he was, scheming ways to get hold of Dick Ruffin's practically worthless two sections of land, with old Dick scarcely cold in his grave. It didn't sound right. It didn't even look right.

Wes started for the livery barn. He had the entire day to kill and he meant to do just exactly that, going over Dick's range, through his old buildings, poking and prying everywhere trying at least to imagine why Ruffin had been murdered like that.

It didn't cross his mind until he was halfway up into the foothills there could be a connection between old Dick's death and Harriman's sudden move to gain control of the land. Even after it occurred to him, he pushed it out of his mind as being too utterly ridiculous. John Harriman was a powerful man with thousands of acres, a big crew of riders, position, influence, wealth. Dick Ruffin had been—well, to face facts—old Dick had been a penny-ante horse rancher on two six-hundred-and-forty-acre sections of pretty damned worthless land. There was a coincidence, but surely no possible connection. Besides, it'd been one of Harriman's riders, Stan Darcy, who'd found old Dick.

He rode past the buildings up into what old Dick had called "the big meadow". It was big by Dick's standards, but by any local range man's standards it would have been called something far less expansive. To get there Wes had to pass through a dark belt of fir trees a hundred yards wide and deceptively thick. But the trail was good and it was pleasantly cool and fragrant in there.

The big meadow itself, which lay just beyond the firs, was probably two hundred acres in size with lush, tall grass, a creek bisecting one corner of it, and ample shade all around where the trees formed ranks again. It was peaceful, secluded, and isolated. It was also the favorite haunt for Dick's horses, and even after Wes rode into sight out of the trees, the animals didn't act too skittery. An old mare trumpeted the warning but the others didn't run; they stopped grazing to look and wonder, but they made no offer to break away in a wild run, which suited Wes just fine.

He eased far around to the left and right never crowding, never getting close enough to stampede the band. Some of the animals he recognized, some he knew only because they had old Dick's shoulder brand, and some he didn't know at all. But when he finally completed his survey and stepped down for a drink over at the creek, he was satisfied it was as Mosley Crawford had said. They were all here. But that didn't help him any. If it did anything at all, it just complicated things more, for he'd eliminated one of the most likely reasons for Ruffin's murder. He made a smoke, lit up, gazed over at the grazing herd for a while, then climbed up and headed back down through the trees again for the cabin area.

He'd already been here once and he'd made a fairly comprehensive search at that time, but he was impelled now by some deeper feeling of anxiety. It wasn't that he thought he'd never find the killer; it was almost as though he thought he would find him, and shrank from it for some reason he could not define.

He went through the old barn, the shoeing shed, and finally through Dick's cabin. He used an old broom to delve under Dick's wall bunk and into corners, seeking the empty casing from the bullet that had killed Ruffin. Not that he expected to find it. Dick had been killed by a .45 pistol; they didn't eject casings. But he looked anyway.

He went over to the old man's handmade dresser and sat down laboriously to go through every little scrap of paper he could find squirreled away over there. But that didn't take long; there were some Morgan registry papers for several horses, some carefully cut out and treasured lithographs of mountains and animals, and a soiled bit of paper with the address of the Nevada Indian school on it. He sat gazing at that last slip of paper longest, and finally decided to take it with him. Not that it was pertinent to the murder, but it was in Dick's handwriting, and it closed, at least for Wes Potter, the last little gate of doubt about Dick's son.

He walked out onto the old porch and cursed to himself. Nothing. No spent casing, no sign of any kind. It was just as it had been the other time he'd come out here. The silence was oppressive, the shadows identical, the pine scent as peacefully pleasant—and the buildings were just a little more forlorn and hushed, and in some way, at least to Wes, haunted. Full of memories of old Dick chuckling as he walked along, or sitting there on the porch in a tilted-back chair, spinning yarns, or riding up on a fine horse as proud as any old-time *ozuye we tawatas*—man of war.

He gave it up, went out to his horse at the barn, mounted up, and rode out. It bothered him that even several days after the killing he still had nothing. Perhaps if he'd been longer at his lawman's trade, he'd have felt differently, but there was no one to tell him that, and even if there had been, Wes was youthful enough still to be impatient. An older lawman would have composed himself for the long wait; sooner or later, if a man has the patience for it, things come out. Sometimes, too, they're right under a man's nose but inhibitions blind him to them.

He rode all the way back to town worrying his problem like a pup worrying an old bone bigger than he was. When he arrived back at the livery barn, it was evening, saloon row was coming to its customary noisy exuberance, and elsewhere Hangtown was turning darkly quiet and composed.

Claude took his horse at the livery barn without much talk, and he afterward ambled down to Stub's place for supper. That empty feeling went right along with him every step of the way.

# VI

He had a little mail to sort and tend to, so he had his after-supper smoke at his desk over in the jailhouse. He hadn't much thought of his meeting with Ben Hedges until, near 8:00 with night fully settled over Hangtown, Hedges and big John Harriman strolled in from the yonder roadway.

Harriman was one of those transplanted Easterners who settled into the ways of the frontier like a duck takes to water. He wore his six-gun as though he'd always worn one. Even his big-brimmed black hat had the sweat stains and dust of a lifelong range man. Only his talk was different. He was an educated man; his English was good, his pronunciations were seldom slurred, and he never seemed to have to grope for the proper expressions. He was a large man, over six feet tall, big-boned and solid. He was nearing his middle fifties now, or at least looked to be nearing them, so a lot of his bulk was turning from gristle to tallow. If he'd ever been married, no one knew anything about it, and he lived as a bachelor out at his Anchor Ranch. He had gray eyes, like oak smoke on a windy winter day, strong features, and a forward, blunt manner. Harriman was the kind of person who inspired respect. His size and heft alone would have done that, but he was also an aloof, driving man who exuded power and authority. It was difficult to be around him very long without feeling somehow less a man than he was in most ways.

Wes was conscious of this feeling the moment he glanced up and saw who his visitors were, because Harriman filled his office doorway effectively blocking out the lawyer until he moved into the office, permitting Hedges to march inside, also.

It only took one look at John Harriman's ruddy, square-jawed face to see that he'd been informed of Dick Ruffin's son, and didn't at all like what he'd been told. Wes nodded without smiling or saying anything, motioned both men to chairs, and waited. The storm would break whenever big John Harriman wished for it to.

It wasn't a very long wait. Harriman sat down and leaned forward to say: "Deputy, Hedges told me what you said about Ruffin having a son. I don't believe it. I lived next door to that old man a long time. Never once did I ever hear him mention having kin."

Wes nodded. He could go along with that because he'd never heard him admit having a son, either. But all that proved was that old Dick hadn't wanted to talk about his son. It didn't prove he didn't have a son.

"He's got one, all right, Mister Harriman," Wes

said. "A tall 'breed whose mother was a northern Shoshone woman."

"Bunk," snorted Harriman, leaning back and throwing one mighty arm over the back of his chair. "Why does he show up now, a day or two after that old cuss got killed? Deputy, this man who claims he's Ruffin's son . . . what does he want?"

"As far as I know, nothing, Mister Harriman. I talked with him a little. I said he should start proceedings to be declared executor of Dick's estate. He said he wasn't going to."

Harriman's hard, gun-metal stare got utterly still. "Wasn't going to?" he repeated. "Why?"

Wes shrugged. "That's what he said. He wasn't going to."

"He doesn't even want the horses?"

"I don't know, Mister Harriman. I don't think, right now, that he knows himself. You see, he'd never known Dick. It was a shock to him to find Dick'd been killed only a day or two before he showed up after all those years. When we talked the other night, I got the impression he's still having trouble understanding that Dick was gone."

Harriman looked at lawyer Hedges briefly, then swung back toward Wes looking a little baffled. "He's up to something," Harriman muttered. "He's got to be. It's too much of a coincidence, Potter. Dick dies . . . and out of nowhere appears this man claiming he was the old man's son. It just doesn't ring true."

"It does to me, Mister Harriman. I saw a letter Dick had written him."

"Forgery, Deputy."

"No, sir, it was no forgery. I've seen enough of old Dick's handwriting to know it when I see it."

Ben Hedges cleared his throat. "Where is this supposed son now?" he inquired.

"I don't know. I told you that before. He was here in the afternoon and evening, then he pulled out."

"Well," persisted the lawyer, "where can he be contacted? Mister Harriman and I would like to interrogate him."

Wes thought back to his own initial attempt at questioning Tom Ruffin and came near to smiling at the vision of Ruffin putting that blank, black stare upon Ben Hedges, and saying nothing. "I don't know where you can reach him. All I can tell you is that he'll be around one of these days."

"Did he tell you that?" Harriman demanded, and Wes shook his head.

"Not in so many words, Mister Harriman," he replied. "But he sure left that impression."

Harriman gazed once more at his lawyer. He seemed stymied. Hedges got up and said: "The next time you see him, tell him to come down to my office."

Wes arose as John Harriman also got up. "I'll

ask him to go to your office," he said quietly. "My impression of Tom Ruffin is that no one tells him anything."

Harriman turned at that, and faintly frowned. He seemed to catch a double meaning to Wes's reply, and the way he was gazing at Ben Hedges. He paused at the door to say: "Deputy, you're an old hand at estimating men. What, exactly, was your impression of this stranger?"

Wes was candid. "That he's no liar, Mister Harriman, and that he can take care of himself in any kind of company."

Harriman leaned in the doorway, eyeing Wes. Finally he said: "What gave you that impression?"

"The way he handles himself, for one thing. For another, he wears his gun for the border cross draw. He's no four-flusher, Mister Harriman, a man who wears a gun like that knows how to use it."

Hedges said: "You mean he's a gunfighter?"

Wes was annoyed. "I didn't say any such a damned thing. What I said was . . . he wears his gun like he can use it. He looks like a man who won't be pushed, and he doesn't say much, but when he talks, it's to the point an' he looks you straight in the eye." Wes turned back to face Harriman again. "It's none of my affair why you want those two sections of land up there, but I'd say this, Mister Harriman, try to buy them from him. Don't try to take them from him."

Harriman's eyes narrowed the slightest bit, then he abruptly turned, stepped outside, and jerked his head at Ben Hedges, who obediently followed him out into the night without speaking another word to Wes Potter.

The sounds of revelry coming from along saloon row were muted by the time they reached the jailhouse. It was a soft-hushed night otherwise, warm and balmy with no threat of the chill that would arrive later. Wes stood in his doorway, watching Harriman and Hedges head on down toward the lawyer's little lighted office for a while, then stepped outside, hiked northward as far as the telegraph office, and sent a query to the Indian school whose address he had on that little scrap of paper he'd brought back with him from Ruffin's cabin.

He'd thought of showing that paper to Harriman and Hedges. But that had been before those two started irritating him. Now, he decided, from here on he'd play his cards close to his chest.

He strolled back to the office to finish going through the mail, and was surprised when he stepped through the door to find Tom Ruffin standing with his hands clasped behind his back over at the wall rack, gazing at the racked-up rifles and carbines and scatter-guns.

Ruffin turned, unsmilingly, and gravely nodded. "Missed you at the ranch this afternoon," he said, moving across to a chair near Wes's desk.

"Read your sign, though, saw where you'd been searching an' where you'd gone up into the pasture to scout the horse herd."

Wes dropped down at his desk, thinking Tom Ruffin's ability to read sign hadn't been learned at the Indian school. He pushed the mail aside and leaned back in his chair to say: "A feller named John Harriman who owns the Anchor Ranch which adjoins your pappy's two sections wants that land. He was in here a little while ago with his lawyer, whose office is down the road an' across the way. His name's Ben Hedges. They want to talk to you."

Tom's very dark gaze lingered upon Wes's face after the deputy had stopped speaking. The expression was that same unreadable look that could mean just about anything, or just about nothing. Wes waited; he'd learned that much. Tom Ruffin spoke when he was good and ready to say something, and not before.

"This John Harriman," he eventually murmured in a low, quiet tone of voice, "is he a rich man?"

Wes nodded. "That's what folks say, but I don't know." He gave Tom a brief thumbnail sketch of Harriman, then fell silent again, waiting. Tom pushed his long legs out and thumbed back his hat as he quietly studied the scuffed toes of his booted feet. He was silent so long this time that Wes got impatient. He knew the Indian way; time meant nothing. But he wasn't an Indian, not even a half-breed Indian, so he didn't have that same attitude. Then Ruffin spoke, his voice just as softly quiet as before, but the words fell like distant thunder, shocking Wes into stunned silence.

"I brought a dead man back to Hangtown with me, Deputy. I don't know who he is . . . or was . . . except that he was riding a bay horse with an anchor branded on the left shoulder." Ruffin dug under his coat, brought forth a .45, and leaned to place it upon Wes's desk. "The initials carved into the handle might mean something to you. They mean nothing to me."

Wes gazed at the walnut grips. Two deeply etched letters stood out: *SD*. He stiffened a little in his chair for a closer look. SD. Stan Darcy! When he raised his eyes, Tom Ruffin was watching him. He said: "You knew him, didn't you?"

Wes said: "Where is he?"

"Tied over his horse out back. Come on, I'll show you."

But as Tom arose, Wes said: "Wait a minute. Yeah, I knew him. His name was Stan Darcy an' he rode for Anchor. But right now I want to know more about how he died and where."

Ruffin nodded. He seemed to have anticipated Wes's reaction. "I didn't do it," he said, standing there, tall and lean with orange lamplight high-lighting his cheek bones, which were prominent, and his long, relaxed lips. "I was well back into the rough country behind that horse pasture where

I met your tracks on the way back. There's a little path up in there. I followed it because whoever made that trail tried to conceal it. I got curious and kept going. About a mile back from the pasture in a rocky place, I found him. His horse was tied to a tree. He was still limp when I saw him, which meant he hadn't been dead very long. Maybe not more'n an hour or two. That's all I know, except that his gun hadn't been fired. It was still in the holster."

Wes let the stiffness leave as he stood up, nodding.

"Show me," he said, and followed Ruffin out into the darkness.

They went around into the alleyway where two horses patiently waited. One animal had the dead man on it.

Wes leaned down and looked. It was Darcy all right. He looked for the bullet hole; it was in the middle of Darcy's chest with powder burns on the shirt front. Wes straightened up, half turned, and met Ruffin's tawny eyes.

"Yeah," Tom said. "Just like the other bullet hole. Plumb center and up close."

Wes stepped back. This seemed to be his time to speculate about coincidences. Unless the same man who had killed Tom's father had also killed Stan Darcy, this was another of those inexplicable coincidences, like having Tom Ruffin show up right at the time his father was shot to death.

"Well . . . ?" Ruffin said.

Wes, who had known the dead man, said—"I'll take him out to the shed."—and reached for the Anchor horse's reins. "You go on back inside. I'll be along directly." He walked off, leading the patient horse. It didn't occur to him until he was unlocking the little shed where the dead were frequently left, pending notification of next of kin, or in case no kinsmen were known were stored until a grave could be dug, that as dark as it was, and as late, perhaps no one had seen Ruffin ride down the back alley with his dead companion.

Afterward, while he fumbled with the lock on the shed, he decided to put the Anchor horse in his own little corral behind the jailhouse and not walk it all the way up to Lucas's livery barn. He had no special reason for doing that except that he wished to talk more to Ruffin, and his corral was much closer. But as he later flung Darcy's rigging over the top corral stringer, an idea came to him. No one knew about the killing but the killer. John Harriman and Hedges wouldn't know, in all probability, because they were down at the lawyer's office and wouldn't have seen Ruffin ride down the dark alleyway.

He leaned on the corral, trying to come to some kind of a conclusion about all this. He was still a little stunned at Darcy's murder—which obviously was what it was, since Darcy's gun hadn't been fired or, for that matter, according to Tom Ruffin, even drawn from its holster. He put the actual killing out of his mind for a moment, turned instead to puzzling over why Darcy had been killed, exactly as he'd puzzled over why old Dick had been killed the same way, in roughly the same part of the country. Suddenly now, John Harriman's interest in those two sections of land became significant. Two innocent men—at least as far as Wes knew they were innocent men—had been murdered out there, and at the same time John Harriman was trying to move heaven and earth to get title to that land. There could, he told himself, be some important connection.

He turned and started back for his office, full of quick, hard curiosity.

# VII

Ruffin had to go over it all again, but slower this time and with Wes frequently interrupting to ask questions. How had Stan been lying, in what direction, how far off was the Anchor horse tied?

Tom finally said: "I'll show you in the morning. I'll even lie down right where I found him for you." He was getting annoyed with Wes's questions. Then the deputy paced once across the room and back, and halted in front of Ruffin's chair.

"He's the one who first found your paw and reported to me old Dick had been murdered."

That brought Tom's flagging interest back up again. He folded one large-boned hand over the other one and squeezed. His knuckles popped. He lifted a puzzled, perplexed gaze to Wes and kept it there without speaking for a long while, but finally he said: "Maybe that's it. Maybe that's why whoever killed my paw killed this feller Darcy. Don't ask me to explain, I can't. But isn't it possible Darcy saw something that day, or heard someone say something, or . . . ?"

"It's possible," agreed Wes. "I was thinking that, too. I knew Stan Darcy well enough. He wasn't a killer. He was just an average range rider, neither any worse nor better than any other cowboy I've ever known. He was like your paw . . . not the kind of a man likely to murder enemies."

"All right," stated Ruffin, "then that's got to be it, Deputy. Darcy knew something."

Wes sighed and went to his chair. "Then why," he asked, "was Stan way up in the forest like that, instead of heading down here to tell me what he knew?"

"You'll have to find his killer to get that answer," said Tom Ruffin, arising, looking a little tired. "What time'll you be in the building come morning?"

"Try me," said Wes. "I'll be here any time you want to show up. Tom . . . ?"

"Yeah?"

"Where you going to bed down?"

Ruffin grimaced. "Out on the range somewhere. I've got a bad feelin' about this place you call Hangtown."

"Well, before you go, if you want to talk to Harriman and Hedges about the ranch, they're still down at the lawyer's office."

Ruffin stepped to the door and shook his head at Wes. "It's not for sale. I've got a feelin' about that, too. Once someone else owns it, I won't be able to prowl those hills back there. See you in the morning."

Wes nodded and sat on for a few minutes after Tom had departed. Then he arose and walked up the opposite side of the road as far as the first saloon. He saw a lot of riders he knew in there, but only had one beer, then left to visit the next saloon, and the next, until he eventually found Mosely Crawford with three other Anchor Ranch men talking and loafing around a poker table where they were sharing a quart of amber whiskey.

He sat down with them and returned their greetings. Mosely yawned. It was getting late. Anchor Ranch had seven full-time riders, including Crawford. There were four of them around this table—and one down in the locked shed out back of the jailhouse. That left two unaccounted for. Wes asked Mosely where the others were. Crawford's reply was indifferent.

"Around somewhere. We all rode in with the boss. He's down at Hedges's office, I reckon. Leastwise that's where he headed when we split off from him."

"The whole crew's in town then," said Wes.

Mosely nodded. "The whole crew. Why, what about it?"

"Darcy, too?" Wes asked, ignoring Mosely's question.

Mosely shook his head. "Nope, not Stan. He wasn't in when we left. Mister Harriman sent him back through the hills after some heifers." Mosely grinned when one of the riders made a tart comment about what Stan Darcy's indignation would be when he got back and found everyone gone from the ranch. "Yeah, he'll be mad. Oh, well, he spends enough time in town anyway. Missin' it one night shouldn't hurt him too bad."

Wes accepted the offer of a drink one of the riders made him and carefully filled a glass and threw back his head. The whiskey burned all the way down and lay like lead in his stomach. Stan wouldn't miss the trip to town tonight one bit, nor any other night from here on. Wes pushed the glass and bottle away, sat a while longer, then left.

He was satisfied about one thing. Neither Mosely Crawford nor any of the men with him knew Stan Darcy was dead. There wasn't a blink or a whisper that passed between them when Wes had mentioned Darcy's name, which otherwise he was confident there would have been because those men were not devious in any way.

He strolled down the darkened roadway, wondering how to exploit this advantage he had. Discerning that the range boss and riders were ignorant of Darcy's passing wasn't enough. He stopped within sight of the lighted window down at Hedges's office, then stepped briskly on again. He could perhaps eliminate two more likely prospects down there.

When he walked in, Harriman was slouched in a leather chair smoking a long cigar, looking drowsy and replete. Ben Hedges was at a roll-top desk working over some legal document. They both turned and looked up as Wes entered, their faces smoothed out and blank. Hedges put down his pen and swung around. In a hopeful voice he said: "You found this pretender already . . . this alleged son of Dick Ruffin?"

Irritability began rising in Wes. He controlled it, went to a chair, and sat down, gazed at Hedges, and said: "Funny thing about Tom Ruffin. He seems to come and go. I saw him a while back right here in town, then he was gone again."

John Harriman's wintery gaze peered wetly through a bluish cloud of cigar smoke as he said: "Deputy, there's not one damned thing funny about this impostor. I don't like wasting my time, either. When I said earlier I wanted to see him, that's exactly what I meant. But maybe you didn't believe I was serious."

Wes studied Harriman's heavy, square-jawed face. "I figured you were serious," he said. "Maybe, if you sent some of your men out to comb the range tomorrow, they'd find Ruffin for you. I've got a hunch that's where he'd be. Either at his place or . . ."

"His place," snapped Ben Hedges. "His place my neck! I'm putting the finishing touches on Mister Harriman's suit for quiet title on the Ruffin land. So far, the only one who claims to have seen this Tom Ruffin is you, Wesley."

For a moment Wes sat there, eyeing Hedges, then he said: "You just called me a liar."

Hedges still looked indignant, but that expression began to fade as he and Wes traded a long, long look. When Wes got to his feet, Hedges seemed to shrink in his chair. John Harriman, looking from one to the other, growled at Wes: "He didn't call you a liar, Potter. All he was implying was that this fake son of old Ruffin's is being mighty sly and prudent."

Wes turned. "Why shouldn't he be?" he demanded of John Harriman. "The gun that downed his father could also down him."

"But you said he was handy with guns himself, Deputy."

"What of it?"

"Well, simply that if he's as gun handy as

226

you seem to think, what's he got to be afraid of?"

"Murder, Mister Harriman. Any man who isn't afraid of being murdered, regardless of how good he is with guns, is a plain fool. And that goes for you, too."

Harriman removed his cigar and peered upward from his leather chair. "Me?" he said.

Wes nodded. "There's a murderer loose around here somewhere. Until I catch up to him, who's to say he's not going to kill others . . . including you?"

"That's ridiculous," stated Harriman, shifting his gaze over to the lawyer. "I doubt if I ever even met the man who killed old Ruffin."

"Or," said Wes, "Darcy?"

Harriman's eyes whipped back and upward. Ben Hedges also looked startled. They sat, staring hard at the deputy. Harriman held his cigar low where its little spiral of rising smoke missed his face, but he still squinted his eyes. Wes felt the coldness come into the atmosphere of that room; he felt their hooded eyes boring into him, but for the life of him he could not make up his mind whether they'd known and were surprised that he also knew, or whether they were genuinely astonished.

"Darcy," murmured Ben Hedges, "dead?"

Wes didn't answer right away. He kept trying very hard to see past the mask of Harriman's heavy face. It was no use; John Harriman had evidently schooled himself to show no emotion under stress. He kept a steady and unblinking stare upon Wes, but it was as blank as a brick wall. Wes turned and went over by the door before he answered Hedges. "Yeah, Stan Darcy is dead. Shot down over on the Ruffin place."

"How?" Hedges inquired in a fading tone.

"The same way old Dick was shot down. Up close and straight through the heart. So close the powder burns scorched his shirt."

Finally Harriman moved. He drew forward in the chair and leaned a little as he said: "How do you know he was killed, Deputy?"

"Because, Mister Harriman, he was brought to town by a man who was up there in the rocks when it happened."

Now, at last, Wes got a reaction from John Harriman. The rancher's slate-colored eyes narrowed, his lips got flat. He said: "Who is this man . . . what did he see happen?" Wes was forming the words to correct the wrong impression his statement had given, but an inner voice told him not to do that, to let that incorrect impression stand. He hesitated so long that Harriman said: "Who is this man who saw Darcy get killed, Deputy? I want to know."

"I'll bet you do," replied Wes, and hauled open the office door, stepped through, and closed it, breathing hard. *He had it!* Nothing he could carry into court; nothing actually he could put his finger upon. But he had it nevertheless. *John Harriman knew!* Wes would have bet his life on that. *Harriman knew Stan Darcy was dead!*

Wes went across to his office and stood in the middle of the room, listening to the dull thunder of his heart. John Harriman had sent Darcy out into the mountains; Mosely Crawford had said that. And Darcy had never come back. Mosely had also said that. Harriman had known Darcy was dead. Wes would stake his life Harriman had known from the questions and the intent way the rancher had looked when he'd asked those questions in Hedges's office. Now, something was beginning to shape up. Wes didn't know why or even how, for that matter, but he was lawman enough to scent a trail. Harriman's sudden, demanding interest in those two sections of land; his prompt appearance at the jailhouse when he heard Dick Ruffin had an heir; and finally, that savagely cold and insistent way he glared at Wes when he'd asked about the man he believed had witnessed Stan Darcy's killing. Another thought occurred to Wes, one that chilled him all the way through. Harriman was no fool. Neither was Ben Hedges. It wouldn't take them long to decide that Tom Ruffin could be the man who'd witnessed Darcy's slaying. Whatever was behind all this was evidently important enough to someone—Harriman and Hedges more than likely—to commit another murder, or have it committed, if they could find Tom Ruffin.

Wes's anxiety drove him to blow out the office lamp and return to the roadway. He locked his office and went around where Darcy's horse and saddle were. He rigged out the horse, tied it, and went up to Claude Lucas's livery barn to get his own animal. After that, he rode quietly back down behind the jailhouse, got the Anchor animal, and led it west of town where there was little chance of being seen, then he struck out in a foraging lope back and forth, trying to find Tom Ruffin.

He never found him. He hadn't really expected to, but he'd ridden with the strong hope that he might. Still a man, such as Ruffin obviously was, wouldn't be found if he didn't want to be, so at least until daylight returned, Harriman couldn't find him, either.

Wes then rode straight for Anchor Ranch. He didn't arrive there until the small hours of the morning, which suited him just fine. He tied Darcy's horse to a corral stringer out behind the barn, mixed expectoration and dust in his palm, and crudely lettered three words in mud across the seat of Darcy's saddle: *What's It Worth?*

He then headed back for town.

Let Harriman sweat. Let him send his men scouring the range. Whatever he did now, except act indifferent or amused, would clinch the suspicions Wes had about him. Hedges, too. He'd never liked the lawyer; he hoped now that Hedges was also deeply involved. He didn't dislike John Harriman. At least up until now he never had. But then he'd never really had any dealings with Harriman until tonight, and now, as he drifted on back through the pre-dawn chill, he still didn't feel any personal dislike, only a powerful suspicion and distrust. He could go after Harriman as impersonally as he'd go after anyone, which was the way for a lawman to go after his prey. Emotions colored things for a man; cold practicability did not.

But he had to see Ruffin. He had to see him as soon as daylight came, too, so he was thankful they'd made that agreement the evening before. When he got back to town, he didn't put his horse in the livery barn. Instead he took him on down to the little corral out back of the jailhouse and off-saddled him there. As he finished, and came around the side of the building, a long, knife-edged sliver of steely light appeared over against the eastern rim of the world. Dawn was very close.

He made a cigarette, sat down on the bench outside his jailhouse, and waited. He should've felt tired, but he didn't. He'd, in fact, seldom felt less tired in his life.

# VIII

Tom Ruffin came up from the south end of town, riding his horse, loose and easy. Wes saw him almost as soon as he entered Hangtown, for there wasn't another moving object anywhere in sight. It was just a few minutes before 5:00 in the morning.

Wes went out to Ruffin at the tie rack, told him to follow along and fetch his horse, then turned and led Ruffin around back where the little corral was. There, Wes explained what had happened the night before with Hedges and Harriman, and the horse he'd left out at Anchor Ranch.

Ruffin didn't seem at all surprised about John Harriman or Ben Hedges, but he scowled perplexedly about the horse. "It's nothing much," Wes explained. "It won't lead me to any murderer."

"Then why did you do it?" asked Ruffin. "I don't understand."

"Well, it works like this," Wes explained. "When you think that maybe someone's involved in something, you get them moving. It doesn't matter what you do it with, but get them to moving. If Harriman knows about old Dick or Stan Darcy, that horse and the writing on the saddle seat are going to start him moving. The thing is . . . which way he moves. If he doesn't know anything, he'll bring that saddle to me in town with the lettering still intact. But if he doesn't fetch it to town, and instead puts his men to combing the hills, I'll have a good enough reason to believe he's somehow mixed up in two murders. Whichever way Harriman jumps, you see, he's going to tell me something."

Ruffin pondered this for a while without comment. Then he turned and looked around. There was no one else close to him but the lawman. He said: "Somethin' just hit me, too, Deputy. Harriman just might figure I'm behind this."

Wes concurred with that. "He might. But if he does, Tom, then that'll satisfy me about one thing. If he suspects you of having killed two men, then I'll know I've got to look elsewhere, that Harriman didn't have a hand in it."

"But you figure he did," said Ruffin, leaning upon the corral stringers and carefully eyeing Wes. "You figure he's . . . ?"

"I figure," broke in Wes, "that if he or any of the men who could be involved in this with him catch you in town, they'll shoot you without a chance."

Ruffin nodded his head. Evidently this possibility had also occurred to him. "Then I leave," he said.

"Not quite," Wes responded. "You'll leave all

right, but I'll be with you. We're goin' up where you found Darcy. We're goin' to ride hard so we can reach that place before Anchor's riders happen along."

Ruffin stroked a bristly jaw. "I figured on getting some grub at that little café across the road," he muttered.

Wes was already moving toward his horse inside the little corral when he said: "There's grub out at your paw's place. Let's go."

They left town, riding northwest so that the chance of being observed would be minimized, and swung off to the northeast two miles upcountry where the land was flushed with a beautiful wave of soft, pale light. They encountered no one, but once they saw a wolf trotting back toward the hills. He had evidently been hunting down through the lower ranges during the night. Range men had no mercy on wolves, but Wes and Tom Ruffin only eyed the beast and made no attempt to shoot it. Gunshots carried for miles in the hush of a new day.

There was a lingering hint of that earlier chill in the air. After they passed beyond the lower rolls and swells where shadows still clung, that cold became more noticeable. Up through the brush and grasslands on the Ruffin Ranch the chill was even more pronounced, because up there giant trees stood sentinel watch, holding back the first quick rush of daylight.

They stopped at the cabin for a little while, ate some cold tinned peaches, discussed making a pot of coffee, decided against it, and went back out to get into their saddles. The lower country was warming up, but where they now went, through ranks of tall trees and through little gloomy, secret cañons, the cold held forth for almost another two hours before heat coming up from the plain brought a comfortable, good warmth.

By then they had reached the spot where Ruffin had found the body of Stan Darcy. It wasn't much of a place for a man to be, either dead or alive. There were rock ramparts on three sides, a narrow slot of land on the fourth side, where grass grew around an old lightning-shriven pine, and the soil underfoot was both gritty and coarse.

The trail to reach this spot, as Ruffin had pointed out, did not come directly through the forest, but angled frequently so that riders still had an excellent sighting down their back trail. Furthermore, again as Tom had said, the trail was neither brushed clear nor easily discernible.

Wes made a comment when he was standing over where Tom reënacted the position and location of Stan Darcy's corpse when he'd first found it. Wes said: "When a rider makes his trail so that he can see back downcountry like this, he has his reasons. When he makes no attempt to keep his trail open . . . he doesn't want it found by others."

Tom arose, dusted off, and looked into the surrounding rank growth of big timber. "And," he dryly added, "if there's a reason why someone doesn't want folks up in this place, where we're standing out here in the grass, all they'd have to do would be lean a carbine barrel against a tree back in there, then there'd be a couple more dead men."

Wes turned to look. The trees northward where the land was steadily more rough and rugged grew in primitive profusion, so close and dense sunlight did not touch the ground anywhere. It was the same to the south and the east. Only on the west where they stood was there any break in the darkness.

"This is cattle country," Wes said. "There's some lumbering and still a little gold mining." He turned completely around. "What good is this spot? Cattle wouldn't stay in here ten minutes. The lumbermen don't have to come this far back, and, as for mining, while I don't know much about hunting gold, I'd say, if there'd been any around here, it would've been prospected long ago."

Ruffin leaned upon a tree, arms folded across his chest. "I did the same kind of reasoning," he told Wes. "All I could come up with was that maybe this feller Darcy just happened up here, and stumbled onto an outlaw in his camp."

"That outlaw," Wes said dryly, "sure camped a long while if that's so, Tom. He's the same one that shot your paw. I never heard of an outlaw who'd stay this close to the scene of a major crime."

Ruffin shrugged. "Then," he murmured, "you tell me."

Wes couldn't. It didn't make any sense to him at all. In the first place, although he believed John Harriman had deliberately set Darcy up to be murdered, he couldn't understand why Darcy had come to this particular spot. It was too awkward to reach, too hard to get to, and with no reason for existing even after a man reached it, unless of course it was some kind of secret rendezvous. But even then, Wes mused, there were many places much more accessible that were just as good, and even better, that were also well hidden.

Giving it up eventually, Wes walked slowly around the tree-shadowed little site. Ruffin remained with their horses, watching and saying nothing until Wes came back on around at the end of his complete circuit. "It doesn't make any sense to me, either," he then stated. "But if they had to meet somewhere, why I'd say this was a good enough spot."

"Why?" Wes asked. "Why meet here, and why kill Darcy here, if they valued this place? Sooner or later someone would find him. The buzzards would see to that."

Ruffin had an answer to that. "They didn't count on anyone stumblin' onto Darcy so soon. They figured to kill him here, then bury him. After all, he's only another cowboy. All they got to do is say he quit and moved on, and no one'd ever be the wiser, after they dragged him back into the forest a mile or two and buried him."

Wes leaned upon a rough-sided rock and started to make a smoke. He thought Ruffin might be close, at that. Darcy's killer meant to return, perhaps with tools, and bury him. Wes lit up, exhaled, and looked at Tom. "You upset someone's little red cart," he said. "I didn't help it any by taking Darcy's horse back . . ."

"Quiet!" Ruffin abruptly hissed, and straightened off his tree at the same time dropping his arms. "Listen!"

Wes dropped his smoke and ground it out. He turned toward the east, the way Ruffin was intently watching, and after a while picked up the bitter squawking of a distant blue jay in the high treetops. Listening carefully to the inflections and decibels, he understood what had captured Tom's attention. Blue jays had a particular pitch to their voices when they were disturbed by men. It was different from their usual garrulous protests at being disturbed by bears or lions or other wild denizens of their patches of forest.

Wes turned, reaching for his reins. "We better get to hell out of here," he said. "If they're from Anchor Ranch, there'll be more than one or two of them. If they aren't from Anchor, I'd like to get a good look at them first."

Tom nodded, stepped up across the leather, and reined off through the westerly forest without another word. He worked back and forth, in and out, until he was nearly a mile away, then he lifted out his carbine, stepped down, looped his reins, and looked over where Wes was also dismounting.

It took an excellent sign reader to pick out tracks over an ancient, foot-thick bed of pine needles. They were safe enough from being tracked down. Tom strolled over and said: "It's your territory. What do we do?"

"Observe them," Wes said. "That's all for now . . . just look and listen." He started back, carbine in hand, treading as lightly as Ruffin also glided along. They heard voices through the gloomy depths long before they were even close. A man's bitter-toned voice said: "Here, take a look at this. An' the tobacco's still fresh. I tell you they were here not more'n a little while ago."

Wes scowled. It hadn't taken them long—whoever they were—to discover that stamped out smoke of his. Men that wary and cautious had reasons to be so leery; it wasn't normal.

"They left here ridin' west," the same bitter-toned voice said. "Two of 'em. Maybe they had Darcy with 'em."

Now the second voice said: "Naw, Darcy was took away last night sometime. You heard what the boss said. That clown of a deputy down at Hangtown knew about Darcy last night. That means someone found him an' hauled him out of here."

"All right," assented the first man. "Then tell me just who the hell done it, and how come 'em to ever find this place?"

For a little while there was no answer, then it came from a different direction, as though one of those men out there was moving around. "The boss told me right after we found that danged horse with the writin' on the saddle that the old feller down at the cabin is supposed to have a kid. He said we got to find that kid, too. And now you know what I'm thinkin'?"

"What?"

"I'm thinkin' this kid of the old man's is skulkin' around in here tryin' to find something. Maybe he figures whoever shot his old man is still in these lousy hills or something."

"You figure this kid found Darcy?"

"Well, who else'd be nosin' around back in here?"

The talk stopped for a while. Wes looked over at Tom Ruffin. Old Dick's son was standing there, gazing straight ahead, his tawny eyes like cold iron. Evidently Tom was having the same thoughts Wes was also having. Whether those two men out there had actually killed Dick and Stan Darcy or not, they almost certainly could name the men who had. Wes rocked his head sideways and started gingerly forward. They had a good long quarter mile of dark forest to cross through, weaving in and out, before they'd be in a position to see those men out there.

They used up a lot of time making their way. Heat was beginning to build up in the breathless hush. A tree squirrel saw them, chattered and flicked his tail at them, then dived into his hole far up a red-barked fir tree. A crow *cawed* somewhere southward, stopping them dead still until they were satisfied it actually was a bird, and not a man giving the old-time Indian warning of alarm.

Wes made the last hundred feet in a steady glide. Tom came up beside him. They had the westerly little grassy spot well in sight, but no one was over there—no men and no horses. Ruffin grunted and took two big thrusting strides forward for a better look. When Wes eased up beside him, Tom turned, wagged his head, and pointed silently over across the secret glade where a light sifting of pale dust hung in the breathless air. Wes understood; the two horsemen had departed, heading over through the yonder trees. He turned, gauged the forest, and after only a very brief hesitation started around through the forest fringe, moving rapidly.

Tom followed. They were not so careful now, for evidently the riders had decided there was no danger of meeting anyone in here and were riding back the way they'd come without much caution. By the time Wes picked up the sounds of rein chains and crunching hoof falls he'd led Tom

Ruffin another thousand yards past the secret place. He cut upcountry, broke over into a little silent jog, and after ten more minutes cut southward again to intercept the horsemen. Where he caught sounds again, he dropped to one knee behind an old pine, and waited.

Tom did the same, but Tom didn't lean on his carbine as Wes did; instead, he kept the gun in both hands ready to be instantly raised and fired.

Someone farther eastward through the trees hooted a high call. At once the two riders Wes and Tom were awaiting called back. That was when Tom suddenly dropped flat down. He had seen the oncoming men. So had Wes, but what he saw wasn't the two men they were after; it was John Harriman with more men coming in from the east. He squirmed swiftly over to Tom, jerked his head, and led the rapid retreat back through the trees.

# IX

They scarcely breathed. Down through the trees beyond their sight the horsemen all came together. Wes recognized John Harriman's voice, but that was the only voice he did recognize. Harriman said—"Well . . . ?"—and another voice answered grumpily: "Someone's been there all right. Only it ain't just that Darcy's gone. Someone's been there this mornin'. And not too damned long ago, either."

Harriman swore, then said: "All right, we'll spread out and comb this forest. We've got to find them. Let's go."

Wes raised up trying to see at least one of those men down there, but they moved ahead too swiftly; he saw nothing at all. When he would have crept in closer, Ruffin put out a restraining hand.

"No time for that," he whispered. "We got to get back to the horses before they find them, Deputy. If they catch us afoot in here, we're as good as dead." Tom jumped up and started cutting in and out of the trees in a swift trot. Wes followed him. He heard the riders spreading out down below, heard two of them swear a little as they caught the backward slap of pine limbs. Those two weren't far away. But he stifled his desire to try for just one glimpse and ran on. Tom was right; if Harriman's crew located their horses, which they'd do unless the horses were moved out of their line of approach, Wes and Tom Ruffin would be set afoot in a country where mounted men had all the advantages.

They reached the horses, but were nearly out of breath from the effort, untied them, and swung aboard, then they sat for a moment, gauging the approaching sound of mounted men. It was difficult to determine just how far southward Harriman's riders were, or, for that matter, how many men he had with him. Tom looked over, and Wes reined off northward. The going would be rougher in that direction, but if they tried to reach open country to the southward, they'd have to ride down the full front of Harriman's men.

It was a good decision. At least for the first fifteen minutes they moved through the forest without interference. Then two blue jays, evidently with a nest in this area, spied them and went into a frenzied, heckling series of swoops to drive them away, squawking at the top of their voices with each dive.

Ruffin swore at the gaudy birds and turned a helpless look over at Wes. The deputy, although he, too, appreciated that Harriman's riders would certainly hear the ruckus and suspect what was causing it, kept right on riding. He felt they had eluded their pursuers, and by swinging eastward now would be able to get far enough away to drop down to open range again, and head for town.

They didn't get rid of the birds for a long time. Even after they did, though, the damage had been done, for the jays had also turned eastward with them. Each cry they made allowed Harriman's men freshly to orient themselves.

But Wes still felt they had an adequate lead. He said to Tom Ruffin: "Unless they can run their horses in here, they won't be able to make any better time than we're making. All we've got to do is hold this lead."

They held it, weaving in and out of the trees, passing around rocky places and cutting across little crooked game trails, never slackening, and unable to hasten, all the time moving through a world of gloom and heavy fragrance, sometimes speckled with diluted light, other times nearly entirely shielded by a darkness almost as heavy as the shades of full night.

When trouble came, they had no warning at all. Wes was swinging to the left around a giant tree; Tom Ruffin was dropping downhill around it. The silence suddenly exploded with a smash of violent, dull sound, and Ruffin's horse gave a violent spring up into the air, and fell dead, heaving its rider a full man's length ahead.

Wes went for his six-gun before his own mount had even responded to the reflex tug on the reins. He saw that little soiled puff of smoke and drove a bullet straight into the center of it.

Ruffin rolled heavily, got both hands under his chest, and pushed half up. He hung there, wagging his head, half knocked out.

Wes turned and hooked his horse hard, straight at the spot where that invisible assassin had been. He let fly with two more shots, one to the left, one to the right. The ambusher had been behind a second-growth pine that was rising up from the charred and ancient stump of an older tree. When Wes was close enough to see over the old stump, he let fly with another two shots. Dust flew, needles sprang upward, and no gunshot came back. He reined his horse around for a closer look. No one was back there, but a Winchester .25-35 lay in the tumbled pine needles with a shattered stock.

Wes didn't wait. He plunged ahead, swinging left and right, but the assassin had fled. Evidently, after having his carbine shattered by one of Wes's slugs, the man hadn't waited to duel it out with six-guns, and this prudence had given him enough of a head start to be well away.

Wes probably could have found the man, but his six-gun was nearly empty, and he didn't like leaving groggy Tom Ruffin back where Tom's horse had been shot out from under him, not with their fierce, brief battle still sending its echoes out and around where Harriman's men would certainly hear them and also double their efforts to ambush Wes and Tom Ruffin.

He went back. Tom was tugging his carbine from under the dead horse. He looked up with a twisted face just as the carbine came loose. Wes kicked his left foot out of the stirrup and leaned down, his hand and arm extended. Tom jumped, hit the stirrup, caught the arm, and swung up aft of Wes's cantle.

"Straight south for open country," he panted, and Wes set his course in that direction.

They did not converse again for twenty minutes, or until Wes could distinctly see dazzling sunlight out through the forward trees. He twisted a little, turned his head and said: "You all right?"

Tom's reply was succinct: "Fair, considerin'." Then he looked back for a while before straightening around and saying: "Where in hell did that one come from? How many men has Harriman got, anyway?"

Wes was slow replying because, as they'd been riding southward, he'd been wondering about something. He knew Harriman's range boss well enough; he also knew Harriman's ranch hands. If that was Mosely Crawford back there, along with Harriman's other riders, none of them was acting at all like the riders he knew. He'd been prevented from sighting any of them. Even the one who had downed Ruffin's horse had gotten clean away. Still, those men weren't acting like Harriman's regular riders.

He eventually said: "There's something here I just plain don't understand."

Ruffin's next comment was sardonic. "Don't you, Deputy? Well, I understand just one thing. Harriman's in this up to his ears, and he's out for blood. Your blood or my blood."

They came to the last fringe of trees and halted to listen hard. The pursuit was still coming, but it was evidently following horse tracks. Since Wes had been forced to do a lot of backing and filling in among the trees, the men with Harriman were making slow progress.

Wes urged his horse ahead. "It won't be long," he said, "before they figure out we're heading for the open country."

The horse carrying them both was a stocky animal, strong and short-backed and durable. But out under that hot sun, with all that considerable weight, he couldn't be expected to run far, so Wes used his knowledge of the countryside to save the animal. He made for a shale-rock surface where the tracks wouldn't be readable, crossed it at an angle, and changed directions as he did so, heading straight east. After that, he headed for the rolling foothills and worked up a veritable maze of tracks passing in and out, back and forth. When he was satisfied he'd laid enough trail to confuse and slow Harriman, he rode southward again, stopped in a bosque of black oaks, got down, and hiked up atop a low knoll to lie prone and study the rearward land.

Sunlight was his ally. It struck against the metal of Harriman's riders as they started combing the low foothills, spread far out and working their way southward and westward. Tom Ruffin cleared his throat, spat dust, and said, as he started to arise: "Five of 'em, Deputy. How many men ride for Harriman?"

Wes got up, too. As the pair of them ambled back to the horse, he said: "About that many. But it doesn't ring true. I know those riders. The range boss and I've been friends for a long time."

Ruffin said nothing but his hard-glowing, dark glance was ironic. He mounted aft of the cantle again, took his handholds, and swayed with the motions of Wes's horse. They passed on down-country that way until Harriman and his riders were lost far back, then Wes looped the reins, made a smoke, lit up, and said: "Been a right busy morning, Tom." His coolness amused Ruffin. He chuckled.

"And I'm still hungry enough to eat the south end out of a bear, if someone'd hold its head."

They saw Hangtown low and ahead where the land leveled out and ran on as far as the eye could see, out to some smoky, far-away, brush-darkened low hills that were ghostly dark against a brassy sky.

"You goin' to get up a posse?" Ruffin inquired.

"No. I'm not going to do anything at all."

Ruffin leaned out to look at Wes's profile. "Why not?" he asked.

"They never saw us, Tom."

"What's that got to do with it?"

"Maybe plenty. They'll go over your horse and saddle for some notion about you. But they've never seen you, either, so they only know they chased two men."

"I don't follow you," Ruffin growled.

"Listen. We need more than what we've got. We need proof against those men for two murders. If I arrest Harriman the next time he shows up in town, that'll tip our hand. I want those men of his, too. He doesn't know it was me back there with you, and what he'll find on your horse and saddle won't identify you for him, because he doesn't know you yet. So, we just hang and rattle for a while."

Tom slouched along right up to the very edge of town turning all this over in his mind before he said: "Well, I sure hope you know what you're doing, Deputy. I'll go along. But I got to get together another outfit an' I'm broke. I couldn't buy a pair of reins, let alone a horse an' saddle."

"That can be taken care of," Wes said, drawing off a little to halt and let Ruffin down. "You walk into town from here," he said. "Head for the jailhouse and meet me down there."

Ruffin stepped down, looked back, saw nothing, looked ahead where the town was going about its usual bustle of trade and commerce, then looked up at Wes. "I think what you need is a drunk cowboy locked up in one of the cells of your jailhouse." He chuckled again in that soft, low way he had of doing it. "I'll see you in a little while."

Wes watched Ruffin move down into a shallow dip and up the far side of it, heading into town from the back way. He looked far into the distance but the only dust he saw was where a coach was beating its way southward along the roadway. Harriman evidently had drawn back into the forest again. He started for town.

At the livery barn, when Wes led his horse in

from out back, Claude and Silas Houseman were in earnest conversation. They saw Wes about the same time he saw them. Claude started down to take Wes's reins, and Silas walked along with him. Silas said: "We been wonderin' where you were, Wes. There's been an accident in town. Mosley Crawford's horse fell on him. He's over at Doc Blake's, unconscious."

Wes halted and stared. "Mosely Crawford?" he said.

Silas wrinkled his face with impatience. "I just said that. What you lookin' so funny for? Don't you think I know Mosley Crawford when I see him? Why, confound it, he's been coming into my store for the past . . ."

"All right," Wes broke in to say. "All right, Silas. It's nothing to flare up about. Tell me, how long ago did his horse fall on him?"

"Couple hours back," the liveryman muttered. "He was comin' out of the post office, y'see, and went to mount up, an', as near as I can figure it, his horse spooked at the mail sack he was carrying, reared up, lost its footin', and fell. Mosley got pinned underneath. He didn't look very good when they packed him up to Doctor Blake's office."

Wes let Claude take the reins to his horse. He looked out into the dazzlingly lighted roadway, then said: "Silas, were any more Anchor riders in town this morning?"

Houseman shrugged. "I don't know whether they were or not, Wes. I just came over here a few minutes ago to see if Claude had heard how Mosley was making it. It was a nasty hurt he got."

Wes started up the cool interior of the barn. "I'll go look in on him," he said, but, when he reached the yonder roadway, he didn't turn left toward Dr. Blake's combination home and office; he turned right and headed straight for his jailhouse.

Silas scratched his head, went up to the doorway, and looked southward where Wes was walking. As Claude Lucas came up, Silas muttered: "That danged character. He said he was goin' up to Doc's, and he didn't even *start* up there. He headed straight for his office."

"Well," Claude said soothingly, "he's got business to tend to first. What's wrong with that?"

"Nothing," agreed Silas. "So have I." He stepped out and went hiking across the dusty road toward his own establishment. He nearly collided with Tom Ruffin and looked startled when he and the dark man exchanged a look. Then Ruffin kept on walking toward the jailhouse, and Silas stood like a statue staring after him, with his mouth open.

# X

Wes told Tom Ruffin what he'd learned up at the livery barn and Ruffin went to a chair, sank down upon it, and raised a questioning look. "You know these folks," he said. "You know the countryside. What does this mean?"

Wes had a theory, but it was no more than that, so all he said was: "I'm going out to Anchor. I want to know if the rest of the crew was with Harriman today."

"Well," stated Tom, "who the hell else would be with him?"

"That's exactly what I want to find out. I can tell you this much, just from association. Mosely Crawford wouldn't have come to town this morning for the ranch mail if there'd been anything worth doing out at the ranch."

Ruffin turned silent for a while, then got up, walked to a window, and stood gazing out into the shimmering roadway as he said: "This Harriman feller . . . would he have another ridin' crew?"

"That's in the back of my mind," Wes replied. "I can't figure any other reason for Mosley being here in town this morning. But more than that, Tom, if Harriman had five men with him . . . well, *someone* didn't belong. Harriman's got seven men

. . . or rather he *had* seven men, counting Stan Darcy. That leaves six men. Deduct one more . . . Mosley Crawford who got hurt in town this morning . . . and you come up with five riders."

"The same number he had with him up there," muttered Ruffin. "What's wrong with that?"

"Just one thing," said Wes. "That feller who shot your horse out from under you was too far back to belong with the other five."

Ruffin turned slowly, gazing back at Wes. "By golly that's right," he murmured. "The others were all together, and a mile east when that one shot my horse. I see what you mean. Someone *didn't* belong . . . or else Harriman's got more men riding for him than you thought he had."

"He's never used more than seven men," stated Wes, who had started for the doorway and now paused a moment as though he'd just remembered something. "I don't dare lock you up and pretend you're a common drunk."

"Why not? No one knows . . ."

"Yes, they do. Silas Houseman, the storekeeper you tried to peddle those guns to, he'd remember you."

Ruffin blew out a big sigh. "This is getting complicated as well as lethal," he mumbled. "All right, fetch me a horse from the livery barn an' I'll slip around into the back alley, get aboard, and slope."

Wes privately debated about that for a while,

then said: "I think you'd better stay with me. You can cut up near Anchor and wait for me in some draw. But I think from now on you and I'd better keep back to back."

Ruffin still looked exasperatedly resigned, but all he said was: "All right. Go get the outfit. I'll step around back."

Wes left the office, went to the livery barn, and stared down Claude who wanted to know who the second saddle horse was for. Claude didn't persist, but he went back to the alleyway and watched the lawman ride southward leading that second horse. He didn't see who mounted the beast, however, because Wes led the animal around the south side of his jailhouse.

The two of them left Hangtown, traveling west because in that direction they had unobstructed open country. They didn't switch direction for two miles. By then they were well beyond sight. But the ride to Anchor Ranch wasn't as uneventful as Wes had anticipated. They saw riders passing from east to west far ahead, moving fast and stirring up dust. They could not make out who the horsemen were and felt no inclination to hasten up and find out.

A mile below the ranch they came upon two cowboys down in a little swale with a roped cow snubbed to an oak. She had a muzzle full of porcupine quills and the men were trying to snub her close enough to keep her from striking them when they went to work extricating the quills. Neither of the riders saw Wes and Tom Ruffin; they were otherwise too occupied. The old cow had horns a yard long and was wise in their use, keeping both men on their toes.

Wes watched a moment from within a stand of scrub oaks, then said: "Well, there are two Anchor riders. Do they look like they're manhunters?"

Ruffin shifted in his saddle and said nothing for a long time. He was interested in how the range men were going about their unpleasant chore. The old cow would bawl, slobber, and roll up her eyes as she fought against being snubbed with all her eight hundred pounds of bone and gristle. Ruffin finally said: "Why don't they just choke her down?"

Wes didn't reply. He turned and continued on toward the home ranch. When he was less than a mile away, passing through a brushy arroyo, he said: "You wait down here. Leave your horse back in the brush, climb up the slope, and keep watch. I'll whistle when I return."

He left Ruffin and moved ahead out of the arroyo, kicked his livery animal over into a lope, and approached Anchor Ranch's buildings without slackening that gait. Two cowboys he knew were out back at the corrals. When they heard him coming, both men turned, leaned on the poles, and watched him lope up. One of them grinned and said: "Hey Wes, you see Charley and Lute down there with that old mossback tryin' to get the quills out of her nose?" The cowboy laughed out loud. "They been fightin' that one old cow since eleven this morning. Slim an' I watched 'em from a hilltop for a while. We figured that was good practice for them."

Wes smiled, drifted his gaze on around, then said: "Where's the boss?"

The grinning cowboys said Mosely Crawford had gone to town earlier, and Mister Harriman hadn't shown up all day. When Wes asked if they knew where Harriman might be, they shook their heads at him. Then the one called Slim, trying hard to be helpful, said: "Last night he come back pretty late. We figured he might be sleepin' in, until we got back from the west range a while back an' seen his favorite horse was gone outen the corral. Maybe he rode down to town, also, Wes."

Potter knew better, but he didn't say so. All he said was: "The whole crew workin' the west range today?"

Slim shook his head. "Naw, just me 'n' Lefty here. The rest o' the crew went over east into the breaks huntin' stray heifers. Them was Mosley's orders before he rid to town."

Lefty turned, raised a hand to shield his eyes, and said: "Wait a second. Don't that look like Mister Harriman comin' in from the west? Sure looks like his big chestnut horse t' me."

Wes squinted to make out movement over on

the western range. He picked up a rider in his vision and watched him. He couldn't make out either the horse or rider, but Lefty said he was certain it was Harriman. "I'd know that big chestnut anywhere," Lefty affirmed. "I ought to be able to. I broke him couple years back." Lefty dropped his hand and turned. "Wes, me 'n' Slim better look busy. Mister Harriman don't like for the hired hands to be standin' around."

Wes turned and rode over across the yard to the porch of the main house, stepped down, tied his horse, and went up to ease down in one of the chairs. He wanted a good look at John Harriman when the cowman came across his yard toward the house.

Wes got that long look. Harriman was in the barn for a short period, then emerged from the front entrance, hiking over toward his residence. He'd evidently been informed by either Slim or Lefty that Wes was over on the porch, for when he stepped out of the barn, he shot a long look straight over there.

Harriman's clothing was dusty and sweaty and brush-snagged. He walked a little wearily, too, which did not surprise Wes. His face was lined with the marks of tiredness. Wes could appreciate that, too, but when Harriman came close, Wes nodded at him, showing nothing in his eyes or upon his face, and said: "You look like you've been in the saddle a long time."

Harriman stepped up into porch shade, cast a hard, probing look upon Wes, then turned and dropped into a chair with a heavy sigh. "No one ever said cattle ranching was child's play," he growled. "What's on your mind, Deputy?"

"Mosley is at Doctor Blake's house in town," said Wes, and watched Harriman's head whip around. "His horse fell on him. He's hurt pretty bad, they tell me. I figured you'd want to know."

Harriman kept studying Wes. The deputy didn't feel that this stony interest had anything to do with Mosely Crawford. Then Harriman said: "I'll send a wagon in for him. How did it happen?"

"In front of the post office," murmured Wes, turning skeptical about Harriman's solicitation. "When he went to get aboard, the mail sack spooked his horse. It reared up and fell, with Mosley underneath. I wouldn't send a wagon for him, Mister Harriman. Not for a day or two, anyway. He's going to need at least that long to be well enough to stand the trip out here."

Harriman leaned back again and said—"Hell."—in a tone of deep disgust. "Next week I wanted to move the cattle over to our marking grounds and put the men to cutting and branding."

Wes stood up. "You still can," he said. "Slim or Lefty . . . almost any of your riders . . . can ramrod things until Mosley is up and around again. They've been with you long enough."

As Wes stepped to the edge of the porch,

Harriman said: "Wait a minute. I want to talk to you." Wes turned, gazed at the older man, and waited. Harriman said: "It's about Darcy."

"All right. What about him?"

"Where is he?"

"In that old shed behind the jailhouse, waitin' for Doc Blake to embalm him."

"I want to know the name of the man who brought him in . . . and when."

"He was brought in last night, Mister Harriman, and the feller who did that is named Tom Ruffin."

Harriman suddenly stood up, his eyes slitted, his heavy jaw thrust forward. "I want this Tom Ruffin arrested for murder," he said. "I'm surprised you didn't figure out he killed Darcy when he brought him in."

Wes hooked both thumbs in his shell belt and calmly gazed at the heavier, thicker man for a long, quiet moment. Then he said: "Ruffin didn't kill Darcy, Mister Harriman."

For a moment Harriman's slitted, smoldering gaze turned cloudy, then it flashed again as he said: "If you can't prove that, Deputy, I want Ruffin arrested. If you won't do it, then I'll bring in some men who will."

"Law officers, Mister Harriman . . . or other men?" Wes quietly asked. "Because if they aren't federal marshals, they won't have any authority here, and the first one to draw a gun in my bailiwick will think the sky fell on him."

Harriman's neck reddened. "Deputy," he said in an icy, very soft voice, "I don't know what you're up to, but let me tell you something. No one plays games with me. No one! If Ruffin didn't kill Darcy, it'll come out at his trial. But I want that man apprehended, and I don't aim to listen to any talk to the contrary from you. Now, either arrest him, or I'll take this thing into my own hands!"

Wes had his reply ready. He said, still standing, loose and easy, and looking Harriman straight in the eye: "You try anything like that, Mister Harriman, and you'll be the first one I lock up." He turned, went over to his horse, untied the reins, and swung up. From the saddle he said: "I realize you're a big man in politics, Mister Harriman, and I sure don't want to tangle with you. But if I have to, don't ever think I won't." He turned and rode slowly back out of the yard, his mind full of anger and overpowering resentment.

He loped back out to where Tom was waiting. The sun was falling away in the west by the time Ruffin got his horse and came up out of the arroyo looking ironic. "I thought you said you would whistle as you came in," Tom murmured.

Wes had forgotten. He said: "Harriman says, if I don't find you and lock you up, he'll bring in outsiders to see that it's done."

Ruffin rode down through a patch of evening shadows beside Wes as he said: "What kind of outsiders did he mean?"

261

Wes snorted. "That's a damned fool question. You know what kind he meant as well as I do. Gunmen. He wouldn't dare bring in any federal marshals. He doesn't even dare ride down to the county seat and try to get the sheriff to come up here for an investigation. He's on damned thin ice and he knows it."

Ruffin said: "How about his riders?"

"It wasn't them," stated Wes, heading across for the open country. "That's what we wanted to know, and now we know. Somewhere hereabouts Harriman's got another crew of men."

Ruffin said dryly: "Yeah, up in the hills behind my father's place. And that begins to make sense about those two killings. Either Darcy and my father came onto Harriman's renegades, or else Harriman had them killed to prevent them from stumbling into his crew."

Wes nodded. "Why?" he asked. "That's what I've been askin' myself all the way down here from Anchor. Why? What is John Harriman up to?"

Ruffin said: "Don't fret, Deputy. You're goin' to find out right soon. I can feel it in my bones. I can also feel somethin' else. Unless I get real scarce around here, I'm goin' to get shot in the back."

Wes raised his eyes toward Hangtown as the shadows deepened and darkened around them. Ruffin was correct; he had to find some way to hide old Dick's son, and it had to be a very good hiding place, too, because after his disastrous handling by Wes and Tom today, John Harriman wasn't going to leave any stone unturned. He didn't want Ruffin arrested for Darcy's murder at all; he wanted Ruffin locked in Wes's jailhouse so an assassin could go and shoot him down in an exposed jail cell.

They came toward town from the east. It was turning dark down there. Along saloon row the usual bright lights came on.

# XI

There was a languid-eyed husky stranger waiting in Wes's jailhouse when the deputy and Tom Ruffin shed their horses and walked on in. He wore a gray Stetson and a loose-fitting tweed coat that hung to his hips. When he got up, there was no sign of any sidearm, although from his general appearance it did not seem likely this man, whoever he was, would be unarmed. He had pleasant blue eyes, a thin, high-bridged nose, and a mouth as straight and unyielding as a sword blade. His entire attitude was one of affability, with a thin facing of iron toughness behind it.

He stood up and nodded at both Potter and Ruffin, then said—"Deputy U.S. Marshal Craig Price, gentlemen."—and offered his hand.

Wes took care of his end of the introductions, then considered his visitor with strong interest. "Been waitin' long?" he asked.

Marshal Price shrugged. "I had supper across the road and a drink at one of the bars. No, I wouldn't say I'd been waitin' long, Deputy." Price repeatedly gazed at dark and silent Tom Ruffin. Finally he said: "Deputy, I'd like to talk to you in private."

"What about?" Wes wanted to know.

"A rancher hereabouts. But it's ticklish business. If it got out federal lawmen were interested in him, it could cause some mighty unpleasant repercussions, providing of course there turns out to be nothing to it."

Tom stood over by the front window through this little exchange, but now he started for the door. Wes stopped him. He then looked at Marshal Price, saying: "What's this rancher's name, Mister Price?"

"Harriman. John Leland Harriman."

Wes and Tom exchanged a look. Wes said: "Marshal Price, Tom Ruffin's mixed up in this Harriman business. Whatever you've got to say can be safely said in front of him."

Price and Ruffin exchanged a look, and the deputy U.S. marshal's blue gaze was just as tough and steady as Ruffin's gaze was. But Price was still careful. He said: "Tell me what you know about this John Harriman, Deputy?"

Wes answered in short, quick sentences. He

talked for a full five minutes without any interruptions. When he finished, Marshal Price raised both brows, puckered his lips, and let off a long, low whistle. After that he said: "Well, I reckon Ruffin *does* have an interest." He pushed back his hat and sat a moment in quiet thought before he said: "Harriman's been busy, but he's running true to form. You see, boys, John Leland Harriman is an embezzler. Oh, he's rich . . . or at least he *was* rich . . . and he's got some power. But where he came from, back in Ohio, he's also known as a man who buys into railroads, gets himself elected to high position through stock ownership, then bleeds the treasury and absconds."

Ruffin looked puzzled. "How come him to use his right name if he's an outlaw?"

Marshal Price smiled. "Well, there are different kinds of outlaws. Harriman's kind isn't usually taken by a posse. He's a smooth operator. He's been under indictment for seven years and has been able to buy his way through enough legal delays to patch hell a mile. You see, falsification of records is a lot harder to prove than simple robbery . . . or even simple murder, for that matter. Particularly when the person under suspicion is a large stockholder in the company which has been robbed."

Wes didn't understand, entirely, but he got enough of the gist of what Craig Price said for it to make sense. Only Wes wasn't too interested in John Harriman's past. It was what he was presently involved in that had Wes's interest. He said: "Is there an outside warrant?"

Price said that there wasn't. He also said the reason he'd come to Hangtown was because of an unusual coincidence. John Harriman had tried to buy into a Nevada railroad line, but someone up there had recognized Harriman, had informed the other stockholders who Harriman was, and he'd thereafter been unable to buy any stock certificates. "But," said Craig Price, "that's when the trouble started. That railroad line has been hit six times in the past two years."

"Robbed?" Wes asked.

Price nodded. "Robbed six times in the past two years, and robbed four times in the past four *months!*"

Tom Ruffin, born and raised in Nevada, asked a question of the U.S. deputy marshal: "What line is it you're talkin' about, Marshal? It wouldn't be the Southern Nevada-Northern California line, would it?"

Price shifted his gaze to Ruffin. "It would," he answered. "You familiar with that line?"

Tom nodded. "I've ridden along its tracks for a lot of miles, and I've also ridden its cars. I remember hearin' it said last year that those robberies were about to bankrupt it."

Wes sat straight up in his chair. "Last year there

was a rumor around here that Harriman was near bankruptcy over some involvement with a railroad. I didn't pay much attention. Small towns got more wild imaginations than any other place. But this is all beginning to fall into place." He leaned forward. "Tell me, Marshal, what do you know about the outlaws who hit those trains?"

"Not too much," admitted Marshal Price, "and that's the hell of it. In fact, when I told my boss I wanted to come down here and nose around a little, he said I was off the track, that John Harriman wasn't that kind of an outlaw."

"Do you have any descriptions?"

Price shook his head. "All I can tell you is what witnesses have told me. About the only two things they all agree on is that there are five or six men in the gang, and that one of them uses good English, that he's a large man, and that the others seem well disciplined as though someone with a good head for planning and scheming has drilled and drilled them until they function almost like a squad of soldiers. They always block the track and either blow the doors off the express cars, or derail them, then dynamite them. Where they go after the robberies has been our biggest mystery. They just disappear, and that's what's kept us from getting any kind of a lead on them. We've had men watching in all the towns, waiting for them to show up. Or at least for some of that stolen money to show up. It never does."

"But you think Harriman might be the big man who leads them and uses educated English," said Wes, making a statement out of it.

Price nodded. "I think so. At least I *hope* so. If I'm wrong . . . we're right back where we were two years ago, and I don't mind telling you fellers that's nowhere."

Tom Ruffin, still leaning on the front wall, suddenly moved over to a chair and sat down. He didn't say anything but he looked over at Wes with a little crooked smile around his tough lips. Wes understood that look. Ruffin was thinking of the hide-out up where Stan Darcy was killed. He was also thinking of the second crew of men who rode with Harriman, and finally he was thinking how John Harriman had fooled an entire countryside for so long in his guise of a successful cowman.

Wes started to make a smoke. None of them had anything more to say until he had the thing lighted. Outside and northward, faint sounds of revelry came down the dark roadway from up along saloon row. They contrasted strangely with the quiet of the jailhouse office.

Wes said: "Harriman had five or six men when he tried to gun Ruffin and me this morning, Marshal. He's out to get title to a piece of land for which he'd have no use whatever . . . as a cowman. And finally he's not a man who comes to town often or mixes much with the local folks, so I think we just might discover, if we look hard enough, that he's not in the country much of the time." Wes smoked a moment, then said: "But I'll be damned if I'd ever thought of him as a hard-ridin' train robber."

Marshal Price smiled. "That's the general idea, Deputy. The really successful ones never look nor act the part." He slapped his legs and stood up. "It's late," he said, "and riding through the Sierras takes a lot out of a man. Suppose we meet here in the morning and do a little scheming of our own?"

Wes agreed, and Tom sat there saying nothing, with only his tawny eyes moving. Craig Price departed, in fact, before Ruffin had anything to say at all. Then it was just one simple statement. "Darcy got sent out to ride the range. He did too good a job of it. They killed him for maybe being where he wasn't supposed to be."

Wes went back to his chair after closing the door behind Marshal Price. He killed his smoke and said: "I'm goin' down the road and ask Hedges a couple of questions. You wait here."

Tom said: "Be careful. He'll get word to Harriman."

"If he gives the right answers," replied Wes grimly, "he won't get word to anyone because I'll fetch him back here an' lock him up. I just want him to confirm a suspicion I've got that Harriman killed old Dick because your pappy wouldn't sell out to him."

Tom sat a moment turning that over in his mind, then he, too, arose from his chair. "Did he know Harriman well enough for him to let him into the cabin?" he asked.

Wes said: "Sure he did. Well enough, in fact, for Harriman to get up within a few feet of him, draw his pistol, and shoot old Dick head-on. But that's not the point right now. What I want is the truth about *why* Dick was murdered."

Wes walked out into the star-washed night, paused to look up and down the roadway, then struck out across the road in an angling way toward the little lighted office of lawyer Ben Hedges. He hadn't quite reached the office when a man in a shapeless black coat and wearing a slouched old hat who was walking northward from around an intersecting roadway corner approached him out of the shadows, looking thoughtful.

"Wes?" the coated figure said, when they were close enough to recognize one another, and stopped in the middle of the walkway.

Wes said: " 'Evenin', Doc. I've been meaning to get up your way and talk to Mosley Crawford. How's he making it?"

"Well enough," stated the medical man. "Considering he has four fractured ribs and some internal injuries. But he'll be all right in a few days. And he wants to see you, too. That's why I stopped. He asked me this afternoon when he came around if you were back in town yet. Seems he tried to see you this morning and you weren't here."

"I'll be along," Wes said, looking past Dr. Blake where the light suddenly went out in Ben Hedges's office. "If not in an hour or two, then tomorrow morning." He started around the medical man as a dark shape farther along stepped out of Hedges's office and turned to insert a key and lock the door. "See you later, Doc," he said.

Blake resumed his northward pacing and Wes got up even with the attorney as Hedges turned, pocketed his doorway key, and took a couple of steps before he saw Wes. Hedges paused, shifted a briefcase he was carrying from his right hand to his left, and peered over at the deputy sheriff. Hedges looked unfriendly. He also looked careful.

"I want a straight answer from you," Wes said, looking and sounding just as unfriendly as Hedges also looked. "This time I want the truth. Why did John Harriman move so fast to try and get title to the Ruffin place?"

Hedges stood like a statue gazing across the little distance that separated them without murmuring an answer for a long time. Finally he said, speaking quietly: "Deputy, you're heading for trouble. You're playing with a man who's got you outmatched four ways from the middle. I told you before and I'll tell you again . . . Mister Harriman's affairs are private. I can spell that for you, if you'd like me to."

Wes took two forward steps and stopped less than a foot from the lawyer. For the second time in the last twenty-four hours something Wes had said or done made Hedges suddenly cave in around the edges, as though he were uncertain and apprehensive. He would have stepped backward to maintain the distance between them, but the office wall was too close.

Wes reached out almost lazily, caught the attorney's coat lapels, and drew Hedges to him. "For the last time, Hedges. Why did Harriman want that land badly enough to kill Dick Ruffin for it?"

Hedges's eyes grew perfectly round, and they darkened with fear. He croaked back at Wes: "You're accusing John Harriman of murder. You're going to lose your job over this, Wesley. Let go of my coat."

Wes tightened his grip. "It's not just one murder, Hedges, it's two. I'm not sure he killed Darcy, but he let it happen or he ordered it done. I don't know which. But I'm satisfied he killed Dick Ruffin. Now . . . why?"

"I . . . I don't know. I don't know anything about it. I swear to you I'm only his attorney. I . . ."

Wes whirled Hedges and gave him a hard shove out into the roadway. "Go on," he growled, stepping out after the attorney. "Go on over to the jailhouse. Maybe if I leave you alone in there with old Dick's son for a couple of hours, you'll feel differently about this privileged information you've got."

Hedges straightened up and said: "You can't do this. I've got legal rights under the law. You've got to prefer charges and I'm permitted my constitutional rights."

Wes took Hedges by the upper arm and started along with him, his grip like a steel trap. He steered the attorney all the way across to his jailhouse door, opened it, and gave Hedges another rough push. The lawyer stumbled into the orange light, regained his balance, looked up, and saw lanky, saturnine Tom Ruffin standing there eyeing him from the shadows, and he collapsed into a chair.

"Is this . . . ?" he whispered, and Wes nodded at him from the doorway.

"Yeah. This is old Dick's son. I'll see you two later."

# XII

Dr. Blake was just leaving the house with his little black satchel when Wes appeared on the front walk. Blake told him to go on in, that Mosley was awake, then muttered something about people who had babies after supper, and went stumping off through the darkness.

Wes remembered something and called after the medical man: "Got an embalming job for you, Doc. He's in the shed where I usually put them. You've got a key, haven't you?"

Blake said that he had, that he'd take care of it in the morning, and resumed his departure.

Wes entered the house, moved quietly around the little soft-lighted parlor, and peered into an adjoining room where a deep voice said: "Come on in, Wes."

Crawford showed Wes where the lamp was. After it was lighted, he said: "I tried to see you this morning, Wes. I tried to see you a couple of days ago, but lately you've been harder to find than the source of an itch."

Wes went over beside the bed. "How're the ribs?" he asked.

"They'll mend. So will whatever inside me got jiggled loose. At least that's what Doc says."

"I told Mister Harriman you'd be laid up for a few days, Mosley. He was going to send a wagon for you and haul you back to the ranch. I told him you shouldn't be moved for a few days."

Crawford's brown eyes were a little sunken, but their brightness was unimpaired. His dark features and thick build contrasted strongly with the pale linen of the bed where he lay, and the spindly legs of the furniture in the room. He said: "Wes, I been a long time comin' to this. Maybe I should've come in an' had a talk with you before. But a man doesn't want to say things he's not damned sure of. 'Specially where someone like Mister Harriman is concerned." He motioned for Wes to draw up a chair, then he said: "The hell of it is, Wes, I'm not certain even now, but still an' all I figure I've got to get this off my chest."

Wes sat down and hooked one long leg over the other. He gazed at the ill man and was quiet. Prompting, even when a man had more than just a suspicion such as Wes had, what someone else was trying to tell him, usually didn't really help much. Anyway, each individual had to face reality in his own way.

Mosley lifted a thick arm and rumpled his dark hair. He looked over at Wes and said: "There's been somethin' damned fishy goin' on, Wes. Once, a few months back, I saw Mister Harriman ride over into the trees behind the Ruffin place and meet a couple of fellers over there. Well, at the time I didn't really think too much of that . . . but then, last month, I went across to the main house sort of late at night to check with him about the work for the next day, and there were five fellers sittin' in the parlor with him, talkin'." Mosley squinted his eyes. "The strange part of it was that there were no horses tied out front, and none of us had seen those men come into the yard."

"They came from behind the house?" Wes inquired.

"Yeah. From around back where no one could

see them comin' or goin'. I know, because I didn't go in, seein' as how Mister Harriman was busy. Then I got to puzzlin', and walked around back. Still no horses, Wes. I walked out as far as the first stand of trees. There they were, five saddle horses tied back in there where no one'd expect to find them."

"Did you ever mention anything about this to Harriman," asked Wes, and got a headshake.

"Hell, no, I didn't want it to look like I was spyin' on him."

"Anything else, Mosley?"

"Little things, Wes. Nothing a man could really put his finger on. Like the last time he went away on business. He told me . . ."

"How often did he go away on business?" Wes broke in to ask.

"Pretty often lately, but before that only a couple times a year."

"OK, now go back to the little things you noticed, Mosley."

"Well, the last time, just before he left, he told me to keep Darcy on the ranch until he got back."

Wes raised his eyebrows. Mosley saw that inquiring expression and nodded on his pillow. "Why?" Wes asked.

"I don't know. I was puzzled when he said that. Stan was a good man, a reliable worker. He'd never had any words with Mister Harriman that I ever heard of. I forgot about it, but o' course I kept

Stan close by. Then, when Doc said he'd heard around town that Stan Darcy had been killed, and a stranger had brought him to town tied belly-down over his saddle, I remembered something else. After Harriman got back a couple weeks ago, he sort of acted like maybe he 'n' Stan knew something or shared something. Like I already said, Wes, none of this stuff was anything you could put a finger on, but it was there never-theless. Stan and I used to play poker after supper with the others. He quit that. He also got sort of quiet around the rest of us."

"Did he and Harriman act friendly?"

"No," said Mosley. "That's just it, Wes. They acted like they scarcely knew one another. Then . . . Stan got killed."

"Up back of the Ruffin place, Mosley. He was shot the same way old Dick was . . . looking his killer right in the eye. His gun wasn't fired. It was still in his holster when he was found." Wes leaned forward. "Mosley, think back hard. Did any-thing ever come up about Harriman getting hold of the Ruffin place, before old Dick was murdered?"

Mosley shook his head. "Not with me," he replied. "Mister Harriman often did things without tellin' me about them in advance, though, and after all he *was* the owner, so I never thought too much about it."

"He never gave you the impression he might want the Ruffin's ranch?"

"Nope. He never did, Wes. All he ever said was that Dick wasn't important enough to bother with, if we kept that old fence between Anchor and Dick in halfway decent shape, we could forget the old cuss." Mosley put a searching look forward. "Who killed Stan?" he asked.

Wes was honest. "I don't know, Mosley. I'm not even sure who killed Dick. But at least I've got an idea there." Wes stood up. "It still looks to me like the same man killed them both. At least they were both killed in the identical fashion. But . . ."

"Yeah, but what?"

Wes put his hat on and considered the pattern in the rug at his feet. "But the feller who I figure killed Dick was right here in town the night Darcy was brought in, and I couldn't for the life of me detect any difference in his face when I told him Stan had been killed."

Mosley kept watching the deputy's face. He said: "Just one last question, Wes. Was this feller you talked to John Harriman?"

Wes nodded his head. "Why?"

Mosley didn't answer right away, but after a little while he said softly: "Stan knew something, Wes. I had that feeling all along. I got no idea what he'd found out, or how he found it out, but he started changin' right in front of my eyes. Then he got killed. He knew somethin', Wes. I'd bank my life on it."

Wes left the house more than ever convinced

that Mosley was right, that Darcy's murder was somehow tied to the unknown secret of John Harriman's double life. He was also certain he knew at long last why Tom Ruffin's father had been killed. The two notions he had were closely allied with what Marshal Price had said, and also with what he had figured out about Harriman by himself.

At the jailhouse Tom Ruffin was sitting by the door staring impassively across where Ben Hedges was crouching upon a wall bench. Ruffin's hat brim shadowed his upper face, showing little more than the whites of his eyes and the tawny, hard glitter of his black stare. He didn't even stop staring over at Hedges after Wes entered, but otherwise Wes's reappearance altered the bitter atmosphere. He gazed over at Hedges. At once the attorney cried out: "Wesley, you're going beyond the law in what you're doing. You'll ruin your career by this. . . ."

"What did he tell you?" Wes asked Tom Ruffin, turning away from Hedges.

"Enough," growled Ruffin, and pointed his chin at Hedges in a little hard jerk of his head. "Tell Deputy Potter what you told me, Hedges."

The lawyer threw out his hands. "I had to," he said to Wes. "If I hadn't, he'd've have shot me, Wesley. I had to tell him what he wanted to hear. It's not admissible. It was gotten under duress. There was coercion and . . ."

"Tell him!" snarled Ruffin, suddenly sitting straight up in his chair. "Tell him exactly the way you told me!"

Hedges recoiled from the pure savagery in Tom Ruffin's voice. "Mister Harriman had to have that land up there. He has been using it for the past couple of years as a rendezvous for some men he . . . works with. They have a hidden camp up there. Once, Mister Harriman took me up there. Only one man was there at that time. The others were on their way over the mountains into Nevada and Mister Harriman was going by coach to join them. He had some legal work for me to do and didn't have time to have me at the ranch."

Hedges ceased speaking and looked imploringly at Wes. He was quiet long enough for Ruffin to say: "Don't make me prompt you again. Tell him *all* of it."

Wes stood there against the roadside door, waiting. He offered no comfort to Ben Hedges at all. He simply stood there.

Hedges slumped. "All right," he muttered. Then, with a little flash of spirit, he said swiftly: "But none of this can be used in a court of law. It was gotten from me by threats and coercion."

"Talk!" snarled Ruffin, leaning as though to spring to his feet.

"I'm talking," said the lawyer, pressing back. "I'm talking. Wesley, they are outlaws. John Harriman is an outlaw. He led them against the railroads and coaches over in Nevada, then they come down here to rest. Mister Harriman goes back to running his ranch, and the outlaws have their secret hide-out . . . only . . . Dick Ruffin stumbled onto it."

"Who told you he found it?" Wes demanded.

"Mister Harriman. We were talking about it the night you walked in and told us Darcy's body was in town. That's what stunned us. Mister Harriman had just told me about Darcy. We were discussing those two . . . Darcy and Ruffin . . . when you . . ."

"You're repeating yourself," growled Tom Ruffin, his voice roughened by deep contempt for Hedges. "Tell him about my father finding the outlaw hide-out."

"Well, Ruffin was a danger. Mister Harriman'd been listening to complaints about Dick ever since his outlaw crew made their hide-out back in the cañon. They kept saying Dick had to be gotten rid of or sooner or later he'd find their hide-out."

Wes said: "And he found out."

Hedges nodded, painfully swallowed, and avoided looking at Tom. "Yes. One day he came down the rearward slopes, caught the scent of a cooking fire, and they caught him scouting them up. Mister Harriman came riding in. He and Ruffin talked, then Mister Harriman made them turn Ruffin loose. The others didn't like that. They said Ruffin would go right to the law. But Mister Harriman said that he wouldn't. Then Mister

Harriman rode out of camp. I was with him. I rode as far as the cabin, then left him and came on to town. I didn't know until two days later that Ruffin had been killed."

"That's obstructing justice," Wes said to Hedges. "It's also complicity, Hedges, and a dozen other things . . . concealing all this knowledge."

Hedges didn't dispute that. He said: "You can't force me to take an oath to any of it."

"Forget that for now," Ruffin muttered. "Hedges, tell him about Darcy."

"He found old Dick," Hedges said to Wes. "He was the one who . . ."

"I know that!" exclaimed Wes impatiently. "He rode to town and told me. What about it?"

"Well . . . ," stated the lawyer, and painfully swallowed again, "well, Darcy came riding into the clearing and saw Mister Harriman walk out of the house putting his six-gun into its holster. It was an accident. Mister Harriman didn't know what to do. He couldn't also shoot Darcy, not right there in the yard."

"So he bought him off, is that it?" Wes asked.

"Yes," said the attorney. "But he told me Darcy seemed to figure he was marked for a bullet, too. Mister Harriman said he did everything he could to keep Darcy around. Then one day he caught Darcy rolling his bedroll. He talked him out of trying to leave, gave him some more money. But he figured he'd have to do something even though his policy was to avoid trouble at all costs around this country so's folks would never wonder about him."

"He sent Darcy back into the forest," said Wes, drawing on his own conjectures. "And sent word to the outlaws to kill him."

"No," muttered Tom Ruffin. "Go on, Hedges. Tell him how he worked it."

Hedges flicked an anxious look from one of them to the other, then said: "No, Wesley, he sent Darcy over to the Ruffin place all right, but he followed him to make certain Darcy didn't try to make a run for it. When they were both over by the cabin, Mister Harriman decided it was safe, there was no one around to hear the gunshot, and it had to be done. He rode out, called Darcy over to him, and, when they were close . . . he shot Darcy just like he shot old Ruffin."

Tom looked up at Wes. "We weren't too far off on the details," he said, then looked forward again, eyeing Hedges with that same bitter, deadly look again. "Nice folks you got around here, Wes. Real nice folks."

Wes slowly straightened up off the door, went to his desk where he scooped up a ring of keys, and jerked his head at Hedges as he headed for the reinforced oaken door at the back of his office, beyond which were his little strap-steel jail cells. "Come on," he muttered.

# XIII

It was past midnight when Wes and Tom Ruffin walked over to Stub Pearson's café for a cup of coffee. They were talked out. They'd spent an hour after Wes locked up Hedges going over what they now knew to be facts. Most of it they'd surmised earlier, but as Wes said just before he reached the café door: "Knowing isn't enough, Tom. Even having half the facts isn't enough. When you take a man into court, it's got to be iron-clad evidence you use just to get him arraigned. To get him convicted you damned near need a notarized confession."

Ruffin stepped through into Stub's café with bright lamplight touching his swarthy features, and said: "I know a lot better way to take care of fellers like that in this lousy world."

Stub was in his back room when he heard the outer door open and close. He came as far as the opening and peered out. When he saw Wes, he said: "I was just fixin' to close up." But he came on through and went after a couple of cups of oily black coffee that he carried down the counter and put in front of the two lanky men sitting there looking solemn.

"A nickel," Stub said, holding out his hand.

When Wes dropped the coin onto his palm, Stub said: "Silas was mad tonight. He worked late on the books, an', when he was finally leavin', here come some fellers with one of John Harriman's wagons to get a bunch of stuff."

Wes looked up. So did Tom Ruffin. Anything that was connected with Harriman's name instantly aroused their interest whether they were tired or not.

"What kind of stuff?" asked Wes.

"That's the part that annoyed Silas. You know that little brick shack out beyond town where he keeps his blastin' powder and excess ammunition? Well, he had to go out there with them, open it up, an' help them load two boxes of dynamite."

Wes put out one hand and firmly pushed the coffee cup away. He got up very slowly as he said: "Who were the men, Stub?"

But Pearson didn't know. All he said was: "Silas didn't say anythin' about that, but he was pretty burned up. It was near ten o'clock, 'way past closin' time. That's how come me to still be open this late. Silas sat there growlin' and cussin'. You know how he gets sometimes when something roils him."

Wes turned for the door. Tom was just one step behind him. Stub stood there, gaping after them. Outside, Tom said: "You know where this Silas lives?"

Wes nodded and struck out without saying a word. They marched southward past the general store to the intersection southward beyond the saddle and harness shop, Ben Hedges's office, then swung to their left and walked past a number of darkened residences until Wes turned in at a white-painted house that sat well back across a neat yard and that was dark except for one lighted window near the back of the place.

Wes rapped upon the front door, waited a moment, then rapped again, harder. Houseman came to the door with a big horse pistol behind his back in his right hand. He peered out first, then opened the panel when he recognized Wes. "What is it?" he asked a little breathlessly. "Someone try to break into the store, Wes?"

"Nothing like that," the deputy replied. "We want some information about those men who bought that powder from you tonight, Silas."

"Come in," muttered Houseman, and leaned to put the big pistol on a little upright table. Neither of his callers made any move to enter the house. He looked out at them again, closer this time, then said: "All right, you look like you're in a hurry." He had, of course, recognized Tom Ruffin, but he gave no sign of it as he concentrated his attention upon the deputy and said: "I never saw them before, Wes. There were three of them. I figured maybe they were riders Anchor had just hired on. They bought two crates of powder an' I had to go down there to my powder house after ten o'clock and help them load it."

"Are you sure it was one of Harriman's wagons?" Wes asked.

"It was," stated Houseman. "They're all branded with his big Anchor mark. I wouldn't have waited on them so late at night if I hadn't seen that thing branded on the sideboards."

"What did they say, Silas?"

"Nothing much. They had a list of supplies that I filled for them at the store. Then they wanted the powder. I was a little annoyed. I told 'em Mister Harriman ought to know better'n send for supplies so late at night. One of them said they'd tried to get into town sooner, but had broken down." Silas stopped speaking and looked from Wes to Tom and back again. "Something wrong?" he inquired.

"Did they head back for the ranch?" Wes asked.

Silas nodded his head. "I watched them go straight out an' around town, heading northeast, Wes. I didn't see anything wrong, except they came so danged late in the night. I don't mind helpin' folks out, but Anchor Ranch's too big to have emergencies like that. There wasn't a thing they bought that couldn't have just as easily been laid over until morning."

"Thanks," said Wes, and took Ruffin's arm as he turned so that Tom departed right along with him. Silas looked out into the darkness after them, but he didn't call out, and, when they were striding back uptown the way they'd come, he finally closed his door, locked it, and went mutteringly back toward his bedroom. Sometimes, folks just seemed to conspire against a tired man getting his rest.

When they were back around on the main thoroughfare, Wes said: "Tom, go to the rooming house up the square and get that deputy U.S. marshal out of bed. Fetch him over to the jailhouse. I'm goin' on over and see if I can get a little more information out of Ben Hedges. If what I'm thinkin' is right, Harriman's about to head over the mountains again for another strike in Nevada."

Tom nodded and walked off, heading northward up toward the brightly lighted and noisy part of town. Wes stepped out into the roadway and hiked across to his jailhouse. He opened the door, took one step forward, and something hit him, half spinning him toward the wall. He was too astonished to do more at first than fight for balance. If he'd been farther into the room, he would have gone down. As it was, he bounced off the wall with both legs fairly set, and dropped low by instinct. Something sailed overhead striking the wall hard. He shot a rapid look upward just as the lamp went out over on the table. He caught sight of a man with something in his hands that looked like a large piece of wood, the leg off a chair or table. He dived straight toward that figure as darkness filled the office, struck out hard, and felt warm flesh yield to his fist.

The stranger gasped and backed off. There was a little weak light coming through the open doorway, but the unexpected assailant who had tried to down Wes with that first wild swing maneuvered so that he was never wholly limned by that light.

Wes's left shoulder hurt where he'd initially been hit that glancing blow. He recovered swiftly from surprise, and sprang forward, both hands searching. He brushed something with one hand and turned toward it at the same time the shadowy stranger took a wild cut downward with his six-gun.

Wes lunged for the man's weapon, missed, fell against the assassin, and pumped two low, solid punches into the man's middle. He heard the gun drop and skitter across the floor. A looping blow raked up the side of Wes's head knocking off his hat and jarring him away. He still had his six-gun but anger more than pride kept him from using it. The other man was unarmed now; he didn't need to use the .45. But more than that, he wanted to beat this man in the same way his attacker had started this fight—by hand.

The stranger sidled away, then sprang. Wes heard rather than saw what the stranger was trying to do, and stepped sideways, pivoted as the dark shape loomed, and struck forward with a blasting fist. It connected. The shock of pain ran all the way to Wes's shoulder. He was rocked back onto his heels by the impact. But the other man did not go down. Wes heard him blow out a ragged breath, heard his booted, spurred feet drag as he came around again. Then the man came at him again in a savage rush.

Wes reached back, caught hold of his desk chair, and swung it violently forward. The oncoming stranger hit the chair with his lower legs, ripped out a wild curse, and crashed down across the chair. Wes moved clear, trying to line the man up with the weak doorway light, saw him rolling over to jump up, and Wes went after him. But the assassin was desperate, and desperation sharpens the wits of the dullest man. He kicked the chair straight into Wes, jumped up, and fled out the open door. Wes braced for the chair, reached out to heave it aside, then also ran outside. But the night was empty; there was no sign of his unknown assailant, not even the sound of running feet. He stood a moment, breathing hard, then felt his shoulder where that club had caught him a glancing blow, and also probed the side of his head where the only telling blow the stranger had landed still throbbed.

He returned to the office, groped for the lamp, and re-lit it. Not until he was lowering the mantle, and raised his eyes, did he notice that the cell-room door was open. He stared at it, his heart beginning to sink. After he'd locked Ben Hedges in for the night, he'd closed that door.

He walked across the room, scooped up his hat, shaped it, and dropped it back into place. He then picked up the six-gun his assailant had lost during the fight, and saw the length of scantling the man'd had in his hands when he'd first attacked. It was a rough piece of board, evidently picked up somewhere and brought along because the assassin, whoever he had been, had meant to avoid the noise gunshots would make if he ran into opposition.

The gun told him nothing; it was an old weapon, worn smooth, with dents and scratches on its hard-rubber grips. He put both gun and club on his desk, crossed to the cell-room, and entered. He only had one prisoner—Ben Hedges—so he stepped up to the first cell doorway and peered in. Hedges was lying out full length on his wall bunk. Wes spoke to him. There was no answer. He spoke again, louder, but still got no reply. He returned to the outer room, took up the lamp, and returned.

Ben Hedges was dead!

There wasn't any blood or any signs of violence. The cell door was still locked. Wes unlocked it, walked over, and held the lamp low. Even then he didn't see the rip until he'd bent far over. Hedges had been killed by one powerful thrust of someone's knife. He'd evidently gotten as far as the bunk before he died.

Wes lifted Hedges's coat, opened his shirt, and looked closer. The blade had been long, narrow, and sharpened on both sides. It had slid past Hedges's breastbone as though the assassin had known his business, and had evidently pierced Hedges's heart. There was very little blood. As Wes straightened up, he murmured: "You damned fool. Why didn't you keep your mouth closed?"

Out in the office two solid sounds of men coming in from the roadway temporarily diverted Wes. He went back out to the intervening doorway, saw Tom Ruffin and the deputy U.S. marshal standing there, and beckoned them on in. They came, entered the cell, and looked hard when Wes held the lamp low enough to reveal the sightless eyes and the knife puncture.

"What . . . ?" Ruffin blurted out.

Wes said: "He was in here when I entered. Right by the roadway door. I reckon he was gettin' ready to slip out and I walked in on him. He had that stick that's on my desk in one hand. He caught me on the shoulder, then we tussled a little. But he got away."

Marshal Price stepped back, frowning. "Why?" he asked.

Wes put the lamp aside and worked his stiffening arm and shoulder up and down and around to prevent the stiffness from becoming too pronounced. "He was John Harriman's lawyer," he explained to the federal lawman. "He told Tom an' me about the murder of Tom's pappy, and a cowboy named Stan Darcy who was also shot to death without a chance. We told you all that earlier, Marshal."

"I know, but why was this man killed?"

"My guess," said Wes, "is that, while Tom and I were out, someone who saw me arrest Hedges earlier . . . and there were some of Harriman's outlaws in town tonight . . . followed us over here and waited. When Tom and I left to go see Silas Houseman, the general store proprietor, he slipped in here. I'm still guessing, but I believe Hedges told this stranger to go warn Harriman, told him what he'd told Tom and me about Harriman's outlaw activities."

Marshal Price said the same thing now that Wes had said earlier, when he'd also been looking down at the dead man. "The damned fool. Why didn't he keep his mouth closed? Of course Harriman would want him killed for telling you all that stuff. Hedges must not have been very smart."

"Well," Tom Ruffin summed up dryly, "smart or not, he sure doesn't get a second chance." Then Tom turned and looked at Wes. "You all right? He didn't hook you with that knife, too, did he?"

"No," answered Wes. "Did you tell Marshal Price about the dynamite?"

Ruffin inclined his head. "And also about those men drivin' the Anchor Ranch outfit."

Wes turned toward Price. "We'd better ride out and take Harriman into custody . . . if we can. I had that in mind before. But now, the feller who killed Hedges will ride hell-for-leather to Anchor, and, by the time we get out there, Harriman'll know how much of his affairs we're familiar with."

Marshal Price said: "All the more reason to head out there, and be quick about it. Harriman just might decide his time's about run out, and try to skip."

Wes didn't believe that, but he made no comment about it. He picked up the lamp, went back out into the outer office, closed and locked the cell-room door behind the other two, then put the lamp aside, and rummaged in his desk until he found what he was looking for—a badge.

"Put it in your pocket or pin it on the front of you," he told Tom, handing him the badge. "I've got the authority to appoint special deputies. You've just been appointed."

Ruffin looked at the badge in his hand and looked up at Wes. "Why?" he asked. "What do I need this thing for?"

Marshal Craig Price had the correct reply: "Because, if you have to shoot someone tonight, believe me, Tom, it's a lot easier afterward explaining it to a coroner's jury when you're standing behind a badge."

Wes went to his gun rack, took out three carbines, and brought them back, then returned for a box of shells. As he returned and broke open the box on his desk, he said: "Carbines are like that badge. If you have to argue, it's a lot easier doing it behind one of these things." He handed Price and Ruffin each a carbine and motioned for them to help themselves to the cartridges, and also filled his own pockets. When the others had done likewise, Wes went over, opened the door, looked up and down, then said: "Come on. I was kind of hoping that butcher was still watching the place, but I reckon he's half way out to Anchor Ranch by now."

The deputy marshal also armed himself with one of Wes's racked-up shotguns and a box of shells. He was the last one to leave the office. Wes locked the roadside door, too, before he led the way up toward Claude Lucas's dark and silent livery barn.

# XIV

The night hawk at Claude's livery barn was sleeping so soundly that, when two efforts to rouse him failed, the three law officers got their animals without his assistance, saddled up, and rode out through the quiet town with no one to witness their departure.

After they'd covered a little distance, Marshal Price said: "Potter, I'm wondering about the other men who work for Harriman. His ranch hands. The odds are big enough without them buyin' in."

Wes didn't believe they'd buy in and told the others so. He also said that, if Mosely Crawford had been up and around, they could be certain the other hands wouldn't get involved. He explained what Mosely had told him; none of it was important now because they were well past the stage of unsupported suspicion, but at least it underwrote how Wes felt about Crawford. Tom Ruffin took no part in any of the conversation. He rode along, gauging the onward night, looking and listening. When Marshal Price asked him about his father, he only said that he'd never met his father, and lapsed back into his silence again.

After a while, when they could vaguely discern the dark, hulking mountains dead ahead, a little shaft of coolness speared its way down through the night. It made the air as clear as crystal. Overhead stars stood out sharply, each facet of their bright shapes different in contour and color. It was one of those magical nights most people sleep through.

Marshal Price said, apropos of nothing but consistent with how all their thoughts were running: "It's interesting how Harriman, who never used violence in the East, adapted himself so well to the ways of the far West frontier. Scheming out here has to be implemented with violence to succeed in lawlessness. Usually, at least in my experience, a man Harriman's age doesn't change his method of operating. If he's an embezzler, he remains one. If he's a gunfighter, he stays with guns."

Ruffin gazed over at the deputy U.S. marshal saturninely. "When I was a kid, I heard a saying about folks being in Rome doing as the Romans do . . . or did . . . or something."

Price looked back and nodded his head. "I reckon that's about the size of it," he agreed. "Harriman couldn't embezzle out here. He never got the chance, so he reverted to the frontier way of making a dollar."

"Speaking of dollars," murmured Wes, "just how much has Harriman's raids netted him?"

Price didn't hesitate. "Eighty thousand dollars in currency and Nevada gold in bars and dust."

Wes was astonished. Even Tom Ruffin looked surprised. Marshal Price saw their expressions in the watery light. He smiled mirthlessly.

"He couldn't have embezzled that much. Auditors would have caught him. Maybe that's why he's perfected his robbing techniques. It's paid off."

"I reckon so," stated Wes. Then he straightened in the saddle. "Hell, no wonder he wanted Dick Ruffin's place. If he's got that kind of money and bullion cached back in those mountains . . ."

Price said: "That's got to be about it, Deputy. As I told you, we kept undercover men watching in every town and camp. None of that loot ever turned up."

Tom Ruffin, looking from Wes to Price, said: "Eighty thousand . . . cached on my father's ranch?"

Price nodded, felt around inside his coat for a stogie, and popped it into his mouth. They were still some distance south of their destination with time to kill. It was getting along toward the small hours of the cool morning. Price lit up and savored the bite of his strong tobacco. It was a small, inexpensive thing, that cigar, but most of the range man's delights and pleasures were like that: inexpensive, savored, hard-earned. Like a drink of cold water on a blistering day or a light, warm blanket over him on a chilly autumn night. $80,000 was a figure, little more. They could off-handedly discuss it, but as for actually conceiving what such an aggregate of money looked like, what it could really buy for a man, or what might be entailed in really earning that kind of money, they could only fall back on a very loose generalization. They had never been wealthy men, and they never would be; their world was a hard place, life in it was elemental and very real. Their pleasures, like their hardships, were sharply cut and clearly defined.

Tom Ruffin sighed, balanced himself in the saddle, and rode along looking straight ahead where the mountains were marching down toward him. After a while he said: "This Harriman . . . if there was a way for his kind to get rich legally, he wouldn't do it. I know the type. And it's too bad, because it seems to me in this life a successful man can be either legitimately successful or otherwise. Brains make the difference, not brawn."

Marshal Price gazed oddly over at Ruffin. He was clearly wondering about a man as obviously the product of the inconsistencies of two races, being that much of a deep thinker. But he said nothing until, a mile more along their way, something on ahead near the foothills caught and held his attention. Then he stopped his horse, lowered his cigar, and sat like stone, straining ahead.

Tom said quietly: "It's riders. I heard 'em a few minutes back. Seems they're goin' from west to east."

Wes heard nothing right away, but when Tom ceased speaking, he picked up the faint ring of rein chains, and, moments later, the ring of shod hoofs hurrying over stone. Marshal Price turned his head. "You know the country," he murmured to Wes, and said no more, but sat there waiting for Wes to make his assessment.

But Tom spoke next: "Maybe that feller who jumped Wes at the jailhouse didn't go directly to Harriman. Maybe he went instead up to the outlaw camp and got his friends in the saddle to go over to Anchor Ranch all together."

Wes nodded. That's what it sounded like to him.

He made some quick calculations. By angling northeastward he thought there just might be a chance of getting over to Anchor ahead of those riders. "Let's try it," he said, lifting his reins. "If we can cut them off, maybe we can scare them off an' still get Harriman before he knows he's in real danger."

They struck out on an altered course, riding in a swift rush. They were soon close enough to the backgrounding hills to be completely lost in the depth of their mighty shadows. Star shine helped, but the moon was too thin and distant, on its way down across the firmament, to add much light. They could see each other fairly well, but not much else.

After a time, Tom called for a halt. They reined down, listened, then Tom flagged forward with his arm, and they moved out once more, loping. The sounds were still up ahead of them, but discernibly to the west. They were close to intercepting those invisible riders. But the cause of survival made all riders of the Owlhoot Trail cautious and wary. Suddenly those other men out there in the darkness halted. Tom heard that and tried to match it, but his horse ran on another dozen yards before he got it stopped. Wes and Craig Price understood their mistake. Someone out there had caught their sound, had called upon his companions to halt, and in the interval between that halt and the halt of the lawmen, the outlaws heard all they had to hear to realize they were not alone in the nearby night.

Wes said: "Well, it was a good try. Now we've got trouble." He lifted out his carbine and laid it across his lap, urged his horse forward at a steady walk with Tom on one side, Craig Price on the other side, and tried to determine exactly where the outlaws were up there in that dark and trackless void.

Ruffin finally edged over, leaned from his saddle, and said: "We better head straight for the ranch. At least there's a chance over there. This way, it could end up in a lousy dogfight."

Wes agreed without saying so, and swerved, but he had no illusions about avoiding a fight. Neither did the deputy U.S. marshal evidently, because he folded his tweed coat inward, exposing a shoulder-holstered ivory-butted six-gun. Tom and Wes saw how Price wore his gun and had an answer to something they'd wondered about much earlier, when they'd detected no sign of a belt gun on the federal lawman.

They stopped from time to time, listening, but apparently the oncoming outlaws were now walking quietly along, too, because they made no noise, either. They were drawing near Anchor Ranch. It wasn't visible yet, but Wes knew this uplands country; they were not much more than a mile out.

Tom Ruffin suddenly hissed for silence and

halted his horse. The second they all became stationary, looking off to their left, they picked up the sound of a solitary rider coming cautiously straight toward them. The outlaws, perhaps uncertain who and where Wes and Tom and the deputy marshal were exactly, had detached one man to scout them. This was something Wes understood very well; he dropped his Winchester back into its boot, stepped to the ground, and led his horse straight northward. Without a word or sign passing between them, Tom Ruffin also put up his carbine, dismounted, and led his horse southward. Marshal Price had the next move; he did exactly what the others expected of him. He got down, ground-hitched his mount, drew his ivory-butted .45, and started walking straight toward the soft sound of that oncoming rider. The outlaw had only one way out—retreat—but if he tried to use it, his chances of living through were slimmer by the second, as he came straight on into the little enfilade.

There wasn't a sound anywhere else. Apparently those other outlaws out there were going to sit back and await the report of their scout. Or at least await whatever reaction his presence stirred up. Wes halted out where he could still make out Marshal Price, but well enough northward also to block the withdrawal of the oncoming renegade in his direction. He couldn't see Tom Ruffin at all, but he knew about where Ruffin was, and what

Ruffin would do if trouble came—kill the outlaw.

Marshal Price suddenly dropped from sight in the grass. Wes, concentrating hard, finally saw what Price had also seen—the moving and bulky silhouette of a mounted man easing cautiously forward, straight for the spot where Price lay concealed. It was a dangerous gamble. Wes hadn't actually expected the federal lawman to take it. He'd thought Price would have only tried to get the drop on the outlaw. Instead, he was going to try the old-time Mexican marauder trick of springing up out of the grass and dragging his foeman off that horse.

The seconds passed. Wes drew his .45, held it low, and tracked the approaching horseman with it, pointing the gun as he'd have pointed his finger. The outlaw was sitting alert, straight up in his saddle, when he came about even with the spot where Price lay. Wes held his breath; if the man's mount caught Price's scent . . .

Wes didn't see the marshal make his lunge upward. All he saw, because he was on the left side and Marshal Price was on the right side, was the way the horse suddenly snorted and violently shied away. After that, the horse was riderless; it swung as though to race away, either saw Wes's horse or smelled it, and paused to look around. Behind it in the grass two men grunted and thrashed back and forth. Wes checked his impulse to run forward; instead, he turned his horse across his own body so the outlaw's mount wouldn't see him, and began inching ahead to capture the outlaw's riderless animal. He did it, got hold of the reins while the riderless horse sniffed Wes's mount, then he could turn back and go across where the battle was in progress.

But by the time he got down there, it was just about over. Tom Ruffin was leaning from the waist, his dark face a mask of willing violence, pressing his pistol barrel into the neck of the grounded outlaw. Marshal Price was getting to his feet, brushing off grass and dirt. The outlaw only rolled his eyes around to where he could see Ruffin bending over him. He didn't seem even to be breathing; the pressure of that six-gun against his neck was a powerful inducement not to move at all.

Price stooped, disarmed the man, and stepped back, beckoning him to get to his feet. He didn't move until Tom Ruffin withdrew his cocked six-gun, and even then, as the man slowly arose, he kept watching Ruffin's gun, not Marshal Price.

"Better check him for hide-outs," Ruffin muttered. "He'll have at least one."

Tom was correct. Marshal Price found a Derringer in the man's right boot. He pocketed it and continued the search, but that was the only other weapon. Wes stepped up and without a word struck the outlaw over the head with his pistol barrel. As the man dropped, Marshal Price swung, his expression showing astonishment and resentment. "What the hell . . . ?" he hissed as Wes put up his .45.

Wes said, gazing dispassionately at the man: "Tie him hard, Tom. Then you two get astride and head for the ranch. I'm going to lead them to you, if my luck is any good tonight." Wes traded hats with the unconscious man, turned, and mounted the outlaw's horse. Just before he turned the beast to backtrack in the direction the unconscious man had come, he said: "Don't waste any time. Head straight for Anchor's bunkhouse and explain what we're up against. They'll either join you or not. If not, disarm 'em and lock 'em in their bunkhouse, then try for Harriman. If you get him hostage, we can still come out on top."

Tom Ruffin's white, even teeth shone in the darkness as he dropped down to truss up the slumbering renegade. "Good luck," he said quietly to Wes. "Give us a couple of minutes."

Wes rode slowly back westward. He did not fear immediate discovery for the simple reason that he had no intention of getting that close to the outlaws. What he *did* fear was that something might go wrong at the ranch; he was positive, that unless Harriman was taken before he could reach a gun, or his riders in the bunkhouse were caught flat-footed, someone over there would get off a shot. If that happened, the outlaws would know instantly they were being trapped, in which case the position of Wes and his companions—between two fires—would be far from envious.

The horse he was astride was a docile beast with a strong streak of laziness in him. Wes was in no hurry, but even so he had to keep nudging the animal to make him step out at a steady walk.

The chill was becoming more pronounced now; dawn couldn't be far off. There was a decided resin-scent in the still air, and mixed in with it was the odor of cattle. Twice, when his borrowed horse pointed its little ears, Wes nearly reined off to a halt, but each time it was cattle. They lumbered to their feet and stood intently watching as horse and man passed along.

The anxiety grew each time his mount carried him farther from Price and Ruffin, closer to the outlaws up ahead somewhere. When he finally saw them, sitting motionless with the back-grounding mountains and sky blacker than their pale silhouettes, he let the horse go ahead only another few yards, until he was positive they'd also seen him, then he halted, turned back, lifted one arm, and lazily gestured. At once the outlaws started moving. So did Wes, but with a tightness like a wire up between his shoulder blades. If anything went wrong now, at this distance they couldn't miss killing him.

He kept his lead and slouched along, hoping with his full ability to hope, that the recognizable mount under him and the old hat atop him would be adequate camouflage. Evidently they were, at least at the start, for no one said anything.

# XV

He got within a half mile of Anchor Ranch, then raised his arm to halt the following outlaws. When he turned in the saddle, one of them softly called ahead: "Make plumb certain, Mack. They got to be around here, whoever they are."

Wes nodded and rode off. So far so good, he thought, but the real test lay ahead. Then the whole scheme, right at the juncture where Wes had thought it might very well succeed, blew apart when someone up in the yonder yard fired off a shot. That solitary long-lancing flame jaggedly tore the night with its brightness and its loud thunder, making Wes instinctively duck in the saddle even though the shot hadn't been fired at him. Then someone ripped out a loud curse and there was the sound of men struggling out of deep slumber and fuzzily crying out in quick alarm.

Wes turned at the sound of riders behind him. The outlaws were coming! He was dumbfounded. He had never once considered the possibility they would come toward the ranch buildings if anything went wrong. But he didn't have any time to wonder about that, because someone back there let fly a wild shot toward Anchor's bunkhouse, and, as though that were the signal, all hell broke loose.

Two men over on the bunkhouse porch fired at gun flashes behind Wes. He had to drop down over the side of his borrowed horse and make a run for it. As he raced toward the yard, other guns also shattered the night. Someone down in the yard let off a high bawl of alarm. Wes saw that man; he'd been crossing from the bunkhouse toward John Harriman's main residence, saw Wes racing into the yard, and turned with a big yell to run for dear life back toward the bunkhouse. As this man fled, he fired wildly over his shoulder. One of those slugs became the fleeing man's lucky shot. It stung Wes's borrowed horse across the sensitive tip of his soft muzzle. The horse slammed all four legs straight out in a stiff slide. Wes, already far off balance down the side of the beast, kept right on going. He was catapulted twenty feet ahead and landed rolling. Someone over at the bunkhouse snapped a shot at him that kicked up dirt. He tried to utilize some of his momentum to reach the bunkhouse porch, but after that close miss he made instead for the log barn north of the bunkhouse, got to his feet finally, and ran as hard as he could.

The outlaws adopted an old Indian tactic. They knew they had enemies down there in the yard, but they did not know exactly how many or where they might be, so they raced around the buildings from out back, firing rapidly as they passed between one building to the next building. It was somewhat the way Indians attacked circled wagons on the plains.

From inside the barn Wes had an advantage neither Price nor Tom Ruffin had. He could step up to the rear doorway and fire pointblank. The trouble was that his shell belt supply was insufficient to withstand a prolonged siege, and it was too dark, the running horsemen too uncertain, for accurate firing. He eventually desisted altogether, re-loaded, and wished he had a carbine.

From the bunkhouse, though, the fight still raged. Wes tried to determine whether the Anchor riders over there were fighting *with* Marshal Price and Tom Ruffin, or *against* them. It was impossible to discern that by remaining inside the barn, so he decided to try and get up as far as the bunkhouse porch.

The moment he inched out the front door, however, someone over by the main house drove a slug into the log wall not more than six inches from his head. He sprang back and flattened behind the nearest wall. If that was John Harriman over there in the dark, Wes was going to have to change his opinion; that kind of shooting, in the dark, was better than most cowboys could duplicate.

It seemed that the outlaws, for some reason Wes could not fathom, were taking reckless and needless chances as they continued their fierce attack. Gradually, though, the gunfire began to assume a definite pattern. The gunmen over at the bunkhouse were beginning to co-ordinate their efforts. They were definitely firing back at the racing outlaws. Wes went back to the rear of the barn and looked out, in order to convince himself that this was so.

Evidently, with their initial surprise past, now, and convinced that whether Tom and Marshal Craig were their friends or not, at least Ruffin and Price were definitely opposing the men who were attacking the ranch. Anchor's range men had aligned themselves with the lawmen and their added gunfire began to make all the difference. Wes was more or less out of it. He tried once more to get out the front door, and was once more driven back by that marksman over at the main house. It didn't occur to him until he'd about decided to leave by way of the rear door to get up to the bunkhouse and his friends that, although the outlaws were definitely and seriously out-numbered, they'd detached one man just to rid the barn of Wes Potter. He hesitated back near the rear exit. The only reason they'd want him out of there so badly was because they needed a horse or two. That was it! They needed a mount for John Harriman!

He drew away from the rear doorway and flattened along a log wall, listening. There was a sudden lull, as though both sides had to re-load. But Wes knew that wasn't it. He edged up where some racked saddles were and poked among them, seeking a booted carbine. He found plenty of saddle boots, but none of them had a carbine in it.

The lull continued. Someone fired from the southern end of the yard. Everyone who was listening heard that bullet strike the bunkhouse log wall with a splintering *crash*. Someone either inside the bunkhouse or upon its little covered porch fired back. But that shot was obviously just as harmless as the other one had been.

Wes heard someone give a hooting, high cry of challenge, from the bunkhouse, then reel off some choice epithets against the attacking outlaws. But that high-spirited man was the only one who cared less about drawing bullets with the sound of his voice than anyone else did, for he got back no replies at all.

Wes looked up toward the yard and back toward the rear exit. He had a feeling someone would sooner or later try to rush him from one way or the other. There were several stalled horses in there with him, two of which were fairly calm throughout all the tumult, but the third one was beside himself with panic and kept moving, shifting his weight, stamping back and forth and softly snorting in his stall.

A carbine *cracked* with its high, sharp sound, from across by the main house. Another carbine slammed a slug straight through the barn from the same general area. Wes heard that bullet sing on through from front to back. Two six-guns made their louder, throatier roars from the bunkhouse, and very gradually the battle brisked up again.

Wes went forward, got down low, and peered out. There were two riflemen across the yard behind Harriman's house. They'd each step out, fire, and step back again. It was impossible to nail those two. All a man could do was wait, try and guess about when either outlaw was ready to step out, then fire. Wes didn't try it; he didn't have that much six-gun ammunition with him. He had a pocket full of carbine shells, but he'd left the carbine on his saddle back where they'd caught their first outlaw.

The dueling went on between those two riflemen behind Harriman's house, and the six gunmen over at the bunkhouse. Wes watched and listened, and waited. Those two riflemen across the yard would be only half the outlaw crew—not counting John Harriman. Where were the others? He turned and uneasily sidled over for a look out the back doorway. That was when the pair of carbines opened up out back, driving lead straight up through the barn's interior to the right and left. Wes dropped flat, but evidently one of those probing slugs hit too close to that terrified horse because he gave a high scream and hurled himself against the low door of his stall. Wood popped and went sailing. The door came all apart under a thousand pounds of panicked horse and Wes rolled swiftly to get clear as the beast swung and charged wildly straight ahead toward the rear exit. Someone out there evidently saw him coming and let off a quick cry of warning.

Wes never saw that man. Neither did he see the other outlaw back there as the blind-running, terrified horse plunged out into the gunshot-shattered night swinging from left to right as it sped onward. Neither of those furiously attacking outlaws out back took up their assault again. Wes waited, his gun cocked and ready, thinking they might be seeking to get in closer by stealth, but they never did. He waited and stood ready until another very gradual lull came, but still the outlaws did not appear. Then the reason they did not became clear. Somewhere, out in the chilly gloom, the sound of ridden horses moving swiftly away became audible.

Wes sprang upright and ran to the front of the barn. Over at the bunkhouse the others had also picked up those abrasive sounds in the darkness. "Hey!" Tom Ruffin's voice recognizably called. "Hey, Wes, you all right?"

"Sound as new money," replied Wes. "Can you see those riders?"

"No," sang out Tom. "They left from over behind the big house."

Wes thought he understood. When the outlaws had failed to get inside the barn to acquire an additional horse for John Harriman, they'd decided to run for it anyway, even though one of their animals had to carry double. He also understood why they hadn't done that earlier; John Harriman was a large man. He would break down any horse, if it had to pack all his weight as well as the weight of its regular rider. But that was only part of it. Wes didn't know about the rest of it right away. Neither, for that matter, did Marshal Craig Price and Tom Ruffin. They were all very cautious about stepping forth from hiding. They eventually did it, though, and no gunshots flamed out at them, so they came together up near the bunkhouse with the Anchor cowboys asking insistent and blunt questions, all of them stuffing in shirt tails and buttoning trousers as they did so, for the suddenness of that initial assault had caught them all flat on their backs in bed.

"You explain," muttered Wes to Marshal Craig Price. "Tell them to fetch horses, too. We can use them." As Wes turned away, Tom also started over toward the main house.

When they kicked open the front door and took two long steps inside where the cordite stench of burned gunpowder made them cough, Tom collided with something and fell, swearing heartily as he went down, caught himself, rolled, and sprang back up. "What the hell?" he snarled.

Wes kicked the object and said: "Now it makes sense. That's a stagecoach strongbox. Now it makes sense why those outlaws attacked the ranch knowing they were badly outnumbered. Harriman didn't have all the loot cached over at your ranch. Look at that strongbox. That'll also explain why they tried so hard to get another horse. Bad enough trying to get clear with one horse carrying double, but that much gold has a lot of weight to it." Wes turned, and nearly collided with Marshal Price in the doorway. He stepped back. Price and the little clutch of Anchor range riders squeezed inside. Tom was fumbling with a table lamp. When he finally got the thing lighted, they all stood gazing at that steel-bound oaken box where it lay open and abandoned upon the floor.

"Hey," one of the Anchor men said in an almost reverent tone of voice, "that there's a stageline strongbox. Must've been full of money."

"Or gold bars and dust," replied Marshal Price. Then he turned on the dumbfounded cowboys. "I thought you fellers were going after horses," he snapped. "Well, get going!" He went forward as though to herd the riders back out into the dark yard, but they readily withdrew and started for the barn and the corrals out back, their astonishment audible in the quick, flat questions and answers they threw back and forth as they withdrew.

Price stood in the doorway, gazing from the strongbox to Tom and Wes. Finally he said: "Well, that couldn't have held more than a fourth of it, boys, so I'm guessin' when they left here, they went after the rest of it. The trick's going to be to spot them in the forest at night."

"No trick," said Tom Ruffin, moving around the strongbox to the doorway. "It'll be daylight in another hour." He left the house walking purposefully toward the barn, leaving Wes and the deputy U.S. marshal looking at one another.

Wes said: "It sure didn't work out like we had it figured. But damned few things ever do."

Price nodded. "Damned few things ever do, Deputy, and now I hope you know those mountains, because I've got a hunch Mister Harriman isn't goin' to waste any time clearing out for Nevada. He won't be using the regular roads. He'll be using whatever secret trails he's been using to disappear over after his successes up in Nevada."

Wes said: "I've never gone through the Sierras from south to north. I know the routes about halfway through, because I hunt in there every fall. But Harriman'll be past the midway point before long, if he does what you think he'll do."

"Well," said Price, "what do *you* figure he'll do?"

"Oh, I reckon he'll head through the mountains for Nevada all right. But I'm also wonderin' if they'll take that damned dynamite with them. If they do, we're going to have to be almighty careful about chasin' them into any deep cañons."

Marshal Price turned that over in his mind for a second, then said: "I'm glad we're teamed up, Deputy. I like brave men who also are cautious. Let's go."

They walked out of Harriman's shot-up house into the yard where the other men were leading forth their saddled horses and calling back and forth, reminding one another to get carbines and extra shells, and jerky to chew on as they pursued the outlaws. Not a single Anchor rider wasn't ready and eager, although none of them fully understood what this was all about.

# XVI

It took a lot of explaining as Wes and Tom rode along on either side of the deputy U.S. marshal. In fact, they were almost over to the Ruffin place before the questions finally ceased, and the Anchor riders rode along digesting all they'd been told. Not until then was Wes able to ask how it was that Price and Ruffin never got inside the bunkhouse before the first shot was fired.

"Easy," grumbled Tom. "The danged door was barred from the inside, and, when we tried to get them to open it, one of them let fly a wild shot through the top of the door."

That, then, accounted for the first shot to be fired, the one that had upset Wes's plans. He looked over his shoulder, but the riders back there were either talking or gazing around with no appearance of knowing anything about that shot.

They found a pole gate leading through the rail drift fence onto Ruffin's range. Someone had hastily flung the poles aside in the grass leaving the gate open. One of the Anchor riders said, as they loped through: "Well, when this cussed fandango is over with, we can come back an' run out old Dick's horses . . . as usual."

They came down to the yard where Tom's father's old log buildings stood, and there came upon a used-up saddle horse standing in soft star shine, his rib cage pumping air in and out at an accelerated and unnatural pace. Marshal Price said, as they loped past this animal, that now either John Harriman had switched to another horse and the outlaws had two men riding double or else they'd caught another horse or two.

Just before they crossed out of the clearing, Tom Ruffin halted, moved his horse up and back a moment while he studied the dust, then he eased off the reins and joined the others where they were jumping old Dick's little creek. On across, Tom said: "They caught a couple of fresh horses right here in the yard."

In the distant east a pale blush of new day was firming up. It brightened all the plain and prairie, but made no impression at all up in the forest where they were heading. "Hell," one of the Anchor men growled in strong disgust, "why couldn't they've stayed out in the lousy open?"

They hadn't, and that was all there was to it, so

no one commented. But when Tom took the lead, he acted as though he could see the tracks anyway, so they made fair progress for the first few thousand yards. Then, when they were nearing the place where Stan Darcy had died, Tom halted them and held his arm aloft for total silence.

There wasn't a sound up through the onward trees. Not even a squawking blue jay.

Wes rode on up beside Tom and stopped, gazing up toward where the first pale light shone upon the little westerly site where Darcy had been found. Tom looked over there, too, and shook his head. "You sure they'd come up this way?" he muttered. "It's awful quiet."

Wes heard something far ahead, but off to the west. "Yeah," he said to Tom wryly. "They almost made it work. Come on. They're up in here all right, but they're playing that start-and-go game, hoping they'll hear us coming without us hearing them."

Wes took the lead after that, and held it, for although he couldn't read sign as well as Tom Ruffin could, he at least knew the mountains, and their few trails, better than any of the others did.

After leaving the place where Stan Darcy had been murdered by John Harriman, they had rough going. There were game trails, but they were extremely narrow, with low limbs overhead, and frequently traversed patches of thorny underbrush.

Wes didn't let any of that slow him down. He

knew Harriman's outlaw crew couldn't be very far ahead. What he also knew, and what was the main reason he wouldn't permit any delay, was that wherever the robbers had their roost in here, they were going to have to stop long enough to load the balance of their stolen loot. He was banking on that delay allowing him and his men sufficient time to corner Harriman and fight him to a standstill, if that was the way Harriman wanted it. Otherwise, he was relying on the fact that he had more guns than Harriman had now, and perhaps the bandit ringleader could be induced to surrender. He wasn't very hopeful about that; he didn't know John Harriman very well, but he thought he knew him that well. Harriman wouldn't surrender; at least he wouldn't, Wes speculated, until it had been powerfully demonstrated to him that he had no other choice.

Tom said from behind Wes: "You know where you're goin', because if you don't, you're likely to take us right smack into a bushwhack, Wes."

That was a possibility, of course, but Wes didn't think the danger would be very great until they got farther along. He didn't answer, but just kept riding along. Still he re-doubled his caution and his watchfulness.

They were strung out one behind the other. There were several trails, but none permitted more than one man to pass over them at a time. Craig Price said: "Deputy, if you know this low country, you ought to have some notion where those fellers have their hide-out."

"No idea at all," replied Wes without taking his eyes off the onward fragrant gloom. "There are a dozen little creeks in here, farther along, and a hundred little glades where five or six men could make a real comfortable camp. But I can't guess which one it'll be."

Tom finally said, sounding irritable: "Wes, let's stop here a spell. I'll scout on afoot. This ridin' strung out like a bunch of Mexicans is givin' me the willies. Just one feller out in the forest could snipe us one at a time like shootin' grouse on a low limb after sundown."

Wes dutifully halted. He wanted to listen ahead anyway. Tom dismounted, tossed his reins to Marshal Price, unsheathed his carbine, and went stalking up ahead. The forest was still slightly cool. It would be some little time yet before the outside heat reached down in here.

"Hear anythin'?" one of the cowboys asked. "Because I sure don't. An' say, Wes, how'd you ever figure Mister Harriman was an outlaw? I been workin' for Anchor four years now, an' s' help me Hannah, I never had no suspicion of him at all."

Another range rider said dourly: "You wouldn't have anyway, Lute, not thinkin' of headin' for town every time a shadow crosses the sun."

Marshal Price looked around. The cowboys

saw his expression and fell totally silent. Not until then was Wes able to concentrate upon the sounds of the waking forest.

There were birds, even a bald eagle floating majestically far above, each making their individual little sounds. There were also the nearer rustling sounds in the undergrowth, but Wes heard no sounds he could match with men and horses. When he finally gave it up and looked across where Craig Price was sitting his saddle, the deputy marshal wagged his head. "We're wasting an awful lot of time here," Price warned. "If they're still on the move, no wonder we can't hear 'em. They'll be too far off."

Tom came back. One minute there was nothing but forest ahead of Wes. The next minute Ruffin was standing there. He took his reins from Price, mounted up and shoved the carbine back into its boot. "Let's ride," he mumbled, and led out northwestward without one single word of explanation. Wes and Marshal Price exchanged a look, each shrugged, then they started out, trailing after Ruffin.

Tom had a definite course in mind, that much was instantly apparent the way he sliced in and out among the trees, always bearing in the same northwesterly direction. None of them said anything; there was somehow an aura of apprehension in this tree-locked, lost world of cool pine fragrance, which wasn't nearly as placid and pleasant as it should have been. Wes kept seeking horse tracks, and, although he saw some from time to time, they looked neither fresh nor as though they'd been made by anyone in a hurry.

Tom halted near a high, frowning overhead bluff that was lichen-covered and naked of even underbrush. He got down, signaled for the others to do likewise, then tied his horse, took out his carbine, and started gliding ahead in close to the cliff face where an ancient game trail lay buried under six inches of pure dust.

Craig Price stepped to Wes and whispered: "I sure hope he knows what he's doing. If he doesn't, we might as well forget ever catching them. We'll have wasted too much time."

Wes had misgivings, but he didn't voice them; instead, he hastened along the little narrow path after Ruffin. The others strung out, moving up, too, that air of uncertainty and peril thicker than ever around them. What bothered Wes was the fact that he hadn't seen any boot or horse tracks. Unless Tom knew something the others did not know, they were very likely doing exactly what Marshal Price was fearful of—wasting time while Harriman and his outlaw crew got clean away.

Tom halted in a small, sunlight-speckled clearing where some alders grew among the pines and firs. He pointed to the roundabout graze when the others caught up, then placed one finger over his lips. The grass was trampled and cropped short. Horses had recently been in this place!

Ruffin twisted to study the surrounding land formations. The frowning dark-stone barranca was still on their right. Dead ahead, where the trees stair-stepped their way straight up, was a large, abrupt hill. But where the barranca and hill came near to joining, to the northwest, there was a marked dip in the land, a readily recognizable break that plunged down separating the barranca from the yonder hill. That, obviously, would offer some sort of trail through and beyond the bulwark hills.

Craig Price stepped up close and gestured. "If they're around here," he whispered, "that'll be their route of retreat."

Tom nodded, looked at the others, then said: "They're around here all right. I tracked 'em up in this direction. The lay of the land told me they had to have their hide-out close by, otherwise they'd have to head straight for that pass up ahead. That's why I brought you here. If they aren't in camp, then we're bound to be ahead of them because we took the shortest route getting here. Either way, in a little while we can close the trap." Tom grinned wolfishly, disclosing large, very even, white teeth. "Let's go," he said, "and be quiet."

They crossed the trampled place, stepped into the forest across the way, and started moving soundlessly again across spongy beds of timeless needles. Finally the morning heat was beginning to build up. It was breathlessly still in the shadowy forest, with heat coming down through the cathedral pines in steady waves.

Tom swung off more to his right, using that notch in the onward hills as his pilot. Wes paced steadily behind him. Behind Wes came Marshal Craig Price and the Anchor Ranch men.

Southward, a blue jay shrilled denunciations at something passing through its private domain. Tom cocked his head, paused just long enough to gauge the distance, then resumed the lead again, moving faster now.

They crossed a clearing that was bisected by a well-marked wide and dusty old trail. Tom pointed at horse tracks as they moved onward. The sign all pointed southward, as though whoever had made those tracks had come down through the Sierras, and had not been traveling northward in the direction of Nevada.

"Damn," whispered Marshal Price, for the first time showing less than high doubt about all this, "Harriman's secret trail from Nevada down to the Hangtown country."

Wes motioned for silence, then pushed on after Tom Ruffin. They left that clearing, turned straight northward, and began to lose ground as the land tilted a little, at first, and tilted more farther along, heading straight down toward that notch in the east-west slopes.

Where Ruffin finally halted, they were in among

a light stand of flood-water ravaged trees looking out over the wide trail where it passed upland and between those two opposite slopes. Wes told the others to wait where they were. He walked out into bright sunlight, looked backward, saw nothing, heard nothing, and went ahead to the very edge of the trail.

Harriman had not yet passed by! All the tracks in that dust were pointing downcountry, back toward the Hangtown country. He went back to the others, reported what he'd found, and beckoned them all over into the trees for the projected wait. It was getting close to high noon with the sun visible over beside the trail, dumping its cauldrons of heat and brilliance straight downward.

They faded back into the hot gloom, knelt in there, and waited. Craig Price had brought his shotgun, but neither Tom nor Wes had anything but carbines and six-guns. The Anchor men turned to examining their weapons and looking intently down where the trail heaved up over a bump in the land before it spilled out across the grassy clearing, and headed straight on over where the land tilted down into the pass.

Tom settled down close to Wes and said: "Good place for an ambush." He smiled.

Wes nodded, but he showed no particular elation. "If Harriman's got a lick of sense, he'll call quits the minute he sees our guns."

Marshal Price had his own private observation

to add to that: "He won't quit. And if he had a lick o' sense, he never would've gotten this deep into trouble in the first place." Price was holding his shotgun lightly across his lap. "I forgot to explain, boys, in the process of acquiring that eighty thousand he had to kill four men. They hang murderers in Nevada. Harriman'll know that. He won't quit, not just so they can hang him in Nevada."

# XVII

Tom got restless and left them to scout southward. Marshal Price asked Wes what was down there where Tom had gone.

"A couple of little meadows, an old Indian . . ." Wes suddenly sat up straight. "An old Indian *rancheria* that hasn't been used in probably fifty, sixty years."

"Why'd you look so startled a second ago?" Price inquired.

"I'd completely forgotten the caves. Down at that old *rancheria* there were some caves back in the face of the bluff behind the sage and mesquite and chaparral. I found them by accident one time years back, but I'd forgotten them until just now."

Price raised his eyebrows. "The *rancheria*?" he

asked. "Are you figurin' that's where they had their camp?"

"I'm thinking it's very likely. I'm also thinking there's no better spot anywhere around for a hideout. A couple of those caves are big enough to stable horses in. As a matter of fact that's what the old-time warriors used them for, when they were hiding, or waiting for someone to go riding past down there on the trail unsuspectingly."

Marshal Price started to arise. Wes reached over to stop him. At the same moment one of the Anchor men said—"Look."—and pointed up the hill in front of them where a lightning bolt in centuries past had cleared a grassy place near the top-out. "A mounted man up there."

They drew back into their shielding forest instinctively, then looked. Sure enough, a horseman was sitting up there motionlessly, studying the onward land up toward the pass and beyond. Someone said it was a good thing he didn't have a spyglass, otherwise he'd have picked them out. That was problematical, but it nevertheless kept them all still and low.

As the stranger began distantly to move off, going back the way he'd come, Craig Price said: "Harriman's taking no chances. He's being shrewd. He knows we're after him by now, and he's wondering if we're trailing him or if maybe we haven't cut clear around him to lay an ambush."

Wes had already deduced that. What he wished

to know was exactly where Harriman was. He got his answer to that moments later when Tom came striding back to them. Tom gestured southward with one hand. "If anyone's thirsty," he said, "there's a cold-water creek down the trail about a hundred yards." Then Ruffin dropped to one knee, hooked both arms around his grounded carbine, and said: "They got a camp down there some- where near a big bluff. It was too brushy and I didn't want to slip in too close, but they're comin'. It looked to me like they were shy a man or two. I'm not sure, but I think I only saw four of 'em." Ruffin glanced out at the trail. "They'll come right past this spot," he said.

"What were they doing?" the federal lawman wanted to know.

Ruffin repeated what he'd said about there being too much brush down there. "All I could rightly make out was that they were watering their horses and striking their camp, rolling bedrolls, gatherin' their war bags, stuff like that, and goin' back up toward the base of their cliff now and then."

"There are caves back in there," said Wes, and Tom looked around at him.

"You know that spot?" Ruffin asked. Wes nodded. "Then tell me something. It's an old Indian *ranchería*?"

"It is."

Tom nodded as though confirming something for himself. "I thought so. There are a couple of cleared places up atop the slopes to the left and right. Indians always kept sentries out when they were hiding in a cañon like this. And something else. Someone a long time ago made a big pool where the creek runs past. They quarried stones and blocked off a low spot backing the water until it made quite a pool."

While they had been talking, one of the Anchor cowboys drifted southward back and forth through the forest until he was some little distance from the others. Where he stopped suddenly, there was an audible sound of oncoming riders. He turned and raced back to spread the alarm. Wes and Tom Ruffin knew a little more of the terrain than the others. Tom said they should divide the crew and catch Harriman from both sides of the trail. Marshal Price was in agreement about that, too.

Wes thought differently. He said: "Tom, take a couple of men and go across the way. Marshal, you stay on this side with a couple. Me, I'm goin' to slip down there an' block off that northward trail. If there's a fight, I don't particularly want to have to chase some riderless horse with saddle-bags full of gold all the way through the Sierras into Nevada." He gestured for the others to get moving. They did; Tom picked his Anchor men at random. So did Marshal Price who didn't know any of the men, either. Wes took the pair he'd spoken to only the day before, the cowboys known as Slim and Lefty. The three of them started quickly for the tilted area just this side of the path, where the trail had to pass between two pinched-down shoulders of land as it went on upcountry. They weren't quite in position when they heard a horseshoe strike brittle stone. It wasn't a loud sound at all, but in the utter stillness of this hidden place it carried to every man lying in wait.

Wes left his cover finally, and trotted quickly over into the rocks at the side of the downward pass. There, as Slim and Lefty crept in beside him, he said: "Watch straight ahead."

The first horseman came into view up over that southward lump of rocky soil. He was riding straight up in the saddle with a carbine balanced across his lap, his right hand curled around the weapon, his trigger finger set in place. Another man came up over the lumpy place, then a third and fourth man. They were riding Indian file, one behind the other. Harriman came next, and one man followed behind Harriman. It was that last rider who suddenly cried out. No one ever knew why; he'd perhaps caught the hard flash of reflected sunlight off a gun barrel, or had maybe sighted movement on one side of the trail. All the ambushers were certain of was that something had alarmed him and he'd cried his sharp, keening warning. Then four carbines lashed their lethal flame at the rider and he was knocked drunkenly out of his saddle, dead before he hit the ground.

Ruffin and his men opened up, along with at least one of the men across the trail where Marshal Price was also waiting.

Wes ripped out a curse. The outlaws, already keyed to instantaneous reaction, exploded into action. They spun their mounts in an attempt to break clear. They opened up with their guns firing both to the left and the right. Price and Ruffin let go another ragged volley. That time a horse went down hurtling its rider head over heels.

John Harriman roared out for his men to make a run for it up the trail. It wasn't good advice, but Harriman didn't know it; none of the outlaws knew yet that Wes was up there, blocking their northward progress. But they didn't follow Harriman's order anyway; all those renegades thought of was getting off their trail, which was entirely exposed, and over into the shelter of the forest.

As it happened, they broke to the west, which was to their left, and charged straight into the flaming guns of Marshal Price's men. But they had a lot of horseflesh to use as protection, plus their abrupt, galvanized speed. Guns crashed and bucked, another horse fell, then the outlaws were into the forest past the initial tier of trees.

Wes's men jumped up as though to race ahead and support the federal lawman, but before they could get fairly away Wes snapped at them to stay where they were and to get back down in the rocks. They couldn't get over where Price and his men were anyway, not in time to do any good.

Wes was right. It had happened too fast. Harriman and his outlaws got to cover after one wild rush, leaving two horses and one dead man out in the clearing where their trail ran northward and southward. Another outlaw, unhorsed and groggy, nevertheless made it to safety while Ruffin and his men were trying to catch the others in their gunfire before the outlaws reached the trees. They didn't get it done; there was too much agitated movement and excitement.

The gunfire briefly dwindled as both sides tried to re-group and get organized for stiffer resistance. The ambush had failed; at least it had failed in Wes's eyes. He'd had hopes they could have gotten the drop on John Harriman, compelling him to surrender without a battle. But in the general sense it hadn't failed, because it had broken up Harriman's race to get through the pass into the wild and trackless depths of the Sierras. Also, it had deprived Harriman's men of two horses, had driven them westward in among the trees, and had them pinned down over there.

Tom Ruffin wanted to rush across the trail, across the open place on both sides of the trail, and get into the yonder trees where Harriman had gone, but each time he or one of his men moved, the forted-up outlaws would rake the yonder and eastward forest with gunfire.

One of the Anchor riders huddled with Wes

said: "Hell of a note. It's a stand-off. We should've had 'em hands down."

Wes felt somewhat the same way, then he observed something that had evidently escaped the men crouching there in the rocks with him. Each time one of the outlaws would fire, he'd be far northward through the trees. "They're heading this way," he told his companions. "They're tryin' to get up here where they can make a run for it through the pass."

"We can stop that," growled one of his men, and started to ease his carbine around the side of a big boulder.

Wes caught the man's arm and shook his head. "Let 'em come," he hissed. "Let 'em get up close enough to try it. Then we'll cut them down."

But that didn't happen right away because Tom Ruffin, grim and unrelenting, began sidling northward on his side of the trail, too, firing into the opposite trees as he and his men did this, until they finally exerted sufficient pressure to halt the outlaws in their withdrawal attempt.

Tom was firing methodically and with unflinching accuracy. He'd try to anticipate the gunshots, and let fly just ahead of the outlaws. This caused many of Harriman's men's shots to explode harmlessly because, as they were moving to peer around a tree and shoot, one of Ruffin's slugs would peel bark or kick up dust a second or two ahead of them.

Wes heard the *rattle* of rocks back on the westerly slope farther in the pass. He twisted to see about that, and so did the Anchor riders cached in those rocks with him. At first there was nothing to see, but eventually two men supporting a third man reached the relatively sound footing of the trail, and Wes recognized Marshal Price and one of the other Anchor men. They were helping another Anchor rider who held one leg up off the ground. Wes sent his companions back to help the federal lawman fetch their injured cowboy on up into the rocks. Then he swung back to watch the onward fight.

By the time Price and the others got that wounded man up where Wes was, Tom had halted the outlaws' withdrawal completely, even without any support from Wes and Marshal Price.

Harriman yelled something to his renegades that was indistinguishable over where Wes turned to lend a hand with the wounded man. Gradually their gunfire slackened off until only an occasional probing shot slashed into the forest over where Ruffin was. It struck Wes that Harriman wanted his men to save their ammunition. He set one of his riders to watching, then crawled back where Marshal Price was making a tourniquet out of the injured cowboy's trouser leg to stop the profuse bleeding where an outlaw slug had ripped a jagged hole through the Anchor man's upper leg. Wes found a stick and inserted it to twist the tourniquet. As the bleeding stopped, the cowboy looked down at his injury, then up at Wes, and said in a husky voice: "Pardner, I sure never expected 'em to charge us. Where are they now?"

"In the forest where you fellers were," said Wes. "You just lean back against the rocks and keep hold of this stick. Slack off every ten minutes or so, but don't let too much blood leak out."

The cowboy nodded, took the stick in his hands, and gazed at his leg. "It's not broke," he muttered. "I can wiggle m' toes. But that feller must've had his gun loaded with harness chain to make a cut like that."

Wes and Price crawled up where the other Anchor men were crouched and waiting. That desultory firing was still going on. It was more a private duel than a battle now. An outlaw would probe with a gunshot, and Tom Ruffin's men would try to catch the renegade while he was still exposed to fire. There was no way to tell how many outlaws were still active; they rarely fired twice from the same place, and they didn't fire in volley formation.

Marshal Price got over close to Wes and said: "We could maybe slip around an' flank 'em."

Wes shook his head. "We're not going to leave this pass," he stated.

Price then said: "All right, but what the hell are we leaving it all to Ruffin for?"

"Because Harriman doesn't know we're over here. When he gets to movin' up this way again, we'll disillusion him about that."

Marshal Price moved away and got down low where he could see a limited section of the southerly woods through a slot between some rocks. Around him on both sides, the Anchor men also lay low, peering around. From among the westward trees a deep voice cried out in a rolling crash of sound: "Hold it! Everybody hold it!" Gradually the gunfire stopped. Hazy gray smoke hung out there in soiled layers. Raw slashes upon tree trunks showed where bullets had hit. The stillness that ensued was almost as deafening, in its own way, as the gunfire had been.

# XVIII

"Deputy Potter," roared that same bull-like voice. "Wes Potter, are you out there?"

Wes answered, but he took his time about it. "I'm here, Harriman. I'm over here, barring your chances of getting through the pass."

"Listen to me, Potter. I'll bring you out ten thousand dollars in cash and gold. All you've got to do is get away from that pass. Ten thousand in gold for you an' your men. It's enough to set each one of you up in . . ."

"Why only ten?" called out Wes. "Why not twenty or fifty, Harriman? You're not going to get to spend a dime of it anyway. Why not the whole eighty thousand?"

Harriman fell silent. For a tense, hushed moment there wasn't a sound. Tom Ruffin broke it, finally, by calling over and saying: "Harriman, old Dick was worth a lot more than ten thousand! Even that feller Darcy you also murdered . . . he was worth something, wasn't he?"

Harriman's answer was bitter: "Darcy was a fool. Who the hell are you?"

"My name's Ruffin, too," answered Tom. "If you'd bought my father out, you wouldn't be over there with your back to a mountain now, Harriman."

"He wouldn't sell," Harriman said. "I tried to buy the old devil out. He said he wanted to keep his land for a while yet, said he'd been waitin' a year for something special, said if nothing changed for him by this time next year, he'd sell. I couldn't wait."

"I reckon you couldn't at that!" Wes called back. "And that something special he was waiting for, Harriman, was his son."

"That's all over with," Harriman called forth. "Thirty thousand in cash, Potter. Split up among your men any way you want, but get clear of that pass up there."

Tom Ruffin aimed and fired in the direction of

Harriman's voice. Instantly Harriman's outlaws drove lead straight back in the direction of Tom's shot. But Harriman yelled out for the firing to cease again. It didn't stop until another couple of rounds had been spitefully thrown back and forth, but after that it stopped and the silence came again.

Now John Harriman said: "Potter, Ruffin, all you men . . . listen to me. We've got dynamite over here. We can set short fuses and heave sticks of this stuff over where you are an' bury the lot of you. Now put down those damned guns and take the thirty thousand, and forget trying to stop us, because one way or another, you can't do it."

For a long moment no one said anything. The Anchor men huddled in the pass while Wes and Marshal Price rolled their eyes at one another. One of the men said: "Wes, what's he talkin' about . . . dynamite?"

"He's got it all right," the deputy replied. "I don't know how much, but he got two boxes of the stuff down in town last night."

"Holy mackerel," a cowboy sighed, and cocked his eyes upward to the loose slopes on both sides of the pass. "He ain't kiddin', Wes. A few blasts up there in them lousy rocks and we'll be buried!"

Marshal Price called out. "Harriman, this is Deputy U.S. Marshal Price! Even if we let you through this pass, you'd never make it on to Nevada. Dynamite or no dynamite, there are posses of lawmen strung out on the far side of the mountains looking for you and your crew. A smart man would've quit long ago. You've pushed your luck too far."

Harriman didn't answer. In fact, for almost a full five minutes neither side had any more to say. Wes huddled behind his rock, speculating. Finally he touched an Anchor cowboy and pointed around to his left. "Go over where Ruffin and the others are," he ordered. "Be damned careful. Stay low in the brush until you get into those trees yonder. Tell Ruffin to watch almighty close for a horse."

The cowboy looked blank. So did Craig Price and the others. "A horse?" said the cowboy. "What horse, for gosh sakes?"

Wes turned and gestured. "Harriman's pinned down over there. He can't throw any dynamite sticks this far. No one could reach us from where he is. Look up along the western slope. It's too open between the brush patches and occasional trees. That only leaves Harriman one alternative. Poke his dynamite into a saddlebag, head the horse toward this pass, and slap it hard over the rump. Now get going. Tell Ruffin to shoot the second he sees any kind of movement over there. Tell him to drop far enough back in the forest so he and his men won't get bowled over by the blast. Now get moving!"

As the cowboy obediently scuttled away, Marshal Price rose up to dart a fast look over into

340

the westerly forest where Harriman and his men were hiding, then Price dropped down and half turned from the waist toward Wes.

"You're no fool," he said admiringly. "Deputy, if you ever get tired of being a sheriff in a one-horse cow town, just say the word an' I'll get you sworn in as a federal lawman."

Wes was concentrating on the hushed, smoke-hazed trees and had no comment to make about Price's offer. Around him the remaining Anchor range riders were scarcely breathing. Time ran on; the tension built up almost to its maximum capacity. Wes tried to locate that courier he'd sent over to Tom Ruffin, and failed. But the man had made it, Wes was confident of that. None of Harriman's men had seen him or he'd have fired. They were too feverishly otherwise occupied, Wes thought, and rubbed sweat off the palms of his hands as he continued to wait.

Harriman called out once more, and this time his voice was swollen with confidence. "Potter, you and that U.S. marshal have one minute to make up your minds whether you clear out of the pass or not. If you don't . . . you're going to stay in that pass forever. Believe me, Potter, I'm not just making a threat."

Price said: "Harriman, what about the thirty thousand dollars?"

Someone else answered Price. The voice was rough and rude-sounding. "Forget the money! You weren't goin' to get it anyway. Just get t' hell outen that pass, or stay in it forever under a couple hundred tons o' rocks."

Price turned and gazed straight at Wes. "You were dead right," he said, picked up his shotgun, and laid it atop the smooth boulder where he crouched.

Wes looked at the Anchor riders. They were concentrating their full attention upon the yonder forest. He gazed around where Tom Ruffin was, and over there, too, not a sound or a shadow of movement was visible. He wiped both sweating palms again, picked up his Winchester, and drew a little solace from the impersonal coolness of its steel.

The sun was sliding off center. Some long, very thin shadows slanted down into the clearing beside the trail. It occurred to Wes that, if Harriman waited until late afternoon to send that doomed horse charging toward the pass, the animal might make less of a target. That thought had no more than uneasily stirred his imagination, when something moved over in the westerly first fringe of trees. He forgot everything else, raised his carbine, and fitted it into the curve of his shoulder. Beside him Marshal Price leaned, picked up his gun, too, and also settled into a crouching, firing position. There was a little ripple of grating sound as the Anchor cowboys who had also caught that faint movement got set.

Someone over there let off a high scream, and struck something hard with a pine limb. The horse gave a violent jump. Wes fired. So did Marshal Price. So did the Anchor men in the pass, as well as the waiting riflemen over where Tom Ruffin was hiding. It was a thunderous, ragged volley that spewed gunsmoke and deafening tumult into the heretofore total stillness.

The horse dropped in its tracks, literally riddled to death before it hit the ground. Over the gun thunder a man hidden in the trees screamed something over and over in a terrified voice. Wes thought that renegade was the same man who had struck the horse; he had probably been knocked down by the wall of lead thrown in his direction, and was now unable to move. If Wes's surmise was correct, what the outlaw was terrified about was fairly simple. He was lying beside that dead horse, with the fuses in the saddlebags fiercely burning!

Wes shot his Winchester empty. He turned to put it aside when the world suddenly buckled and heaved, a great breath of rushing air lifted off his hat and carried it away, then a roar so deafening it left him temporarily numb and unable to hear, rose upward accompanied by a blinding flash of violent orange light brighter even than the sun.

He dropped in close to his protective boulder and remained there, his head twisted, his mouth open for air. Craig Price wasn't next to his rock; he was tumbling backward. One of the Anchor men flung both arms over his head and dropped down on both knees.

The avalanche of pine limbs, clods of moist earth nearly as heavy as lead, cascades of pine needles and cones rained out of the sky. Wes was pelted unmercifully, and put his hands over his head, too. The air rushed back into the area of implosion, making a sound like a gigantic tidal wave. It bent tall trees and uprooted clumps of sage and thorny chaparral. It stripped limbs of green needles and pinecones, sending both hurtling through the air. A slip of earth began sliding down into the pass from up the westerly slope. Wes heard its ominous rumble and looked up. Then he sprang to his feet, yelling for Price and the Anchor men to get out of the pass. Most of them staggered to their feet and groped their way clear, but the federal lawman was lying flat, floundering heavily as though dazed. Wes fought against the tearing wind to reach him. The avalanche was gathering slow momentum. He got to Price, grabbed his coat, and wrenched the deputy U.S. marshal to his feet, then ducked down, flung Price over one shoulder, and turned to stumble and stagger out of the rocks. He made it, with his lungs near to bursting, dropped Price out in the clearing, and looked back. The avalanche came lazily and inexorably, its rolling rumble increasing as it gathered up more tons of rock, earth, whole trees, and fell finally into the pass, blocking the trail and sending up choking clouds of ancient dust.

Tom Ruffin was standing beside Wes when he turned away to see whether all the Anchor men had made it or not. Someone had gotten that wounded man out. He was sitting there on the grass beside the trail, still holding the stick to his tourniquet, with his mouth hanging open and his eyes bulging, looking back down into the pass where he had been.

Ruffin touched Wes. "You all right?" he inquired.

Wes nodded, completing his turn. Over where that rigged horse had been, there was nothing but dust, falling parts of trees, and an impenetrable pall.

Ruffin said: "No use to look."

Wes started across the clearing anyway. The Anchor cowboys were congregating around that wounded man, stunned and numb and speechless. They watched Wes and Tom walk over where a crater had been gouged out of the earth, making no attempt to go over and look at that spot themselves.

There were two dead men over there, all that remained of the outlaw crew. One was a pock-marked, dissolute-looking dark man. The other was John Harriman. He didn't have a mark on him anywhere. He was leaning with his back to a big fir tree, the entire front of which had been stripped of bark, both eyes open, his gaze fixed on a massive granite boulder fifty feet in front of him.

Ruffin leaned, touched Harriman's shoulder, and the dead man toppled over, all loose and limp.

Wes walked over to the granite stone, stepped around it, and made a grunt. Ruffin came over also to look. " 'Be damned," he muttered, and looked back where Harriman lay. "Do you reckon he had time to do this?"

"Must have," murmured Wes, and bent to heft one of the swollen saddlebags back behind that boulder. He could hardly lift the thing. There was another set just as swollen beneath the ones he'd tried to lift. "Better get Marshal Price over here," Wes said. "It's his eighty thousand."

Price came, when he was no longer so groggy, and stood staring at the hoard of stolen gold and currency, then he went through the blasted forest for a quarter mile trying to locate the other outlaws. They never found them. They saw a torn shell belt hanging fifty feet up in a blasted tree, and one of the Anchor men found a carbine twisted completely around into the shape of a letter U, but they had only three bodies to take down out of the mountains with them; one belonged to John Harriman. Another was that pock-marked outlaw with the cruel cast to his face. The third was that first renegade to stop lead; he was lying back down the trail where the initial exchange of gunshots had taken place.

They were slow getting ready to go back. For one thing they didn't have enough horses. For another, they were still too badly shaken by what they'd seen, had lived through, to act normally for more than an hour. It was, in fact, late afternoon before they finally got under way.

They were working their way back down the trail in the direction of old Dick's cabin when Tom Ruffin said to Wes: "I didn't figure to stay around here, when I first arrived."

Wes nodded. He remembered the bitter things Tom had said about the Hangtown country. "And now?" he inquired.

Tom looked on ahead where red sunlight faintly brightened the clearing down where old Dick's cabin and barn and grave were. "Reckon I'll stay, Wes. I've met some good men around here." He turned and smiled. Wes smiled back. They rode on out of the forest side-by-side, saying nothing more. Behind them came the burdened horses of the Anchor men and Marshal Price.

# ABOUT THE AUTHOR

LAURAN PAINE who, under his own name and various pseudonyms has written over a thousand books, was born in Duluth, Minnesota. His family moved to California when he was at a young age and his apprenticeship as a Western writer came about through the years he spent in the livestock trade, rodeos, and even motion pictures where he served as an extra because of his expert horsemanship in several films starring movie cowboy Johnny Mack Brown. In the late 1930s, Paine trapped wild horses in northern Arizona and even, for a time, worked as a professional farrier. Paine came to know the Old West through the eyes of many who had been born in the previous century, and he learned that Western life had been very different from the way it was portrayed on the screen. "I knew men who had killed other men," he later recalled. "But they were the exceptions. Prior to and during the Depression, people were just too busy eking out an existence to indulge in Saturday-night brawls." He served in the U.S. Navy in the Second World War and began writing for Western pulp magazines following his discharge. It is interesting to note that all of his earliest novels (written under his own name and the pseudonym Mark Carrel) were published in the British market and he soon had as strong a following in that country as in the United States. Paine's Western fiction is characterized by strong plots, authenticity, an apparently effortless ability to construct situation and character, and a preference for building his stories upon a solid foundation of historical fact. *Adobe Empire* (1956), one of his best novels, is a fictionalized account of the last twenty years in the life of trader William Bent and, in an off-trail way, has a melancholy, bittersweet textaure that is not easily forgotten. In later novels like *The White Bird* (Five Star Westerns, 1997) and *Cache Cañon* (Five Star Westerns, 1998), he showed that the special magic and power of his stories and characters had only matured along with his basic themes of changing times, changing attitudes, learning from experience, respecting Nature, and the yearning for a simpler, more moderate way of life.

**Center Point Large Print**
600 Brooks Road / PO Box 1
Thorndike ME 04986-0001 USA

(207) 568-3717

US & Canada:
1 800 929-9108
www.centerpointlargeprint.com